Praise for Laura Jarratt

"The fantastic writing kept me hooked from the very first page."
—*The Guardian* for *Two Little Girls*

"Tense, twisty, and compelling, *Two Little Girls* asks the questions no mother wants to answer."
—Lisa Hall, bestselling author

"Laura Jarratt is a fabulous new voice on the crime fiction scene. More like this, please."
—Lesley Thomson, author of
The Detective's Daughter, for *Two Little Girls*

"Ambitious and articulate."
—*Daily Mail* for *Two Little Girls*

T0044417

Also by Laura Jarratt

Two Little Girls

Without Saying Goodbye

A NOVEL

Laura Jarratt

Copyright © 2023 by Laura Jarratt
Cover and internal design © 2023 by Sourcebooks
Cover design by Ploy Siripant
Cover images © Lynn Whitt/Arcangel

Sourcebooks and the colophon are registered trademarks of Sourcebooks.

All rights reserved. No part of this book may be reproduced in any form or by
any electronic or mechanical means including information storage and retrieval
systems—except in the case of brief quotations embodied in critical articles or
reviews—without permission in writing from its publisher, Sourcebooks.

The characters and events portrayed in this book are fictitious or are used fictitiously. Any
similarity to real persons, living or dead, is purely coincidental and not intended by the author.

Published by Sourcebooks Landmark, an imprint of Sourcebooks
P.O. Box 4410, Naperville, Illinois 60567-4410
(630) 961-3900
sourcebooks.com

Originally published as *Disappeared* in 2022 in Great Britain by Orion Fiction, an imprint of
The Orion Publishing Group Ltd. This edition issued based on the paperback edition published
in 2022 in Great Britain by Orion Fiction, an imprint of The Orion Publishing Group Ltd.

Library of Congress Cataloging-in-Publication Data

Names: Jarratt, Laura, author.
Title: Without saying goodbye : a novel / Laura Jarratt.
Description: Naperville, Illinois : Sourcebooks Landmark, [2023] |
   Originally published as Disappeared in 2022 in Great Britain by Orion
   Fiction, an imprint of The Orion Publishing Group, Ltd.
Identifiers: LCCN 2022050968 (print) | LCCN 2022050969 (ebook) | (trade paperback) | (epub)
Subjects: LCGFT: Thrillers (Fiction) | Novels.
Classification: LCC PR6110.A755 W58 2023 (print) | LCC PR6110.A755
   (ebook) | DDC 823/.92--dc23/eng/20221028
LC record available at https://lccn.loc.gov/2022050968
LC ebook record available at https://lccn.loc.gov/2022050969

Printed and bound in the United States of America.
WOZ 10 9 8 7 6 5 4 3 2 1

Dedicated to the memory of Elizabeth O'Brien

THIS HAD TO END HERE, ONE WAY OR ANOTHER.

Her head was a jumbled mess of chaotic panic. All her senses were running on maximum alert as she hurtled forward.

No, this could not be happening. Not now.

Her heart pounded almost too hard to bear, not from exertion, but utter terror, as she took in everything around her.

They say time slows in events like this, but it didn't slow at all. Instead, everything assailed her all at once. Overwhelming, horrific. The chill of desperation holding back the sweat of fear.

The gleam of sharp metal as the car headlights glinted off the blade of the knife. The smell of the burning rubber where the tires had skidded to a halt on the cobbles. The scream of terror piercing her ears as the blade came toward her.

She could die here. Worse—so could they.

Then she could feel the cold, hard metal in her hand again, and the heft of the shotgun to her shoulder came easily.

The taste of hate was bitter on her tongue. All those life-changing months that had gone before tonight, months of confusion and worry, but also of discovery mixed with newfound freedom. Those memories all scrabbling like rats in a barrel to win out against her past life. Driving her into action, giving her the strength to do this. All that fear. So much fear. Now turned into power. Turned into the will to fight back.

A mother would die to save her children. And sometimes she would kill.

The gun fired—a crack cutting through disordered senses. Then there was the heavy thud of a body slumping to the ground.

1

Five months earlier

LET IT BURN.

The explosion shattered the night as the car windows and tires blew out.

Shock waves of noise echoed out across the hills, but there was no one to hear them.

No one except her.

Cerys huddled on the rocky outcrop, her arms wrapped around her body as she watched the flames from the car lick up into the darkness. The drizzle falling around her wasn't enough to put them out. There'd be little left of that comfy old SUV soon. And that was okay—that suited her.

She'd heard the crackle when the rear of the car had first sparked up and then the crash as the windows had blown out. She hadn't even flinched. For eight years, this car had been hers. It had carried her to work every day, run their old dog to the vet for that last time, and taken two of her three children off to university; it had been a reliable comrade, and she'd resisted changing it for a newer model every time Gavin tried to persuade her it was getting old and shabby, but right then she hated it.

Let it burn.

Along with the rest of her life.

She'd considered staying in the car and going up with it, rather than sitting here watching, but she was a coward and afraid of the pain. Afraid she might not stay the course, might get out—screaming and horribly burned—to die in agony on this cold hillside. No, that wasn't for her. Far better to end it like this and let the cold take her down slowly. A farmer's daughter like her knew that was a kinder death. She just hoped it would drown the blackness out as she went under. She didn't want that to follow her down. It had kept her in its clutches long enough now. Time to end that.

Cerys had grown up in these hills. A night out here in this weather would finish her, painlessly. It wouldn't take long for her shivering to stop. Maybe a couple of hours, and then she'd become sleepy and drift off. Once she got to that point, the worst was over. They wouldn't find the remains of the car, or her body, for a good while. Long enough for the winter weather to finish its work. Cerys had chosen her spot well. She might not have been here in over a decade, not since her father passed, but she still knew this valley like the back of her hand.

Her bones would be found in this hallowed land of her childhood, and that was fitting. Her dad would understand her reasoning, even if nobody else did.

Suddenly another explosion ripped through the quiet of the soft falling rain. She felt as if it juddered through her very bones as a flash of light tore the dark apart.

Cerys shook like a wet dog. She'd been so lost inside her own head that she hadn't noticed the flames reach the fuel tank. For a brief moment, she felt a faint warmth as the heat traveled through the night, but then it was gone. The fire raged inside the car, a November bonfire, burning up all the heartache of these last few years—the loss of the people who'd mattered most that still ate away at her—until there was nothing left but twisted metal and emptiness.

If she took her coat off, maybe it would be over quicker, but she couldn't move. Her limbs were lead and her head too sad and sore to force the effort. Never mind, it would happen soon enough anyway.

She hadn't written a note for them. That had been a deliberate choice. Because what could she say? She didn't have the words to explain why, just that deep, deep blackness wouldn't leave her no matter how hard she tried to get rid of it, and she couldn't live with that any longer.

Words couldn't make it better for those she was leaving behind, so it was as well not to try. They were better off without her. She'd only drag them down if she stayed. A nuisance, that's what she'd become to them all.

Oh, this darkness inside her had hold of her good and tight. But not for much longer. Not now. This way she'd be rid of it for sure.

She lost track of how long she sat on the hard rock, but the car fire burned out completely while she did. Thoughts galloped through her brain, but she waved them away, turning them from her so they raced off into the night.

Numb. Empty. That was how she needed to be to carry this through. No memories to pull her back, no thoughts of the future. Just a nonthinking machine whose power supply would shut down soon.

She'd thought sleep would come much faster than this though.

Lily closed the door behind her softly, so softly, her fingers trembling as she prayed the slight click of the lock wouldn't give her away. The sleeping child, draped like a blanket over her shoulder, stirred and snuffled into her neck but didn't wake. Shifting the carryall in her palm to get a tighter grip, Lily tiptoed down the drive, her breath held, picking up speed only as she escaped into the street.

She made a silent, desperate plea that the cold wouldn't wake her child. A frost had settled on the branches of the trees already, and she could hear the crackle of twigs snapping beneath her feet as she hurried along, trying not to slip on the icy patches along the wet pavement.

The car was parked on the next street; she just had to get there safely. Only one street. She could do this, right? Even she could do this much.

When she got to the end of the road, she dared to look back. Her heart raced as she searched for signs she'd been discovered missing, but there were no lights on in the house, no open door. She swallowed down the nausea brought on by the adrenaline swirling in her blood, and she hurried on.

That precious weight across her shoulder kept her going. This was why she had to succeed. Nothing else mattered.

She got to the car, finally. It was an old white hatchback bought yesterday for a few hundred quid. A cash buy before he noticed the hole in his bank account.

She placed the sleeping child gently in the car seat. "Shush, sshhh," she soothed, but the four-year-old was deep in sleep, and she was able to get in and start the car to the sound of soft snores. She pulled off down the street and headed out of the city, still trying not to retch. It would take a while for that adrenaline to ebb away. For now, it was still doing its job and aiding her flight.

Nothing and nobody was going to make her go back there.

She didn't have much of a plan, but she knew where she was going. She had a scribbled note of hasty road directions beside her on the passenger seat. Lily had a destination, and for now, that was enough.

She gripped the wheel harder and followed the blue signs for the highway.

2

THERE WAS AN OLD LEGEND in these remote hills that if you slept here through the night, the faeries would steal you away to their country while you slumbered. And when they returned you to wake to a cold dawn, you'd either have gone mad, or they'd have blessed you with a gift.

It was an old story her *nain*, her dad's mother, used to tell her, cuddled on her aproned knee in front of the open fire in the farmhouse.

That was the first thought that came to Cerys when she woke.

The second was why the hell *was* she still alive.

She uncurled her stiff, freezing limbs from where she was huddled on the rock. The morning greeted her with a faint light and a soft, mild breath that answered her question. The temperature had shifted in the night. She looked west to where the sea lay over the mountains. A warm front had blown in, dismissing the rain and stoppering Jack Frost's bottle.

The faeries' gift? Not a gift but a curse.

She buried her face in chilled fingers. Now what was she going to do?

I'm fifty-three years old, and I can't even succeed at killing myself. Dear God!

How had she got this useless? She didn't used to be this way. Did she?

Or is that why Gavin had no time for her? Her kids too. Because she was this powerless, drained lump who'd given up on everything. But she hadn't even been able to get giving up right, had she?

She couldn't go back. She couldn't. What would she say? And it'd all just be the same.

But what would she do now?

She waited for the blackness inside to rise and overwhelm her.

She waited a long time but it didn't come. In its place was something else instead.

The blackness was a dragging, sinking thing that sucked *her* away.

This new feeling wasn't like that. This was different. Pain—sharp and screaming pain inside that split her head and made her want to yell out.

Or was it fear? Was that what was hurting so much?

She was shaking. And it wasn't with the cold. It was the shock that she was still here, and she still had no answers. All her bridges were burned, and there was no way back.

But no way forward either.

She let out a sudden shriek because it hurt too much not to. But only the hills were listening. She wanted to scream it all out, but then she thought she might be screaming forever because it kept coming and coming, as if there was no end to it. All that rage inside that she hadn't known was there. What even was this?

What have I become?

The hills couldn't answer her.

❧

Lily stretched her legs out. She was still cramped after driving for so long. It had taken hours and hours to get to this point. The solemn face of the little boy opposite her was smeared with hot chocolate. Lily forgot her aching legs and smiled. "Was that good?"

He nodded, smiling back. *I can do this*, she told herself. *I can be who I need to be. For my child.*

She smiled more tremulously, hoping she could make that thought true just by wishing.

Because if she couldn't, what would they do now?

She split a doughnut in half and pushed the plate to him, but he shook his head. She wrapped his half in a napkin and put it in her bag. "Have it later then," she said and immediately felt guilty when she looked over at a table nearby where a woman maybe ten or fifteen years Lily's senior was having no difficulty persuading a spotlessly clean girl of about five to eat a pot of fruit salad.

Lily couldn't even get her child to eat a doughnut, let alone a healthy breakfast. She looked at his little cheeks, still pudgy in that baby way, and her heart hurt. What had she done to him? Dragged from bed and towed across the country, cramped up in an old car, and all he had was a mother who couldn't cope with life even at the best of times.

How did she ever think she could do this?

Panic rose like vomit in her throat.

Desperation had driven her to believe she could do this, but the hard reality of a crappy breakfast in a highway service station brought her back down to earth and to who she really was.

An unfit mother.

That woman at the next table, she could do it. Not like Lily. Her child was one of the lucky ones. She would grow up secure and happy, looked after, protected.

"Mummy?"

Lily blinked hard, pushing back tears. "Sammy?"

"I've finished now. I'm bored. Can we do something?" He ruffled his short brown hair, frowning. "What happened to my…? Oh, I forgot, sorry."

She was useless, couldn't even notice when her own child was wriggling with frustration after being driven around for hours, with longer to go, and she had no solution to that. Never mind that he shouldn't have to be here in the first place. And that was her fault too.

Unfit mother.

She could hear those words spat at her like they were being said right now, right here.

A shudder ran through her.

And remembered pain. She could feel the tight fingers on her throat, choking. The look on his face as he tightened his grip. The look that told her she was nothing—she was dirt.

She couldn't let herself remember that. She'd lose what little nerve she had. It had taken her too long to pluck up the courage to do this. She had to hang on.

After all, if she went back, it would be worse than ever now. Her child deserved better, even if she didn't. This one deserved a future free from fear.

"Come on, back to the car." She got up and lifted him into her arms.

"You can have another sleep soon while Mummy is driving if it gets too boring."

She strapped him back in the car and hid her tear-filled eyes from him as she wrestled with the seat harness.

"Sorry," she whispered as she closed the car door and he couldn't hear her. "So sorry. I hope I can do this right for you. Please forgive me for all this mess."

3

CERYS LET HER HANDS HANG limply at her sides as the sharp winter sun rose over the horizon gaining strength. She still had no answers.

I can't just sit here.

But what can I do?

None of this felt real; it was as if she wasn't really here. As if this wasn't her anymore. As if she was someone else entirely now, but she didn't know who that was.

No, that wasn't quite right. But she wasn't sure what version of her old self remained. It was like parts of her were lost and parts were found, but she didn't know which yet.

And then finally a calm, quiet voice spoke inside her. It was the kind of voice you'd hear even through a storm.

You get up and walk out of here.

Really? That was impossible.

No, you do it.

She got to her feet, unsteady and uncertain, but that voice was the first thing she'd heard inside her head for months that sounded sane. It was miles and miles across the mountains to get out of this place, so sane probably wasn't the right description, but at least the voice didn't sound like the chaos and destruction that had been screaming inside her before.

That was enough for now. Small comfort, but comfort still.

She knew this land. If she walked to the west, and walked and walked, eventually she'd come to the sea. It might take days, but that's where that path would take her. Through these hills, between the mountains, and down to the sea.

Cerys pulled her coat tighter around herself because it might not be cold enough to kill out here, but it was still chilly, and she started walking. No, this wasn't sane, but it was all she had.

And sometimes when there was nothing else left, you had to go with that.

⟋

Lily glanced into the rearview mirror at her sleeping child. His tousled hair stuck up at the front like hedgehog spikes, and his little mouth quivered occasionally in sleep, responding to his dreams.

She didn't know now where she had found the strength to do this at all. Desperation had given her wings that she never knew she had.

Because if I don't fly away, I won't make it.

And then what would become of her baby?

She knew the answer to that. That was why she kept driving, even though the tide of despair was beginning to rise and overwhelm her. That was why she'd keep on. She might be a crap mother...the worst...but she had to be better than the alternative.

She had to be.

She could hear his voice inside her head. It was always inside her head, whispering, threatening, telling her how she was nothing without him. The stench of burning flesh was there too—she could always smell that when she heard his voice speak in that way.

She took a left at the next ramp from the highway, going where they'd never find her.

4

IN THE END, CERYS DIDN'T have to walk the whole way to the sea, but she did walk for four hours without stopping. Somehow she'd once again found that loping country pace she'd had as a child. Though it made her legs ache from disuse and the atrophy of middle age, it still ate up the miles until she came to a village with a bus stop. It wasn't somewhere she'd ever been but typical of the area, with a few scattered farms, a collection of terraces along a main street, and a small post office in the middle. She checked the bus times on the board in the shelter. There was one due in twenty minutes, which was good timing, because then there wasn't another for three hours.

She pulled the cords on her hood so it tightened around her face and went into the post office.

"*Bore da*," the shopkeeper called.

"*Bore da*," she replied, and the woman smiled, recognizing her accent as local despite the time that had passed since she'd used her Welsh. She quickly bought a chocolate bar before the woman tried to engage her in further conversation. After all, she didn't want to be remembered.

Cerys wolfed the Snickers bar down at the bus stop while she waited. She was the only one there in the shelter, which was a relief. She counted the money in her purse. Fifty-six pounds and eighty-two pence. She'd thought she had less, but then she'd found a twenty-pound note jammed down behind some receipts. Goodness knows how long it had been there. Not that it would get her far.

The sugar in the chocolate hit fast on an empty stomach, and it lent her a glimmer of warmth until the bus pulled up. The driver was deep in conversation with a man in the front seat, and they obviously knew each other, so she was able to pay without either of them paying her much attention and take a seat near the back. There were only a couple of other people on the bus. One was a teenager with headphones in and her eyes glued to her phone and the other a man in laborer's work gear who was reading a newspaper. Neither looked up at her.

Good. Nobody to notice me here either.

She watched the hills speed by through the bus window. They cut off onto another road to travel through the mountains on a route she dimly remembered going on as a child on an occasional treat to the seaside. She made her mind stay empty—no thoughts to trouble it, just noticing the clouds over the mountain peaks, the bare skeletons of the trees, and the little silver streams that ran down the mountainsides. She shut out everything else.

Her mind felt still in a way it hadn't for so long.

Dod yn ôl at fy nghoed.

It was a Welsh phrase meaning to get back to a balanced state of mind. What it literally meant was "to return to my trees."

Tears sprang suddenly and unexpectedly in her eyes, and she focused determinedly on the view outside and blinked them away.

Not now, not here.

She concentrated on the trees until the bus rolled out of the mountains and climbed down the coast road. The gray Irish Sea lay ahead, white horses riding the choppy waves. She used to say that to Katie when she took her to the beach when she was small—"Look, white horses riding."

A barb of pain, swift as a dagger under the ribs, penetrated her careful shield.

She turned her eyes from the cold sea. A harsh sea, that stretch. Always had been, always would be. Maybe she shouldn't have come here.

Or maybe she should.

Maybe this sea was the answer for her.

The bus pulled into a turnout and drew to a stop. On impulse, she got up quickly and alighted. She didn't want to travel this road any longer. Time to get off. Her thoughts were illogical, and she was a creature acting entirely from instinct now. It had been so long since she hadn't had to consider anyone else in everything she did, that getting off that bus—just because she felt like it—was an act of rebellion.

The rain was falling heavier here, and she all at once felt very cold and old and tired. Her stomach growled, reminding her how long she'd been going, fueled only by one small chocolate bar. She looked around her. Houses stretched down the length of the road opposite the sea, but there was no sign to tell her what this place was called. It looked as if she could be on the outskirts of a small town, but she couldn't see far enough to be sure. The wind whipped up sea spray and drove it into her face, and she blinked at the salt sting.

She couldn't see anywhere she could buy food, so she guessed she'd have to walk again. She set off down the road, a long straight stretch that bent to the right a mile or so further along. The pavement was separated from the sea by a short section of pebbles and guarded by a white railing that ran the full length of the road as far as she could see.

God only knew where she was. But He probably didn't care any more than she did.

☙

It was midafternoon as Lily parked up in a side street opposite the seafront. This was their third stop now, and she was tired of driving. She'd laid the false trail though, heading across from the South West as far as Kent on the highways, making sure that if she was seen at all on CCTV, it would appear that she'd be on the other side of the country completely. Then she'd left the highway and the cameras, and wound her way through the connectors to head into Wales and the North. It had taken forever to get here, longer than she'd thought, and Sammy was fretful and desperate to get out of the car.

She zipped up his coat. She didn't have a hat for him. Of course not—she was too stupid to have thought of that. She pulled his hood up and tried to fasten it closely enough that the rough wind wouldn't yank it off. They walked back over the road to the burger van parked at the seafront. There wasn't much else there except the small toddler playground Sammy had spotted as they went past. He tugged at her sleeve, but she led him on toward the food van. "Later, if you eat all your food," she told him.

She bought burgers and chips and cans of fizzy drinks and they sat down at a battered picnic bench by the side of the playground. Sammy picked at his food, and she felt her irritation growing. Why couldn't he just eat it up? It was freezing here, and the light levels were dropping as if it would rain torrentially soon. It had been drizzling steadily until recently and although she'd tried to wipe the bench seat with some napkins from the burger van, she could feel the wet seeping through her jeans.

"Mummy!" Sammy wailed and she looked up to see he'd tipped all of his food onto the ground.

"Oh, for God's sake!" she yelled. He flinched back away from her, his mouth trembling in a way that betrayed tears were on the way. At the sight of that, she beat him to it and broke into sobs herself. She was a shit mother. She didn't know what she was doing. She'd dragged him here. It was freezing and wet and they had nowhere to go. And she just couldn't do this, and now she'd made him cry. She was shattered from the driving and the endless feeling of being afraid, as if at any moment *he'd* find them, and she'd tried so hard to prevent that. "Just no more, please," she sobbed, "I just can't do this…"

Cerys walked tiredly along the seafront. Her eyes were on that gray, chilled sea. Waiting for it to tell her. Wanting a sign that here, that now, this was what she should do. A cold pull from the waves, taking her toward them, would be all it took.

The smell of fried onions wafted through the damp air from a nearby burger van, making her mouth water. She passed a picnic table as a small boy accidentally tipped his food tray onto the ground with clumsy, still-baby hands. The young mother with him, who Cerys judged to be no older than Matt—early twenties—snapped at him in that worn-out and desperate way Cerys remembered feeling when her own were that age. As if your every last nerve was shredded and you just couldn't carry on anymore. Then the girl burst into tears and a second later, predictably, the little boy followed suit.

Cerys swooped down under the table and scooped up his food tray. Most of it had gone into the lid and little had been lost or in contact with the muddy grass. She discarded anything that looked as if it had touched the ground and placed the tray back on the table. The little boy sniffed as the tears rolled down his cheeks and he looked up at her with big green eyes. "See, everything's fine," she said, automatically smiling at him as she would have done at Matt when he was this age.

His mother didn't hear, her face still covered by her hands and her shoulders shaking with her sobs as if her heart was breaking.

Exhausted, Cerys thought. She put her hand lightly on the young woman's shoulder.

The girl jumped, startled, revealing her tearstained face. Eyes just like the little boy's, though her hair was more dark blond than nut brown.

"It's okay." Cerys smiled at her too and nodded at the boy poking a chip into his mouth and watching them curiously. "No harm done." She patted the thin shoulder reassuringly. "Sometimes they just wear you out, don't they? I know mine did."

Fresh tears sprang in the girl's eyes and she bit her lip and nodded.

"No harm done," Cerys repeated.

⌒

Lily stared up at the woman through her tears. A middle-aged woman with a capable face, the sort that meant she'd never been as hopeless as Lily was. The sort that put a roast dinner on the table every Sunday and thought nothing of it. The sort of woman Lily would never grow up to be in a million years.

The sort Sammy should really have as a mother.

"Thank you," she said tremulously, realizing the woman had rescued her son's food for her.

"Is it any good?" the woman asked, nodding at the burger in front of Lily. "I was just going to go and get one."

Lily grimaced. "Not great, but there's nothing else round here. I drove round and round this place looking for somewhere to get him something, but this was all I could find."

"Oh well, it will do," the woman said and gave her a last smile before she went to the van.

Lily shifted uncomfortably as she saw the woman get her food and then stand to one side, trying to balance the polystyrene tray and her can of Coke at the same time. On a reluctant impulse born solely out of gratitude to a stranger who hadn't needed to help her, Lily called out to her. "The seat's wet, but you're welcome to sit here." Sammy waved at the woman and grinned, still eating his chips.

She came over hesitantly. "I don't want to intrude."

"It's fine," Lily replied. "Sorry it's so wet."

"That's not your fault," she said, sitting down. She ate as if she was very hungry. Lily noticed that—she knew how it felt.

The stranger didn't ask any questions and Lily was relieved.

"My bum is wet," Sammy said, squirming around.

"I'll get you some fresh clothes when we get back to the car," Lily said hastily. At least she'd managed to bring a few changes of clothes with her. She hadn't been able to carry much though, or risk packing ahead and being caught out.

"Occupational hazard of living in Wales, having a wet bum," the woman said to him, and Lily finally registered she had a soft Welsh accent. "It rains a lot here, especially on this coast."

She'd taken them for tourists, Lily realized, and that was no bad thing.

Sammy was still eating, slow as only a four-year-old can be, and he wouldn't hurry up for all the weather conditions. Lily shivered in the wind. She wasn't sure how far they had left to go, and it was getting late. She had to find somewhere to stay, and that probably wouldn't be easy.

She cursed herself silently. Why couldn't she have thought about that earlier? Why couldn't she have planned? Instead of bolting blindly as she had done. *He* was right—she was useless. She'd sorted the car and the money. Why hadn't she finished the job properly and booked somewhere to stay?

Because courage and sense had deserted her when she'd got that far. She'd managed this much but more had proved beyond her.

Her hands began to tremble with the familiar fear, and she could feel her eyes beginning to well up again.

"When will we get there?" Sammy asked, chewing a bite of burger with frustrating slowness.

"I don't know," Lily answered, trying not to snap, "but a lot quicker if you hurry up and eat."

He huffed at her and carried on chewing at exactly the same speed. "Where are we going?"

Which was exactly the question she hadn't wanted him to ask in front of this woman. She didn't want anybody knowing where they were headed but she couldn't not answer or it would look suspicious. "There and back," she said, which was something her dad used to say way back when she was Sammy's age. Before he cleared off and left them.

The woman beside them finished her food and dusted her hands off, getting up. "Thanks for letting me sit here. I must be off."

"Us too," Lily said with a sigh. "I think I'll just wrap this up, and he'll have to eat it in the car. It's starting to rain again." She'd been trying to be a good mum and give him a break from the car seat after he'd been cramped up in it all night and day, but this was ridiculous. He wasn't even halfway through his food yet.

"I want the playground," he said with a wail, recognizing he was about to lose freedom.

The woman hid a smile. "Better finish that superfast then," she said. "Quick as you can."

Sammy began to gobble, and Lily could have screamed in frustration. Why couldn't he have done that for her?

"Sorry," the woman whispered to her, looking guilty. "I shouldn't have interfered. It just came out, like an instinct. My daughter was a slow eater too, you see."

"It's okay," Lily said, through clenched teeth. Yes, an instinct—one she didn't have and never would.

It must have shown on her face because the woman's expression turned to concern. "Are *you* okay though?" she asked. And on receiving no answer, she reached out and put her hand on Lily's coat sleeve. "You know, being a mother is the hardest job in the world, and there's no manual for it and, most of the time, nobody to tell you if you're doing a good job. And it's the most terrifying job you'll ever have, because all you want is to do the best for them, and ninety-nine percent of the time you won't know for sure what that is."

How did this woman know? How did she know how exhausted and useless Lily felt? Was she so bad at hiding it? Or was she just so hopeless that it was obvious to everyone?

The woman smiled at her and patted her arm again. "We're all winging it."

And oh God, she wanted to believe that. For it to obliterate all the crap in her head. All the failure. All the fear. She wanted someone to help her, to tell her how to do it right. To be her mum.

Her mum. Yeah, right—like that would help.

Lily sank to the ground on her knees and covered her face and sobbed. She had nothing left. No reserves. And she didn't know what to do next.

She was down to empty. And inside was that fear he'd been right all along about her.

5

CERYS STARED, APPALLED, AS THE young woman slumped to the ground. She glanced quickly at the little boy whose face had crumpled at the same time as his mother's legs.

"Oh dear, Mummy's a bit tired. Don't worry, she'll be fine. Why don't you pop over onto the playground before the rain comes in proper? Mummy just needs a cup of tea and she'll be all better." The child nodded hesitantly. "Off you go then—the gate's open, and we're right here."

He scampered off and Cerys crouched down beside the sobbing girl. "Oh *cariad*, what's wrong?" Because there was something very wrong here. She hadn't been a mother for twenty-seven years without knowing that.

"I can't do it," the girl sobbed, and Cerys recognized that she was only being told this because the girl was broken down to nothing. Cerys knew that place herself.

"What can't you do?" she asked as if it were Katie she was dealing with. She rubbed circles on the girl's back.

"I'm a crap mother. I can't do it. I can't," and the girl sobbed even louder.

"Of course you can; now tell me—what's your name?" Cerys put her arms around the girl, enfolding her.

There was a pause before the girl answered. "Lily."

"You listen to me, Lily. We all think that. Sooner or later—and usually sooner in my experience—we all think we're useless. We all break down, and we all realize how weak we are in the face of the magnitude of looking after a little person whose whole life and spirit is so dependent on us."

Lily looked up at her, her face red and puffy with tears. "You don't understand. I really am rubbish. I don't have any mother's instinct. I get everything wrong. I don't know how to be a mother. Not at all."

Cerys looked at her, trying to read what lay behind this. "Who told you that?" The girl shook in her arms as she tried to suppress breaking down again. "Never mind, now," she soothed. She somehow knew not to push any further. This girl had had enough. "I'm going to go to the van and get you a hot cup of tea. And we can watch your little boy play. Trust me, that'll cheer you up."

She helped Lily to her feet and went to get the tea. When she got back with two Styrofoam cups, she was standing by the playground gate watching the little boy rocking on a car on a spring. "Thanks," Lily said, taking the tea, her voice still thick with emotion. "I don't know why you would help me. I don't even know your name."

"Cerys," she replied because it didn't occur to her to lie in time to think of another name. "Why wouldn't I help you?" she found herself asking because it struck her as a curious comment for Lily to make.

The girl looked at her as if she didn't understand the question, or rather she found it unfathomable, then she shook her head and took a too-hot gulp of the tea.

"Have you got far to go?" Cerys asked because the afternoon light was fading fast.

"I don't know," Lily said miserably. "I think so. I think I've messed up."

"Why?"

"I didn't sort anywhere to stay, and it's going to be dark by the time we get there, and I don't know where to try."

Cerys frowned. It certainly wasn't how she would have planned a holiday trip with a little one. "Will you be staying at a hotel? You can check in quite late."

"I don't know." Lily chewed her lip. "I was going to…to…oh, I don't know really what I was going to do. I'm so stupid. I should have sorted this, but I need to make sure Sammy and I have somewhere to stay tonight."

It seemed bizarre more than stupid, but she strongly suspected Lily hadn't organized a holiday with a small child before, and criticism was the last thing the girl needed now.

"Holiday planning with little ones is never easy," she said, looking as reassuring as she possibly could. "Maybe I can help. You could always call ahead now and book in." From Lily's utterly blank look, she knew she was right: this girl had never booked anything herself before. She had a brief question in her mind about whether Lily had ever stayed at a hotel at all, she looked so baffled by the prospect. "Let me help," she said gently. "Where are you going?"

Lily took a deep breath. She looked nervous, maybe even scared, Cerys thought, which was even more strange. What was going on with this girl? It made Cerys uneasy, and suddenly she was very sure she didn't want Lily and Sammy driving off somewhere until she knew they had somewhere safe to stay. She had a bad feeling about whatever was going on with these two, and while Lily seemed caring but lost, there was a young child here and his safety had to be a priority. People weren't always what they seemed.

Sammy went whizzing down the slide.

"Careful," Lily called to him. She turned back to Cerys and sighed. "Anglesey. We're going to Anglesey."

Cerys nodded. "Beautiful place for a little holiday, especially with young children. Whereabouts?"

Lily shrugged, looking away. "I don't know. I hadn't got that far. I told you I was crap."

In normal circumstances, Cerys might have agreed in frustration at her lack of forethought, but she wasn't convinced that Lily was entirely as limp as she seemed at that moment. Her feeling that all wasn't well with these two wasn't abating.

"Beaumaris?" she suggested. "It's this side of the island, so the shortest drive, and there's lots there for little ones. Sammy will love it."

Lily shrugged. "I don't know it."

"Have you got a phone? I'll show you."

Lily went pale. "No."

"You don't have one?"

The girl hung her head and stared at her feet. "No."

Cerys drew a long breath. "Lily, what's going on here?"

Lily shuffled her feet, reminding Cerys of Katie when she was little and had been caught out in a lie. "I lost it."

"Lily, a mother doesn't take her child on holiday—with no place to stay—lose her phone, and just carry on into the middle of nowhere with no way of communicating with anybody. That just doesn't happen."

"I know," the girl mumbled. She looked up, her eyes brimming with tears again. "Can I borrow yours to look for somewhere to stay? Please? Please don't ask me anything else, but I need to find somewhere for us to stay tonight."

Cerys met her eyes steadily. "You could," she said, "and I'd lend it to you gladly, I really would, but—" She paused and held Lily's gaze. "But I don't have a phone either, you see."

6

IT DIDN'T FEEL LIKE A fog, the depression, or a mist—how Cerys had seen some people describe it—or even a sea.

It was like tar. Thick black tar that stuck your limbs together. That pulled you down inside yourself. Too viscous to get free. Everything too heavy, way too heavy, so you sunk lower and lower and nobody saw. Nobody noticed. It seemed nobody cared. You could give your whole life to looking after people, and then, when you failed, they left you alone inside your tar pit to drown.

Sooner or later she would sink completely, and then the black muck would fill her lungs and finish her.

And that's what had finally happened. That evening when she and Gavin had that final row. The tar rose over her head and filled her lungs until she couldn't breathe any longer.

Did some faerie on that mountainside pump her lungs free of it so she could live to breathe a little longer?

Crazy thinking. But no crazier than today and what she'd agreed to do.

That girl's face though. So young to be so broken. What had happened to her to make her feel like this? Like she was nothing.

That kind of feeling, that was for old crones like Cerys, not a girl just at the start of her adult life.

She'd looked at her and couldn't bear to see that pain reflected back. And Lily had asked for her help.

Too many years now of "Mum, stop fussing," and "Cerys, I'm busy—not now," meant the girl's plea was like a clarion call, and she'd responded instinctively. It was absolutely out of character, of course, and risked far too much. Not least that she'd be found and then what would she say? A bit different from not having to be there to face them because she'd ended it all.

How had everything got so muddled?

And what on earth was she going to do now?

She'd visualized them at home, eventually finding out she was dead. And they'd grieve and be sad for a short time. But secretly there'd be relief too, that she wasn't there to hold them back. They could be free and independent like they wanted, without the guilt of a mother clinging on when she really should let go gracefully.

Gavin had shouted that at her a few months ago when she'd ventured a complaint that they hadn't all been together for much too long. "For Christ's sake, Cerys, let them breathe! Let *me* breathe!"

She'd hated him that day, and hated herself too.

He'd seen it in her eyes as the exasperation faded from his face, and he'd reached out a hand to her in shock at what he'd finally said. And she'd turned away from him and left the room.

He was right. Her kids only wanted what she'd wanted at their age. It was normal and natural for them. But it didn't feel normal and natural for her.

That night in bed, she'd pushed him away and hadn't bothered to make an excuse that she was tired or anything like that. She just said, "No," flatly. He got the message. He didn't try again.

She didn't know whether she was sorry about that or not. But it didn't matter now. They were done.

7

LILY DROVE THE CAR DOWN the last stretch of road toward the Menai Suspension Bridge. Her eyes were tired from driving in the dark on unfamiliar roads. Sammy was muttering in the back about being hungry, despite his performance at the burger van.

"Not far now," Cerys told him and he seemed to take it better from her.

Lily didn't know what to make of her at all. Originally she'd taken her for some local woman, possibly a farmer's wife from the bedraggled appearance and the sensible waterproof jacket. Although she wasn't sure what farmers' wives wore or whether bedraggled would be a fair assumption as she'd never actually met one to talk to.

But then Cerys had pulled that line about the phone, and Lily suddenly knew…really *knew*…that there was a lot more going on with her than she'd thought.

They'd looked at each other in silence for a little while, each taking in the import of the other's lack of phone out here in such an isolated spot and what that might mean.

She knew the danger she was putting herself and Sammy in, but what else could she do? She had no way of finding accommodation now without help, and let's face it—she didn't know what she was doing. Lily had felt lost a lot in her life. It was sort of her default setting really. But right now, she felt as alone and confused and bloody useless as she ever had. Right now, she was all out of everything, and Sammy was at more risk if she didn't get help because she didn't know where she was going, and more importantly, what to do when she got there.

She'd just bolted like an idiot.

Yeah, but you did *it*, a little voice inside said. *You might have done it wrong but you did do it.*

And then Cerys had nodded at her, as if finding something in Lily's face that gave her an answer to a question Lily hadn't even known she was asking. "No names, no pack drill," she said to Lily, and held out her hand.

"Sorry?" Lily asked, not following.

"I won't ask you and you don't ask me," Cerys replied with a laugh. "I suppose you're too young to understand that phrase. It means mention no names or specific details, and then no blame or punishment—that's the pack drill part—can be given."

"Oh, I see," said Lily, who didn't entirely understand, but she got the general gist.

"Shake on it? You have things you don't want to tell and so do I—that right?"

Lily nodded and held her hand out cautiously. Cerys clasped it in hers and shook gently. Her hand was warm. It felt safe, Lily thought, although she also felt that was probably a stupid thought that didn't really make sense. But it made her feel better.

"Do you want me to help you find somewhere to stay?" Cerys asked.

Lily sighed. "Yes, please." She shouldn't need this help. She was a mother. She should be able to do this, but actually she had no idea where to start.

"Come on then." Cerys got up and walked with her to the car.

"But where were you going?" Lily asked.

"Nowhere," Cerys replied.

Lily almost asked what she meant but something in Cerys's face stopped her. *No names, no pack drill indeed.*

Cerys knew which way to go so they headed out down the road out of Bangor until they got to the Menai Suspension Bridge. Lily got confused at the roundabout, so Cerys told her to go round again and then talked her through the exits so she came off at the right one this time. Lily's knuckles tensed on the wheel at her mistake, and she could feel her knees shaking even when they were on the right road and following a sign that said Beaumaris. She realized she was waiting for the shouting to start, for the abuse, even though he wasn't there.

Sammy was still grumbling in the back of the car, but it was easier to tune out as they got closer to their destination.

It was too dark to see the coastline, but it seemed she hadn't been driving long after the bridge before they wound into streets of picturesque Georgian houses painted in fondant colors. Although Lily was concentrating on negotiating the narrow streets, she couldn't help but be charmed. "Oh, it's pretty!"

"Pretty colors," Sammy chimed in from the back.

"Isn't it?! It's just like I remember it," said Cerys. "I haven't been here in a long time, but it's as lovely as I remember. Now, if I'm right, there are hotels down here. Take a right. It's okay, don't worry—take your time."

Lily steered around a tight bend and out onto a wider road with a lamplit pier stretching out ahead as the road curved. She followed the line nervously.

"Left into this drive here," Cerys said and Lily was so intent on steering that she didn't look up at where she was going. "Park there," Cerys said and Lily pulled into an empty bay.

"I remember this place," Cerys said. "I can check here for you to see if they have any vacancies."

Lily looked out and gasped. They were outside a hotel with a grand Georgian frontage, with stone balconies and ornate windows. "Don't worry—it's not as expensive as it looks," Cerys said with a laugh. "Or at least it wasn't. I'll check the prices before you commit. But it was always known for being very family-friendly. Somebody I know stayed here not too long ago and said it was still the same."

Lily couldn't speak for a moment. "I can't go in there," she stuttered finally. "What would I say…? I don't know how to…"

Cerys reached over and held her hand for a second. "Don't worry. I'll do it. Come on. And you don't have to stay here if you don't like it. We're just checking it out."

They got out of the car, Sammy shivering in the brisk wind off the sea. Cerys shepherded them in through the grand doors into a thickly carpeted hall. Lily looked around her. She'd never been anywhere like this in her life. An impressive staircase rose in front of them with turned balustrades. There were alcoves set into the walls with enormous decorative vases. She gulped.

"Come on," said Cerys, ushering them through to a room with a terrifyingly large wooden counter. A man in an equally terrifyingly formal uniform stood behind the desk, typing something onto a computer screen. He looked up as they approached and arranged his features into a professional smile.

"Good evening, ladies." He looked down and saw Sammy. "And gentleman. Can I help you?"

"Hi," Cerys said with a confident smile, and Lily blinked at how at ease she seemed to be with what appeared to Lily to be a fearsome situation. Cerys might be standing there in a travel-stained raincoat with bedraggled hair, but she sounded completely at home here. "Do you have any rooms available?"

"Certainly," the man replied, smiling back in a way Lily knew he wouldn't have if it had been her approaching the counter. "We've got a few rooms vacant at the moment—suites and doubles. How long are you wanting to stay?"

"Not sure yet. Maybe just the night but possibly a few days. What's your rate for a twin room?"

Lily tugged on her sleeve. "You are staying too, aren't you?" she hissed urgently.

Cerys smiled at the receptionist. "Just give us a moment," and she stepped away from the counter. "I wasn't," she whispered back.

"You can't leave me here," Lily begged. "Please."

Cerys seemed to deflate in front of her. "I didn't bring much money with me," she admitted. "I wasn't planning on this, you see. And I can't go to a bank because…"

Because she had no money, or because she'd be found? Lily had a funny feeling that Cerys was hiding from something, or someone, too. Maybe she was wrong, maybe she was projecting, but that's how it struck her. And maybe, actually, she was exactly right because it took one to know one, right?

"I have enough," Lily said, pulling herself up to her full height, which she was aware wasn't very much, but it felt important to stand tall in this place. "And I don't think I can do this without you. I've never stayed anywhere like this before." She swallowed hard. "I've never booked a room before. I don't even know how to."

"I can't impose like that," Cerys said, but Lily saw an opening. Cerys did look genuinely torn.

"It's not imposing, it's helping," she pleaded. "Just one night. Please? I really can't do this on my own."

The man at the counter was watching, and it was starting to get uncomfortable. "Okay," Cerys said, "but I'll get you the cheapest option."

She turned back to the counter and gave him that smile again, the one that said she knew what she was doing, the type that Lily would never acquire.

Ten minutes later, they were standing in a suite with twin beds and a sofa that pulled out to make another bed for Sammy. The paint did look a bit tired in places, and the en suite bathroom looked more "old" than "period," but it was still the grandest room Lily had ever stayed in. Cerys had booked them in for a three-day stay in the end because there was a special discount deal on, so it worked out as a very good value.

"This place needs some money spending on it," Cerys said, looking around with a critical eye, "but never mind, because that makes it a good value for now, and that's why people come here."

At that, Lily wondered what kind of places Cerys normally stayed in.

"Do you want to eat in the restaurant, or nip round the corner for fish and chips?" Cerys asked, looking out of the window onto the street below. Sea views were more expensive.

"Fish and chips," Lily replied fervently. Facing a restaurant with an exhausted child who should be in bed wasn't a prospect she fancied at all.

"Come on, then," Cerys said. "We can eat in. Let's get him fed and to bed as soon as we can before he gets cranky."

She let Cerys navigate to the fish and chip shop and deal with the order. She found a table and settled Sammy down. Fortunately at this time of year, the place wasn't filled and they didn't have to wait long.

She looked Cerys over again now that she had more time to study her. Sammy snuggled up under her arm and coiled little fingers around hers. She'd place Cerys in her early fifties, perhaps? And although her dark hair looked like she'd spent the day in rough weather on the hills, Lily realized when Cerys smoothed it down that her hair was a precision-cut bob. It wouldn't have been cheap, and Lily paused for a moment to appreciate the workmanship of the unknown hairdresser. Mature hair wasn't the easiest to handle either, but with a good blow-dry, she knew that it would look great. No trace of gray there at all, carefully covered by tonal highlights in varying shades of honey and chestnut. That outdoor coat of hers had been soaking wet when they'd first met, but now it had dried out Lily could see that it was relatively new, and she suspected it wasn't cheap either.

No handbag, or indeed any other kind of bag. Just a leather purse shoved in her pocket. What had she been doing when they met? Was she even from that area?

Lily shook her head at her own impulsiveness. She'd never learn. She'd just taken this woman in her car, knowing nothing about her, and driven off. Not that she had bad vibes about Cerys; far from it. But what was she doing out there?

What's your story?

8

THIS GIRL DIDN'T HAVE A clue, bless her. Even Katie, only a year into university, would have more idea than her how to go about things. Cerys couldn't quite make her out; though she strongly suspected that there was a lot more to the girl's story than was immediately obvious. That was a given, really. She'd long since worked out that this wasn't really a holiday, no matter how Lily might try to make it appear. Nobody, no matter how clueless, went on an unplanned holiday with a four-year-old and had nowhere to stay and then appeared terrified of actually going to deal with that when she got there.

Cerys paid for the fish and chips and cans of pop from her meager stash, then watched as, this time with a better-cooked meal in front of him, the little boy dug into the food with the usual enthusiasm of a child faced with chips. Cerys wasn't surprised when his fatigue took over and he slowed down after a few mouthfuls. Lily was obviously hungry, which again reminded Cerys how young she was because she devoured hers in the same way Cerys's boys used to attack their food as teenagers. Alex and Matt have a little more decorum these days, though she wouldn't put it past Matt to wolf food like this if she wasn't around.

"Let me," she said quietly to her as Lily tried to coax him to eat more while trying to eat her own food too. "You've had a long drive—take a break and eat your dinner."

She scooted onto the bench next to Sammy and cut his fish up into easy bites. "Sip of lemonade, bite of fishy," she said, laughing as she gave him a slurp from his pop, carefully decanted into a plastic cup so he didn't cut his mouth on the can, and then followed by airplaning a forkful of fish into his mouth. "Om-nom-nom!" He chewed obediently. And that was the key with them at this age when they were tired or grumpy—make everything a game. He was too old for this kind of treatment normally, but children seemed to regress when tired and appreciate the comfort of being babied, and from Sammy's cheerful acquiescence, she knew she'd made the right call.

She caught an odd look from Lily as she wolfed down her chips. Hard to read, but not hostile. Perhaps wistful, and it almost appeared that the girl might cry again.

"I want him to have a good holiday," Lily said. "I want that more than anything."

The unspoken words "I don't know how to make that happen" were almost audible, almost slipped from her mouth, Cerys thought.

"How old is Sammy—three? Four?"

"Four last month."

She looked so young and crestfallen, Cerys just had to ask, "How old were you when you had him?"

"Eighteen." She looked ashamed. Someone had made her feel that way. Cerys wondered who.

So very, very young. At that age, her Katie had been packing her suitcase to leave for uni, not becoming a mother. Cerys had been teaching her how to cook well for herself and budget her shopping, not how to change nappies. That made Lily twenty-two now, younger than Matt. The thought of him looking after a four-year-old on his own! No wonder Lily felt a little lost with it all. She wondered how much help she'd had with the little boy from her own mother. Those early years were so very hard, no matter how old you were, and Cerys remembered how much her mother had helped out, especially when her eldest, Alex, was born, and she felt helpless and clueless. The fatigue of those first weeks was still etched in her memory, and her mother had left the farm in Wales and installed herself in the spare bedroom. Before Alex was born, she'd scoffed at the suggestion. She wouldn't need her mother there. She was twenty-six, and she had plenty of energy. And she knew what she was doing. She'd helped out with her sister Rhiannon's babies often enough.

"Mum wants to come and stay," she'd told her sister, still slightly aghast at the news. "How do I tell her no?"

"Don't," her sister had replied firmly. "No matter how much you think you won't need her now, trust me, you'll be sobbing with gratitude that she's there after a week."

And Rhiannon, proud mum of four vigorous children under ten, was absolutely right, it turned out. Cerys's mother came to stay for a while after the birth of each of her three children. and Cerys was profoundly grateful for every minute of it. She remembered three days after Alex's birth, sitting there at six a.m. trying to feed, exhausted because he'd hardly slept, and her mother bringing her a cup of tea while Gavin slept on peacefully and oblivious in the room next door. Her eyes filled with tears as her mother took the baby to give her a break and let her drink her tea, and she rocked him as Cerys snuggled into a blanket, cold from lack of sleep. She looked up at her mother and her son. "I'm sorry," she said, a tear rolling down her face. "I understand now."

Her mother smiled and chuckled softly as she rocked her grandson. "I said the same to my mother," she said, "after Rhiannon was born. You can never know what it's like until you have your own."

And she was right. Suddenly Cerys had become part of a secret club that it was impossible to understand before initiation, but one which utterly changed your life forever.

She realized Sammy had come to the end of his chips. She'd been feeding him the entire time she'd been lost in thought without realizing it, so automatic was it still for her, even though her kids were long grown past that. Lily had finished too and was watching her thoughtfully.

"Penny for your thoughts," the girl said.

"I was thinking about my mother," Cerys said. "She's been dead four years now and I still miss her every day." That loss had devastated her at the time, and still did in so many ways. She wasn't sure she'd ever be the same again. She'd felt adrift without a compass on a strange, unfathomable sea ever since she lost her.

Something unreadable crossed Lily's face and her mouth pursed. Normally people made a polite comment on hearing of a bereavement, so it was surprising that Lily said nothing at all.

"Past his bedtime," Cerys said softly as, now that his tummy was full, the child beside her began to droop against her arm. "Shall we get him back?"

Lily seemed to return to herself. "Oh yes, we should. And thank you so much for your help. I don't know what I'd have done without you today. I really don't," she said with such utter sincerity that it struck at something inside Cerys.

They went back to the hotel and settled the little boy into the sofa bed. He was asleep almost as soon as his head touched the pillow. "Is he an easy sleeper?" Cerys asked as she smiled at the sight of the child snuggled down under the covers, only the shock of brown hair and the tip of his nose visible.

"He is," said Lily watching him, with that kind of quietly fierce protection in her face that Cerys recognized. "I've been lucky that way. And once he's down he doesn't often wake."

"Would you like a hot chocolate?" Cerys asked, nodding at the hospitality tray on the bureau.

Lily looked at it as if she didn't know what it was. "Oh!" she exclaimed and went to examine it. It reminded Cerys of the first time they'd taken Katie to stay in a hotel and she'd run to look at what was in the selection in excitement, only Katie had been about seven, not a grown woman. "Oh, there are biscuits too!"

Cerys's heart broke a little for her.

"You get ready for bed," she said as if Lily was her seven-year-old Katie. "I'll make you a hot chocolate, and—I tell you what—we'll rebel and eat biscuits in bed! Who's to stop us?" She winked conspiratorially and was rewarded with a grin from Lily.

What a pretty girl when she smiles, Cerys thought. She hadn't realized that about her before, seeing her so worried and careworn and damp with the rain. But with a smile on her face, she looked like a different girl. Too thin though. It didn't suit her. It made her face pinched and harried.

Sitting in bed, eating the biscuits, and sipping the hot chocolate, Lily looked lost. Cerys wondered how they would go on in the morning when she had to go. This room was booked for three days, and she'd thought that would give Lily time to sort herself, but she was quickly realizing that maybe Lily might not know how. Cerys had wrapped herself in the complimentary bathrobe to sleep in as she had no other clothes, of course. Borrowing something from Lily was out of the question. She was tiny, and even a T-shirt wouldn't stretch over Cerys's middle-aged spread. She pulled the bathrobe glumly around herself so she didn't have to see the result of too many lonely nights on the sofa with only a tub of ice cream for company.

She took the cup from Lily when she'd finished. The girl's eyes were heavy with fatigue, and she brushed the crumbs from the duvet for her. "Thanks," said Lily, almost as though Cerys's actions pained her, but her face told a different story, one of gratitude. Why did her voice break on the word then?

Cerys was too tired herself to make more sense of it. She got into her bed, and at least the mattress was comfy. She hated hotel beds with bad mattresses. If you were going to get one thing right as a hotel, it should at least be a decent bed.

It was a strange thing to go to sleep knowing by rights you shouldn't still be here, but at least now she could sleep for a while and deal with the morning when it came. One hour at a time, that's how she would get through this. And if that got too hard, she'd take it minute by minute. That way she didn't have to think about what lay behind her.

When she considered what happened this morning, and the shock of waking up at all, she could feel her body begin to tremble. The whole point had been to make all the pain stop, but when that hadn't worked, the option of just sitting there and waiting for it to come more slowly, days maybe, hadn't actually been an option at all. Her body simply hadn't let her. It had programmed her to flee senselessly, as if she could escape the pain and emptiness that way. Of course, she couldn't—life didn't work like that.

But Lily and Sammy had been a distraction from it, had thrown her right back into practical mode and given her something to do. Something that felt normal and like the old her.

It had been a long, long time since she'd felt like someone she recognized. It almost felt good.

9

DANNY STARED OUT OF THE front window. So, she was gone. Really gone. And he had no idea where. He hadn't seen this coming. Not at all.

She was okay yesterday, wasn't she? She'd seemed fine, just her usual self. He racked his brain for evidence of anything different or out of the ordinary. There was no sign of a note, and he could only see a few clothes missing. He wasn't sure if she'd taken a suitcase or not.

Why? Why would she do this to him? He'd given her everything. She hadn't wanted for anything. A nice house, her own car—that she hadn't even taken with her—decent clothes. Everything she'd never had before him. And it obviously hadn't been enough for her.

When he woke yesterday morning, she was up already. That wasn't a surprise. She was usually up first. She'd be showered and have done her hair and makeup before he stirred. He liked her to keep herself smart, and he took pride that she'd not let herself go after having Sammy. Running a small business like his was tough, and appearances mattered. This was a small town, and people talked. It was important to keep standards up, and that included his wife.

He had showered and gone downstairs. He had to be off soon, a meeting a couple of counties away, trying to get a contract for cleaning a big firm. It would be a coup if he could land this, but he knew there was strong competition for this one. He'd need to be on top form to talk them into choosing him, as he suspected he was the smallest and least well-known of the companies bidding. Even at his best, he wasn't sure he could do it, but Fortune loved a trier, and that's what he'd always been.

The house was oddly quiet as he went into the kitchen. He had hoped she'd got the coffee machine on already and that she'd remembered what he had on today and got his breakfast ready. Not that she should have forgotten because he'd mentioned how important this was enough times in the past week.

But there was nobody there. The lights were all off, and it didn't look like she'd been down at all. Puzzled, he went back upstairs and checked into the little 'un's room, but it was as empty as the kitchen, the covers thrown back on the bed. He put his hand on the mattress, beginning to have a bad feeling about this, but it was cold. Hadn't been slept in for a while.

His heart began to thump painfully against his ribs as he hurried through the house, looking for them, his sense of dread growing. They were gone, but the car was still there, so maybe he was overreacting. Maybe they'd gotten up early and gone for a walk or something. He'd never known her to do that before, but it was more likely than her taking off.

Wasn't it?

With a sick feeling in his stomach, and with sweat slicking his palms, he got his phone and checked his banking app.

And then he sank to his knees in shock.

No, she couldn't be gone! She couldn't have done this to me! No!

10

LILY SURVEYED CERYS RUBBING HER freshly showered hair dry and pulling out the tangles with her fingers. Sammy was still asleep. Cerys picked up the hair dryer and was about to rough-dry it when Lily stopped her. "Let me? Please."

"Okay," Cerys replied, surprised, but she sat down in front of the dressing table. Lily picked up a brush from inside her carryall and began to dry Cerys's hair, first with a quick allover blast and then section by section, lifting and volumizing and smoothing.

Cerys gave a grin of delight. "You're a hairdresser!"

Lily grimaced. Maybe she shouldn't have given so much away, but she couldn't resist the chance to pick up a brush and give something back to this woman who'd done so much for her yesterday. And it was such a small thing, but who didn't feel better when their hair was properly done? "I used to be," she admitted. "I haven't been for a while now." She could hear the longing in her voice.

"Well, you're very good," Cerys said, watching, impressed, as her bob became her stylist's original intent again under Lily's fingers. It had been beautiful when it was first cut, and she'd had the same style for years now, but she'd lost interest in looking good. She went to the same hairdresser by default, but in between cuts she made little effort with it. Her limbs seemed so heavy these days and her head so tired. Getting old, she supposed. Somehow she hadn't thought aging would come so soon. Or so hard. It didn't seem to have hit her friends as badly, and she was so jealous of the energy they still had.

Lily blushed at the compliment and said nothing, focusing determinedly on Cerys's hair and adding a final shine with a cool blast from the hair dryer.

"Mummy," a sleepy voice said from behind them. "Mummy?"

She put the hair dryer down quickly. "I'm right here," she answered, hurrying over to the little boy who was poking his head out of the covers.

"Where am I?" he asked, sounding fretful.

"On holiday, in the hotel. We're on holiday—remember?"

"Oh yes." He snuggled back down again drowsily, but Cerys knew it would only be minutes before he was up and bouncing around in that way only children can first thing in the morning.

Her clothes had dried out and had a good airing in the bathroom overnight, and she'd washed her underwear in the sink, but she would still have liked a change of clothes this morning. Never mind; her shiny, perfectly groomed hair lifted her a bit when they went down to breakfast. Sammy held her hand on the way down the stairs while Lily followed behind, nervous and out of her comfort zone again.

She was even less comfortable when they got into the large dining room with its ornate drapes at the long windows looking out over the sea and the tiny harbor. She shrank behind Cerys when the waitress came over and asked for their room number to seat them. Cerys picked a table by the window so Sammy could watch the boats. There weren't many in the dining room yet, just a number of elderly couples making their way slowly through large plates of full Welsh breakfasts. Cerys smiled; it never ceased to amaze her just how much food those tiny old ladies could pack away.

It was the usual hotel breakfast buffet arrangement. Cerys scanned the options with Sammy by her side and talked him through the choice of cereals and hot food. Lily hovered beside her, silent and biting her lip. "It all comes with the room rate," Cerys whispered to her, "so take advantage and get whatever you want."

"What are you having?" Lily whispered back as Sammy surveyed the options of Coco Pops or cornflakes.

"I'd normally go for the continental option and get some yogurt and fruit and muesli, then maybe a pastry," she said with a chuckle. "But I don't think this place has quite grasped the principles." She pointed to the tiny selection of unappetizing sliced cheese and salami, meager yogurts, and tinned fruits decanted into a bowl. "It looks like something from the seventies, but I suspect they think their guests will only go for the traditional options, given the age of most of them in here, so they don't make much effort. I think I'll have to give in and join them and get a cooked breakfast instead. Why don't you have one too? It does look very good."

Lily's eyes turned to the trays of sausages and bacon and eggs with all the accompaniments. "It does look a lot nicer, you're right," she answered. "Will they let Sammy have a sausage? He likes those."

"Sammy can have whatever he wants. He's on the room rate too. He can have cereal first and then a sausage. How about that, Sammy?"

Sammy pointed to the Coco Pops and Lily started to fill up a bowl for him. A woman of around Cerys's age bustled past them with a small boy of about five. "No, Michael, absolutely not. You're not having those—far too much sugar," she said when he made a move toward the Coco Pops too.

Lily recoiled as if she'd been bitten, her face paling as she watched the woman pour muesli from the dispenser instead, deaf to the wail of "But Grandma..." and sail off with the child in tow.

Cerys nudged her. "I always let mine have whatever they wanted on holiday. That's what holidays are for. Anyway, it teaches them that treats are for certain times and healthy eating for the rest. If you never let them have anything, they just rebel when they're old enough and do it behind your back."

Lily smiled tremulously with relief and carried on filling the bowl with chocolate cereal.

Back at the table with a view, Sammy ate and gabbled between mouthfuls about the boats he could see from the window. The weather was bright for November, with a clear sky. "Chilly but sunny," Cerys remarked.

"You can go crabbing on that pier," she said to Lily. "That'll keep him busy for a while. I expect he'll love that. Last time I was here, there were lots of little ones doing it."

"Will you come?" Lily looked up from her breakfast with hopeful eyes, and the words of refusal dried up in Cerys's throat.

What difference will one more day make?

"Yes, if you want me to."

"Oh, I do! Sammy will too."

Sammy had his mouth full of sausage and tried to smile through it.

His mother didn't have the confidence to do this on her own, and the child deserved a nice day, didn't he? The relief in his mother's eyes helped dam that pool of blackness inside that so often threatened to drown Cerys completely.

⌒

Lily didn't know what she was going to do after their time in the hotel ran out. She stood on the pier and looked around this place, Beaumaris, with its pretty fondant-colored houses and the view back toward the Welsh mainland, and then ahead out to sea. She could taste the salt on her lips. Cerys was sitting on the wooden boards beside Sammy, their legs dangling companionably over the edge of the pier while they strung the crab pot and lowered it down to the sea. She knew how to play with him in a way Lily didn't understand. She knew how to be with him to make him happy.

For a brief moment, Lily considered that the best option for Sammy was her running away down the pier, disappearing, and never coming back. It was a dream where he'd stay with Cerys and she'd look after him the way he should be looked after and he'd never miss his useless mother. But that would never happen—they'd never let Cerys keep him, even if she wanted to. And what did she know about Cerys anyway? Even the idea showed what a crap mother she was, and a stupid one.

Yeah, she'd got no idea what she'd do in two days' time, and all she could think of was trying to make a nice day for him today. One day to make up for the rest of this bloody mess and the shitty life she was giving him.

She remembered when she'd first held her baby in her arms and that rush of emotion that she was going to give her child something so much better than she'd ever had. Then reality had set in and soured that dream. Like all her dumb dreams. She was just one of those people in life who for some reason didn't deserve any better than the shit she got. She didn't know why—that's just how it was. Some girls grew up with big houses and ponies and glittering, charmed worlds full of happiness, and she got what she'd got.

Not a thing she could do about it. It was what it was, and always would be. When she watched Cerys with Sammy, she knew how far away she was from that stupid dream of giving him a better life. She couldn't get out of the starting blocks with that one.

Oh, but she wanted to, something inside her cried. So, so much. Why? Why couldn't that dream be his life? It just wasn't fair. All because he'd been born to a dumb bitch like her.

"Are you okay?" Cerys asked. They'd set the crab pot and come back to her side.

"Just thinking," Lily said, unable to stop the sour twist of her mouth.

"Can I get him an ice cream?" Cerys asked, "and do you want one?"

"Yes, sure, but not for me."

Cerys sniffed. "Well, I'm getting one. Are you sure?"

Lily needed to watch her weight. What if she got fat? She wasn't supposed to get fat.

And then she stopped herself, a little bubble of anger rising inside her. What the hell did that matter now? She could get fat if she wanted, couldn't she?

Yes, she could. Screw him!

She smiled at Cerys. "Yes, please. Raspberry ripple's my favorite, if they've got it."

Cerys took Sammy to choose his, and he skipped down the pier beside her. Lily watched them go. How did you get to be a woman like that? A woman to whom motherhood came easy. A better woman. She wished she knew.

She realized people probably thought that Cerys was Sammy's grandmother, and that realization hit her like a physical blow in the stomach. If only he really did have that. If only that was her life too.

Cerys came back with a double cone of raspberry ripple with chocolate and sprinkles. "All the trimmings," she said, and something in Lily hurt again but also warmed at the gift. Such a little thing to some people but not to her. And it was then she started to formulate a plan of sorts. Or one of her dreams. She wasn't quite sure which, but it made sense to her right there and then. It felt good and so little did feel good these days that maybe, just maybe, this was worth trying for. But she kept quiet while she ate her ice cream and got her thoughts together.

Later. She'd talk to Cerys about it later.

They went to the park then and took turns pushing Sammy on the swings. Or at least Cerys started that and Lily watched again, until Cerys said something to him and laughed and turned to Lily. "He wants Mummy now. Come on, your turn and my arms can get a break." And Lily tried to push him just the way Cerys did, smiling the same way as he squealed and asked to go higher. But she was acting, always acting. It didn't feel natural, not like it did for other women, but maybe if she copied Cerys she'd learn to understand.

It was odd. She wanted to make him happy, in fact the happiest child on the planet, if she had her way. But she could never see any way to do that with her there. When she was with him, it was as if everything was at a distance, as if there was a barrier between them, and she couldn't break through it. Maybe even as if she wasn't real, as if she wasn't there. Whatever it was, she knew it was wrong. Mothers weren't supposed to feel that way.

No maternal instinct.

Now, Cerys had that in bundles. She was so lucky. Luck wasn't really a thing though, was it? Just some women deserved it and others, like her, didn't.

But despite everything life had thrown at her and how broken that had made her feel day after day, she would kill to keep her child safe. Oh yes, she would. She would die herself without a second thought, but she would kill too if she needed to.

He didn't know that about her. She wondered if he'd ever known her at all.

11

IT HAD BEEN A LOVELY day. Magical, really. Cerys hadn't felt this way in what seemed to be forever, as if the blackness was so far away it might never have existed. The winter sun had burned bright, and they'd wrapped up warm against the wind coming in off the sea. Sammy had found some crabs in his pot, and his face had lit with that joy that made Cerys want to cry, because all that treasure seemed so long ago in the past, those moments that had made her days worth living and the sleepless nights and arguments over fussy eating seem unimportant. From the moment she knew she was pregnant with Alex, she had lived her life for her children. God knows she hadn't always got it right—far from it—but she had given them every scrap of her energy, her commitment, her time. And she'd never begrudged a second of that. Moments of frustration, yes, where she'd snapped at them because she'd gotten tired, like every mother in the whole world. But if she stopped and took stock, she didn't resent a second of it. They were her whole life.

She had remembered the joy of those days as she'd watched Sammy eat ice cream, as she'd pushed him on the swings, as she'd helped him examine the crabs, as they'd all walked out together down the pebbly beach and scrabbled about in the rock pools. Just the pudginess of little hands was a pleasure to be around again.

At three o'clock, they went back to the hotel for afternoon tea and ordered little sandwiches and cakes. It transpired that Lily had never had a scone with clotted cream and jam, so she didn't know what to do with hers.

Cerys had to show her. It seemed such a simple treat to have missed out on, and Cerys wondered what else this girl had missed in her life. Lily didn't look like she smiled a lot. She looked like she'd forgotten how, and Cerys knew how that was.

But not at her age; that was the sad thing about this girl's melancholy.

Still, it was time for Cerys to go. It had been a beautiful day to finish on, but it had to end. She had no idea what would come next, but this couldn't go on forever.

She needed to be alone to decide where she went from here.

"I need to get going soon," she said as Lily took the final bite of her scone. She looked as if she'd enjoyed it, and that gave Cerys some satisfaction. A first cream tea wasn't remarkable as a gift, but she thought maybe this girl hadn't had much, so every little thing gathered more importance than for other people.

Lily gasped and put the remains of the scone down. "No! We're booked in for another two nights, aren't we?"

"The room's booked, yes—" Cerys was startled by the look of horror on the girl's face "—but I need to go."

Tears started in Lily's eyes. "Why? Did I do something wrong?"

Cerys was horrified. "No, *cariad*, of course not! It's been a lovely day. I've enjoyed being with you. More than you can possibly imagine, in fact. But I never intended to come here, and I can't impose on your generosity any longer."

"It's not imposing," Lily hissed urgently, dashing tears away before Sammy saw. "It's helping! If anyone's imposing, I am by asking you to stay here and help us. And I know that and I'm sorry, but I don't know how to do this on my own."

Cerys handed her a napkin. "Do what on your own?"

Lily's face screwed up in a pain so real that Cerys could feel it inside her too. "Be a mother!"

Sammy looked up from his cupcake in surprise, distracted from his task of licking all the icing off before eating it. "Everything's fine," Cerys reassured him. "You eat your cake."

"See?" Lily said in a broken voice.

"What I see," said Cerys firmly, "is a young mum trying to do her very best for her little boy. We're not born knowing how to mother, you know. We learn it. We learn it from our own mothers, and then from our mistakes, and we spend every day hoping to God we don't make any mistakes that matter too much. And you know what, sometimes we do and then we do our best to fix it. You're doing fine."

"But I didn't learn it from—" And then she stopped dead and shook her head in despair. She took a deep, shuddering breath and looked Cerys in the eyes. Cerys could see it took all her courage to do that. "So what are *you* doing here? You've got no phone, no bag. You were just walking when we met you. Where were you going before I dragged you away?"

"Nowhere," Cerys said. "I was going nowhere." She wouldn't lie to the girl. She could see how much it cost her to ask these questions, and she wondered who had taught her to be so afraid of others.

"Do you live in that place we met you?"

"No, a long way from there."

"Then why were you there? Just walking in the rain."

Cerys stared out of the window at the sea. "I tried to kill myself the night before and it didn't work." She spoke quietly so the child didn't pay attention to her and would have no comprehension of what this was about. "I walked because I didn't know what else to do. I think I was probably going to try to work out how to do it again and succeed this time, but I hadn't gotten that far. I was numb."

Lily gasped, her hand flying to her mouth in horror. She had thin little fingers, Cerys noticed. There looked to be no strength in them, like a child's. Clever little fingers though, she thought, remembering them drying her hair that morning.

"*Why?*"

Cerys shook her head. "My life stopped being of any value," she said.

Lily nodded miserably. "I understand that. Not the dying part, but that feeling."

Of course she did, poor girl; she had her own secrets to keep—that much was very clear.

They sat in silence for a while. Sammy helped himself to another cake, and Cerys couldn't help but smile just a little as he bit into it with satisfaction. "He's a lovely kid," she said. "You must be very proud of him."

Lily frowned in confusion. "I don't think I am." Her lip wobbled again. "I don't think I can get past the guilt to feel anything like that."

"Oh, Lily, you shouldn't feel that way—not at all."

"Mostly I don't feel anything. Just numb. I wanted to be a good mum."

"And you are." She sighed as Lily shook her head. "Why are you here, Lily? You're not really on holiday."

Lily closed her eyes, her teeth biting down so hard on her lip that Cerys was surprised she didn't draw blood. The girl rocked slightly, like a child trying to shut the world out and comfort herself. It was painful to see. "To give him something better than I had," she said finally. "But I can't. I'm too stupid." Her eyes flew open. "You know how stupid I am? Out there today, I had this idea and I was going to tell you and try to convince you, but there's no point now, because you're going to leave." She trembled with something that looked like betrayal in her eyes.

"What was your idea?" Cerys said softly, and she had no idea why she asked that because it really wasn't helpful to her own situation. Except she couldn't stand to see that look on Lily's face.

"No, it's stupid."

"It doesn't matter. I still want to hear it. It's important because it's what you wanted."

"Yeah, but I'm an idiot."

"I don't think so. Please tell me." She reminded Cerys so much of her own kids when they were disgruntled teens trying to wrestle with emotions too big for them to manage. It hurt her to remember them. Every moment of their childhoods was so precious, no matter how frustrating it had felt at the time.

Lily's eyes were empty of hope, empty of everything. "I thought you might stay with us, for a while, maybe a few months or even longer if you don't have anywhere you need to be. I thought I could find somewhere to rent, and a job. And you might like to take care of Sammy while I was at work, and he would like that because he really likes you and spending time with you. I had this stupid, thick idea in my head like we were a little family and it looked great. But that's because I'm a dumb bitch."

Cerys sucked her breath in sharply and her eyes flew to Sammy, who was staring at his mother in alarm. Lily looked down at him with that awful blank look in her eyes, and then she got up and walked out of the coffee lounge and out of the hotel doors beyond.

"Mummy?" Sammy said uncertainly.

"Mummy's gone to check if it's still warm enough for you to play outside," Cerys told him brightly, still in shock but determined to hide it from him. "Let's go and see."

She wiped his sugary fingers with a napkin and followed Lily out of the hotel, Sammy's hand in hers. They crossed the road to the little playground by the paddling pool. Lily paced up and down on the pavement, pulling at her sleeves with agitated fingers, her mouth moving silently.

"There, Sammy—you go and play. It's not too cold out here yet," Cerys told him.

He cast a worried glance at his mother, but the lure of the little slide and the rocking chickens proved too much, so he scampered off.

Cerys shut the gate behind him and made her way over to Lily, a few yards away. "It wasn't thick and you're not dumb," she said softly.

"It was stupid," Lily said with bitterness.

Cerys shook her head sadly. "No, not at all. It was maybe the sanest thing either of us have said all day."

Lily looked up, frowning. Cerys could tell from the suspicion in her eyes that she didn't expect she was being honest.

"Come and sit with me and we'll watch him," she said, putting her hand on Lily's too thin arm and giving it a gentle tug. "I want to explain."

Lily wouldn't throw her hand off, but she didn't believe her.

"Come," she repeated.

Lily gave a defeated shrug and followed her to the bench just inside the playground gate. They were the only people there.

"It's not stupid," Cerys reiterated. "It's what you need, and that, Lily, is never stupid."

"Stupid to think it might be possible," Lily muttered, picking at the skin around her nails in what looked to be a painful exercise.

Cerys laid her hand over Lily's. "Stop, you'll hurt yourself."

"That's all people like me get," she said. Cerys wasn't sure exactly what she meant, but she followed the general gist.

"So you wanted to stay here, for a while at least, and get a job, and for me to stay? Is that it?"

Lily nodded in that sullen way Cerys understood was without hope and full of shame.

She watched the little boy playing happily on the slide now that he could see his mother sitting only a few feet away. All his worry had evaporated like mist on a summer morning field as it only can do when you're four. And then she looked beyond him to the sea, to the cold gray waves, and then back to his mother.

Somebody needed her. Really needed her, and she didn't fully understand why, but did that matter?

It had shifted, that blackness inside, with the recognition that she was still needed. That a child, a young woman, might need what she could give.

Lily was right, and she had no idea how they could make this work. And Cerys knew nothing about her, and was that dangerous?

But she knew no one this age should have eyes so hopeless, and her boy shouldn't have to grow up with that.

She also knew that she could never go back home now. Utterly and irrevocably, she had burned a bridge, not just a car. There was no way back for her. In that past lay the feeling of being so alone and miserable that she wanted to die, and she never wanted to return to that. There was no future, not really. She hadn't wanted one either—but Lily did, and maybe Cerys shouldn't think about what it meant for her too deeply. Maybe she should just do what she could see needed to be done.

Utterly unlike her.

And maybe the sanest she'd been in months. A creature of instinct, not reason—that's what she'd said to herself yesterday. No names, no pack drill.

"Okay," she said, looking Lily straight in the face. "Let's do it."

The girl looked back at her in disbelief. And then slowly, slowly, a kind of desperate hope, the kind that hardly dares believe because it's been disappointed so often, began to rise in her eyes and dispel any of Cerys's lingering doubts (or were they good sense?). "Really?"

Cerys nodded firmly and squeezed her hand. "Absolutely!"

Instinct; yes, that was it—mother's instinct.

12

IT HAD BEEN A SHOCK to learn what Cerys had been doing in that village where they met. It had taken the wind from Lily. Cerys had seemed like a rock to weather any storm, so much wiser than her. It had knocked Lily sideways to find out she was in such a state that she wanted to end everything. She lay back in the bed, trying to make sense of it all.

But that was the mark of what an amazing woman Cerys was. She was in such a way herself but hadn't let it show and had looked out for them, got them here, taken care of them.

That was a real mother.

She said she had kids. My God, did they know how lucky they were? What would Lily's life have been had she been one of them?

Maybe being around her could rub off on Lily? Maybe she could learn to be the mother she'd always wanted to be. And Cerys was giving her that chance, which was incredible beyond anything. Lily didn't get chances though. She'd learned that even when she thought she was, it'd turn out to be something else. Usually something shit. That was how things rolled for her.

Maybe, maybe, maybe this time it could be different though.

Please let it be. For once, please let her catch a break.

And she didn't know what was going on in Cerys's life, but maybe it would also be good for her out here. Perhaps she had stuff she needed to get away from. Lily knew how that felt. She couldn't imagine Cerys allowing herself to have stuff to run away from, but anyone could make a mistake. Life had certainly taught her that.

As far as she was concerned, Cerys was the real deal—a proper mother and a woman who could get stuff done. Look how she handled that terrifying guy at the hotel reception. She'd been bedraggled with rain and mud splashed, and it hadn't even occurred to her to be intimidated by him. That was a real woman, a grown-up, and Lily had decided right there and then that this was the kind of woman she wished she could be. Though she knew that would never happen.

Maybe she could be a bit more like her though. Just a tiny bit. If she hung around her for long enough, some of that polish might rub off.

She had no idea what the morning would bring, but she was going to the hair salon down the street from the hotel, and she would see if they needed anyone, even if it was just reception and sweeping up. If that didn't work, she'd try the shops next, then the cafés, and she'd keep tramping round this town until she found somewhere to take her on.

She'd never have had the courage if Cerys weren't here, but somehow Cerys's admiration of the simple little blow-dry she'd given her spurred her on to try. *What would Cerys do?* That's what she'd secretly started to ask herself now when she didn't know what to do next, and she was sure Cerys wouldn't give up trying if she had a child to feed. *When you get nervous, pretend you're her*, she told herself with a rueful laugh as she slid down under the covers.

She felt quite excited about tomorrow, in a way she hadn't been excited for a long, long time. Nervous too, of course, but as if the morning might be full of possibilities and a new dawn.

The bad thoughts, they were still there behind everything, and when she had a happy idea, they pushed up inside her and jostled to take over, but tonight she wouldn't let them.

Somebody cared enough about her to stay for her. That was an incredible thing.

13

"DAD, WHAT DO YOU MEAN? She's been gone two days, and you haven't called the police? I'm coming home right now!"

Katie hung up and, with shaking hands, rifled through her shoulder bag to make sure she had her purse and car keys. She chucked her phone in beside them and grabbed a carryall from the top of the wardrobe.

She should have called Mum earlier. Why hadn't she called her?

She felt sick to her stomach. She threw some jeans and T-shirts and underwear in her bag and then locked her room and ran downstairs. It was a two-and-a-half-hour drive home.

When she stopped at the services off the highway to refuel, she texted her mother. "Mum, where are you? Please get in touch. I'm worried. Love you xxx"

She grabbed a coffee and drove the rest of the way without a break. It was past ten p.m. when she burst in on her father sitting in the living room in silence with his phone in his hand.

"Have you heard anything?" she demanded.

He looked up at her with exhausted, shocked eyes. "No, nothing. Nothing since she went." His face was gray, and the lines of middle age seemed more deeply etched than the last time she'd been home a few months ago.

"Call the police, Dad. I can't believe you haven't already. What possessed you?"

"I thought she'd be in touch. I thought she just wanted some time. I didn't think she'd still be gone," he said, his voice breaking on the words.

"When have you ever known Mum to want time?" she demanded. "Have you told Alex and Matt?"

He shook his head. "If she'd gone there, they'd have called me already."

And she wouldn't go to them. It'd be to Katie she'd go if she'd gone to any of them. Why hadn't she been in touch? This wasn't like her at all. The grip of fear around Katie's throat tightened a little more.

"What happened, Dad?"

"We had a row, a terrible row," he said, miserably. "I went to bed, and when I got up in the morning, she wasn't here."

Katie took a shuddering breath. "What did she take with her?"

"Nothing. Just the car."

"Nothing? No clothes? A suitcase?"

"Nothing." He stared at his hands as if he couldn't really see them there, as if he was looking at something else entirely. "That's why I thought she'd come back."

Katie realized her legs were shaking, and she sat down in the armchair abruptly. "Dad, you need to call the police now. What if something terrible has happened to her?"

"I can't," he said, still staring at his hands. "I keep trying, but I just can't move."

He was in shock, she thought, though she didn't really know what that looked like. She just knew she'd never seen her dad in this state ever. "I'll do it," she said. And she couldn't bear to do it in front of him, so she took her phone up to her old bedroom and sat on the edge of her bed while she made the call.

Afterward, she wanted to throw up. The taste of the bile in her mouth was sharp and acidic. The questions they'd asked about her dad—she hadn't expected that.

There was an officer on the way to the house right now to take statements. They wanted to know why Dad hadn't called this in, and she could hear the suspicion in the voice of the person taking down details. "He's known she's been missing for two days, and you've only just found out?" It sounded so much worse when they said it. "And this is out of character for your mother?"

"Yes, she's usually the most reliable person ever."

"I see." A pause. "We'll get someone over to you now. Don't go anywhere, please."

And suddenly she was scared about more than what had happened to Mum. What would the police say when they saw the state he was in? They'd make assumptions, and he was in no position to defend himself right now.

She called Matt. "It's me. Yes, I know what time it is—this is an emergency. You need to come home now. We need you. Mum's disappeared."

14

"MY WIFE HAS DISAPPEARED, AND she's taken our four-year-old with her. I'm seriously worried about their safety. I don't think she can be in her right mind, or she wouldn't have done this. We need help." Danny sat forward in the chair to emphasize his point. The police officer frowned slightly, and Danny held up his hands. "Look, I don't care about anything but getting them back. If Kayleigh needs mental health support, I'll get her that, but you need to help me before she does something awful."

The officer leaned back, still frowning. "And what makes you think she's going to do that?"

He knew they'd likely suspect him. He wasn't stupid and that was par for the course. Wife goes missing—is it the husband? But he needed this guy onside. Kayleigh thought she was just going to slip off with his child and his money. Nope, not in a million years was he going to lie down and take that. And, what's more, she'd know he wouldn't.

"Look, I love my wife, but she's troubled. I've always known that, and I've tried to help her. When I met her she was up to all kinds, drugs…men… you know…" Danny held his hands up to illustrate how he hoped he didn't have to explain further. He got him, right? "I thought she'd straightened out, but it looks like I was wrong."

"You think she's gone off with another guy?"

He hadn't, up until now. Actually, that hadn't occurred to him at all, or that she was using again. It hadn't even entered his head. No, his immediate reaction was she'd screwed him over for the money and legged it in her flaky, stupid way that she wouldn't have planned properly at all. He was amazed she'd got it together enough to take his money. Been playing dumb, obviously. What he really thought was she'd got pissy about that fight they had last week where he'd had to remind her who was boss, and she'd decided to get all pathetic about it. Wanting attention, and for him to feel guilty. And it had been her fault—if she hadn't wound him up like that, it wouldn't have happened. She'd made out it was way worse than it was too.

Was this policeman right though? Had she legged it with another man?

Danny felt his face and neck color with rage at the thought of her with someone else. She wouldn't, would she? No, this was surely just about her getting back at him over a few more disagreements recently.

"Officer, she's not the most stable of women. And I am really scared for my kid with her. She can't be trusted to look after herself when she's in a state of mind like this, let alone a child." He hesitated. "And if she has taken up with some man, it's not going to be the kind I want my kid around. Trust me on this. He'll be pumping her full of shit, and she'll be doing anything to get a fix. She's been there before. Please help me get my family back—you have to understand, a child is at risk here. If this was yours, how would you feel?"

The policeman thought for a long moment, and then nodded. "Okay, I'll see what I can do. Wait here."

"Thank you," Danny said in relief. "Thank you so much."

A nationwide alert out on her—that's what was needed. That'd bring her back. And when he did get her back, he'd make her regret this. Every last second she'd made him suffer—she'd pay for that.

15

CERYS TOOK SAMMY FOR A walk down the shoreline to look for shells while Lily went off on her job search. She smiled at the determined look on the girl's face as she set out. This kid had grit. She might look like she was going to collapse half the time, but the girl didn't give in. She'd get knocked down and she'd get up again. Cerys's smile took on a winsome note. A shame she'd been knocked down so much, and it was clear she had. She deserved better than that.

Some kids just didn't get a fair deal in life. She'd always tried to make sure her children had a gilded childhood, and it broke her heart to see what some had to go through. Life was so bloody unfair. A cruel, cruel world.

"Found one!" Sammy shouted excitedly, and she turned her attention back to him in relief, away from the thoughts that would drag her down.

"Oooh, watch your fingers on that! It's a razor clam, that one. It's huge. Well done, Sammy—good spot."

He grinned and put it in his bucket. "I'll show Mummy."

"She'll love it!"

He skipped off into the shallows again, splashing the sea up in the air in kicks and whooping as he looked for his next find.

She hoped they were kind to Lily in those shops. She hoped it with a fierce and sudden passion. "They'd better cut her a break," she muttered as she followed Sammy.

"Paddle?" he said to her, and she grinned back at him and kicked off her shoes and joined him. It was absolutely freezing, and her toes might possibly drop off, she thought, but then the shallow water warmed slightly as they splashed around in it. She bore it for the grin on his face.

Because why not? Sometimes the world needed a four-year-old to show it the way. Needed that purity and that joy. That could save anyone, she really believed.

She should be suspicious of Lily. She should wonder what she was hiding and if there was anything there she should be concerned about. Her fifty-three years told her to be careful, but, at the moment, her instinct told her to believe, and while she had no evidence against that, she would.

That's what mothers did.

❧

Lily breathed in, as if by doing so she could suck courage deep into her lungs. Then she entered the hair salon. There was a woman of about forty behind the reception desk, but aside from that, the place was empty. The woman looked her up and down, assessing her.

Lily felt herself flush.

Pretend you're Cerys.

She tried to squeeze Cerys's polite and in-control smile onto her face. "I've just moved into the area…" Yes, she could imagine Cerys saying that, keep going. "And I'm just starting job hunting and spotted your salon." These were definitely Cerys's words, not hers, just like they'd rehearsed before she left. "Are you in need of any help at the moment? I'm a qualified hairdresser but I can do admin support too."

The woman blinked at her. "You're qualified?"

"Yes," she said with a bright smile, still channeling Cerys. Oh my God, so much channeling of Cerys going on because she totally didn't have the courage to do this. Any minute now she was going to get blown out badly here.

The woman got up off her chair and moved with difficulty out from behind the counter. She leaned her elbow on the hatch and said dryly, pointing at her swollen belly, "Well, in about three months I'm definitely going to need help, as I'll be too far along then to manage on my own. I'll be huge by March and still another month to go, then when the baby arrives I'll want at least six months off. So I guess I could try you out now. If you're useless, mind, I won't think twice about getting rid of you." Then she grinned. "But if you're any good, then this might just work out. Do you want a coffee?"

Lily beamed, her face blushing with relief and pleasure, but for once she didn't mind someone seeing that. "Yeah, that'd be great."

⁓

Cerys looked up in surprise as Lily hurtled back into their hotel room like a mini whirlwind. "I did it! I got a job! I did exactly as you said and she's giving me a two-week trial."

Cerys felt as if she'd caught a ray of the girl's joy, and it warmed her. "Well done, I knew you could! And you'll be great. I guess now we have to find somewhere to live then." She pushed down all thoughts of her old life, of her family. This wasn't real time. It was a suspended life, one that would end when she'd done what she needed to. Some fragment carved out of reality and so what happened here didn't affect what had been left behind. She had ceased to exist that night on the hill.

Lily blanched a little at the idea. "Oh, I don't know where to start."

Neither did Cerys really, but at least she knew she could do this kind of thing. "You've got your job. I'll take care of this part."

Lily beamed in relief. "I honestly don't know what I'd have done these last few days without you."

And that was why she was still here, because Lily really didn't know. And she couldn't just leave her like this now, her and Sammy.

She absolutely refused to think of what was going on at home. Every time the thought came to her mind, she sent a steel shutter crashing down on it. In that life, she was dead. This here, now, was just a brief interlude. Keep it that way—she wasn't strong enough to bear anything else right now.

"Let's get some fresh air," she suggested brightly. "It's stopped raining for a bit. I think we'll have to nip out between showers today. You can take Sammy onto the playground by the castle and he can have a good run around. I'll check out the estate agents."

What the girl needed right now was to get up and on her feet. She could decide the course of her life after that. At the moment, she just needed a taste of success and happiness. Lily's eyes looked mostly as if she hadn't known what happiness and contentment were in a long time. It was Cerys's job to make sure that all changed.

It wasn't good news in the estate agents, though. They were in holiday cottage territory, and small properties were therefore few and far between. Some of the cottages were available for a month or so to get through the winter season, but Cerys didn't want to settle just yet. She wanted a more stable solution for Lily than that, and she wasn't about to give up on the first day of trying. Although time was running out on the hotel, and they were due to check out in the morning. Doubtless, they could book in for longer, but she'd rather Lily didn't waste too much of her money, so she needed some kind of solution soon. Perhaps one of them might have to do. She harrumphed though—they were still overpriced. Lily had talked to her about how much she could afford in the short term, but she needed a sustainable solution in Cerys's view—one that she'd be able to afford from her wages without eating into her savings further—and that wasn't going to be easy.

God, she needed to wash her clothes. She felt rancid now.

Actually, what was she going to do about that? She couldn't keep washing them every night, and she had no money to buy more. There had to be a charity shop somewhere on this island. She'd have to look into that tomorrow.

She trudged back toward the playground and passed a little kiosk on the way back that sold sweets and ice cream. There was a village bulletin board in the window. She stopped to look at it. Lots of cards placed by local tradesmen about plumbing and gardening services, and bundles of kids' clothes for sale, but no houses or flats to rent. She sighed and scanned again to make sure she hadn't missed anything. In the top corner of the board was a newish-looking postcard scrawled in cursive script.

"Help wanted with housework and sheep. Cottage available."

Nothing more, just a phone number. Cerys frowned at it for a while and then popped into the shop to speak to the woman behind the counter. "*P'nawn da*! The postcard in the window about help with housework and sheep? Do you know anything at all about it?"

"Oh, that's Dilys," she replied. "Broke her leg, she has, and can't get about proper."

"She lives on her own then?"

The shopkeeper looked her up and down, eyes narrowing. "You thinking of applying? I've not seen you before. You not from round here?"

Cerys recognized the element of protectiveness in the way she was being assessed.

"No, I'm not. I've come up to help my daughter look after my grandson, and I spotted that postcard. I grew up on a sheep farm near Betws-y-Coed, you see. Wondered if I could be any help."

"Hmmm, well, Dilys is a sharp one. She'll either like you or she won't. Shall I give her a call for you?"

Again, the protectiveness of local people for their own; Cerys remembered that with fondness. It'd been years since she'd seen it. She almost laughed when the woman switched to Welsh on the call. She could understand enough of it to know that she was questioning the unseen Dilys about whether she felt safe, and to call her back as soon as this visitor had gone so she knew she was okay.

"She says you can go up there now," the shopkeeper told her. "I'll write the directions down for you."

With them in hand, Cerys hurried off to meet Lily and Sammy. "We're going for a drive," she said. "Checking out somewhere we might rent."

They drove out of Beaumaris, Cerys reading out the directions from the roughly drawn map. After twenty minutes of winding lanes, they turned off down a narrow track.

"Bumpy!" Sammy said, his eyes widening as he was jolted about. "B-b-b-ump!"

Finally, they came to a Welsh longhouse painted white. "Bryn Terrin," the name on the wooden sign declared. "This is it," Cerys said. To the side lay a little stone cottage signed "Yn Terrin" with a small courtyard and patch of lawn in front.

The farm door swung open, and a flurry of barking black and white fur flew out at the car. Sammy cringed in his seat. "Leave it to me," Cerys said. "You wait here."

She got out of the car. "Come by!" she said to the dog sharply, and it paused to look at her. She clicked her fingers at her heel and walked toward the door. It dropped in behind her watchfully. As she neared the farmhouse, she could see the old woman lurking back in the doorway.

"I'm Cerys," she called. "I've come about the job."

The woman hobbled forward and stepped out into the yard awkwardly. She was on crutches with her right leg in a full cast. Cerys estimated her to be in her late seventies at least. She could well have been older from her weather-beaten face. No wonder the shop woman had been so protective. Dilys must be remarkable to survive up here on her own at this age.

"Have you now? And what makes you think you're suitable?" Dilys eyeballed her. She'd been a tall woman once, and even now her eyes were on a level with Cerys's. Cerys suddenly got a vision of her when she was younger—a strong and vital woman running this place on her own terms.

"My dad was a sheep farmer. I grew up on a farm like this. And the housework—well, I'm a mother. I've been doing that the rest of my life," she said with a laugh.

"There's not so many sheep now," Dilys replied. "But what there is I can't look after with this leg."

"What happened?"

"Gate hinges broke, and it cracked me on the thigh, then landed on me."

"How did you get help out here?"

She shrugged. "I was pinned there till the post came, then Kip alerted him." She fondled the collie's ears. "So, what are you doing here and why do you want the job? Don't give me no nonsense, mind; I'm not a fool."

"I'm here to look after my grandson," she said, pointing back at the car. "My daughter's got a job in Beaumaris. Quite honestly, we need somewhere to stay, and we can't find anywhere. I passed the shop and saw your card. He's a good kid, so he'll be no trouble—only four so he'll tag along with me. Is that the accommodation there?" She gestured to the cottage by the longhouse.

"Yes, used to use it for holidaymakers but not for the last year. It's in decent condition though. Three bedrooms, though they're not big." Dilys peered at the car. "Why're you both here with nowhere to live?"

Cerys met her eyes steadily. "She needs a fresh start," she replied, "and I need to make sure she gets one."

Dilys looked back at the car again. "Bring her over."

Cerys walked back to the car. "She wants to meet you both," she said to Lily as she coaxed Sammy out. "No, the doggy won't bother you now. He was just doing his job and keeping watch."

Lily approached Dilys nervously, a few steps behind Cerys.

"You've got a job then?" Dilys rapped.

"Yes, at the hair salon," Lily replied with a nervous smile.

"Oh, Angharad, yes—I knew her grandmother. She was flighty too," Dilys announced.

Cerys stifled a laugh. Anyone not farming was flighty, she guessed. Poor Lily just looked confused.

"And who are you?" Dilys demanded, looking down at Sammy.

He glowered at her and stepped behind his mother. Cerys looked anxiously to Dilys, who bellowed a laugh. "Good lad—don't talk to strange old women!"

Sammy poked his head out and gave a tentative smile, then retreated behind Lily's leg again.

Dilys looked over them all again. "I don't suppose I have much choice if I want the sheep fed. But if you try to rob me, I'll put a bullet through you."

Lily blanched and put a reassuring hand on Sammy's head.

"Well, you won't need to," Cerys replied firmly. "There'll be none of that from us; we're decent people. Now, when do you want me to start?"

16

IT WAS THEIR FIRST NIGHT in the new cottage and a full week after they'd first met Dilys. They'd stayed on at the hotel a little longer, and Cerys had negotiated a reduced rate without much difficulty as it was quiet in the trade at this time of year. Lily lay there in the dark, staring up into it as sleep slipped away from her again and again.

"We're decent people," Cerys had said to the old woman. Well, Cerys was but she didn't know what Lily was. She couldn't have said that if she did know.

She was eight years old when she realized what her mother was. It was a kid at school who told her and not in a nice way. It was screamed in her face as the other girl pulled her hair and shoved her to the ground and kicked her. She hadn't done anything to the girl—she just hated her because her mother was a whore.

She'd seen the needle tracks on her mother's arms. She'd seen her shooting up. She'd seen the men come and go when she was younger, but they were boyfriends. She hadn't understood what her mother did when she was gone all night. When she locked her in her bedroom at night so she couldn't get out. Her mother would sleep in too late to get her to school in the morning, so she learned to get herself up and eat cereal and walk herself there way before other kids walked on their own. She was careful about that though. She knew school would ask questions, so she used to time it so she met the kids next door but one, whose mother always took them, and she'd tag along so it looked like their mum was taking her too. That mother wouldn't say anything to the school—she had her own issues to keep quiet.

Still, everyone on the estate had known about her mother, it seemed. That's what Lexi had said when she'd shoved her face into the asphalt and spat in her hair.

When that had happened, she'd wished her mother would die so they'd take her away and get her adopted. And one time when she'd got mad with her mother because she'd forgotten her birthday when she was off her face on a bender that kept her in bed for three days, she'd shouted that at her. "I wish you were dead so I could live with a proper family."

"Get real," her mother had spat back, groggy and spiteful with it. "Nobody would ever want *you*. Useless little bitch!" And then her mother had passed out back into sleep again, and she'd spent her birthday on her own, watching TV in the front room, her stomach aching with hunger because there was no food left in the house. She'd wished she was brave enough to go to the shop and steal some.

But she hadn't been yet. She would be later. She'd had to be to survive.

17

THE SOFT CRUNCH OF THE frost-covered earth beneath her boots.

The quiet pant of the dog at her heels.

The click-snap of the gate latch closing.

All familiar from years back. The sounds of home from long ago. They should be no part of who she was now. Another time, another place, really another person. Or that's what she'd thought.

Cerys was a mother, a wife, a suburbanite. No part of the farm girl remained.

And yet here it was, etched into her DNA. It's where she'd returned to the source, to end it all, and when that hadn't worked, it's like that part of her had been reborn again on that hillside.

The sounds of a quiet farm early morning—a sense of rightness deep down in her very bones.

She headed down the track away from the farmhouse, a puddle of ice in a wheel rut snapping under her boot, and away up the hill. The air was sharp and still with the frost hanging low over everything and spiking the trees. She could taste its tang.

The black and white collie clung to her heel as it was bred to do, and she strode up the steep path, her breath coming faster and harder than it would have done when she was a girl, and almost painfully so at points. "I'm out of condition," she whispered to the dog, though there was no one to hear but a robin in the dark of the hedge, caught against the tangle of the branches in the beam of her flashlight.

She toiled up the hill, ignoring the burning of unfit lungs; the old woman had done this every day until she'd snapped her leg, and so she'd be ashamed to slow or stop when Dilys would have kept going despite having three decades on her. The dog trotted beside her, keen and eager, knowing the job even though it wasn't his beloved mistress beside him.

When they got to the top of the hill, the faintest glimmer of light lifted the darkness on the horizon over to the east.

Toward home, Cerys thought, and, as she must in order to survive, she turned that thought swiftly away. Even turned her head from the sliver of light.

Her first task was to walk the bounds and check on the dispersed flock. She needed the collie for this without the luxury of light. But the young dog knew his job, and he'd find any sheep in trouble. Her dad's old dog had been skilled at this—he had a nose for stress, her dad always said. Maybe she should have left it until the sun had come up with such a youngster as this, but she wanted to be back to take over with Sammy before Lily had to leave for work.

She'd done this job in the dark with her dad on their hills many times. She followed the line of the hedge further up the hill and gave the dog the instruction to get out and search. Kip scampered forward without hesitation. She'd half wondered if he'd obey her out here, as she wasn't Dilys, but as she watched his crouched pose in the lightening gloom, his slow creep forward, she could see how strong his bloodline was. He'd literally do this job for anyone.

But it was only Dilys he'd rest his head on by the fire when his work was done, and that was the difference. She knew dogs well enough to know that this was the way this one operated.

She walked the bounds of the field, letting the dog range out and scent. A sheep gave a grumbling "Baa" and moved out of her path in the disgruntled way she remembered from her dad's old ewes. The trudge through the frosted grass had a mesmeric effect on her senses. She could feel the peace flowing from the frost-hardened ground into her boots, through her, settling inside her in a deep, still pool of calm.

She walked the hill.

As someone had done for centuries, men, women like her, tending the sheep in the same way day after day, year after year, following the rhythms of the seasons and the land.

She was round the other side of the hill when the dog picked something up, with a prick of his sharp ears and a low whine. She followed his low creep across the grass to a thicket of thorn and bramble. And deep in the center, a sheep was caught fast and dragged half over onto its back in its struggle to free itself. They could easily die like this if left too long, which was why a good dog really was a lifesaver. She gave the shaggy little head a pat, and pulled some cutters from the pocket of Dilys's borrowed shepherding coat and waded in.

For a moment, she wasn't quite sure how to get hold of the sheep, which kicked out at her despite its plight, as these hill ewes always did. The woman she was back in her pristine five-bedroom suburban house couldn't quite remember how to deal with this, or how to cope with getting soft hands ripped by brambles. But then instinct kicked in. She took two strategic handfuls of wool and twisted the sheep to clamp it between her thighs, gripping firmly while she snipped away at the thorn-tangled wool in the light of the rising sun.

The dog lay on the grass and waited patiently, its tongue lolling, watching her work with a vague interest.

It had been easier thirty-odd years ago with younger joints and stronger muscles, but she gritted her teeth as the ewe strained against her and hung on and kept clipping. Finally, she clipped the last of the long, trailing brambles from its fleece, and it sprang free, kicking its hind legs in the air as it went.

She sniffed and rolled her eyes at Kip as she stuffed the clippers back in her pocket and picked her way free of the thicket. "No gratitude!" she said, and gestured the collie forward again to finish their work.

By the time they made their way off the hill and down to the farmhouse, the sun was weakly shining in that peculiar faint beauty of winter light. She lifted the thumb latch on the farmhouse door, and the collie broke from its obedient place at her heel and rushed past her. Dilys was sitting by the range in the kitchen, the fire stoked within, and Cerys was met by a welcome surge of heat. The dog fussed round Dilys and then settled against her legs, its head cradled in her lap, its keen eyes watching her face.

"*Bore da*," Dilys said. "Did it go all right out there?"

She had a terse voice, Cerys concluded, probably born of speaking to too few people on a daily basis. She took a closer look at Dilys. Her imagination, surely, but the old woman looked somehow diminished since yesterday. Cerys frowned and put the kettle on the hob.

"All fine. There was a ewe caught up in some brambles up the top, but the dog found her well enough, and once I cut her free, she was on her way with no harm."

Dilys grunted. "Good." She fondled the shaggy head on her knee. "He's a great little dog. Should never have got him really, because I won't outlast him, but he's such a wonderful worker that he'll have a home somewhere. I don't think you'll like leaving here much though, will you, Kip?"

The dog's fiercely determined stare was fixed on her face.

She meant he wouldn't like leaving her, though she wouldn't say it, Cerys realized. She frowned again. The old woman's words took her by surprise, and she wondered if maybe she wasn't wrong about her initial thought that she didn't look too good this morning. She made the tea silently.

"Breakfast?" she asked when she handed Dilys the mug.

Dilys grimaced. "I don't like all this waiting on," she admitted. "It grinds my bones something awful."

Cerys shrugged. Sympathy wasn't the way with this one. She knew the type; she'd grown up around them. "You'll be back on both feet soon. What do you want?"

"Toast," she replied grudgingly. "Bread's in the crock there."

Cerys didn't waste words on her but got about making the toast. It wasn't long until Lily would have to leave.

"Bring the boy over," Dilys said, seeing her glance at her watch.

Cerys looked at her in surprise.

"It'll save lighting another fire," she said.

Cerys buttered the toast. "Anything on it?"

"Honey, there on the windowsill."

Cerys obliged and handed her the plate.

Dilys raised a sparse white eyebrow at her. "Need some sweetening, don't I?" And she chuckled to herself. "Go on, get the boy so his mother can get off. He'll come to no harm over here."

Cerys slipped out of the farmhouse as Dilys fed a crust scrap to the collie. She wasn't sure about this at all. Sammy was bound to be bored in there, and Dilys didn't strike her as the type to have much patience with a young child.

Inside the cottage kitchenette, Lily was waving a cereal box at a bleary-eyed Sammy.

"I don't want that," he whined. "Can I have toast?"

"Sammy, I haven't got time," Lily said, her voice edging on a wail.

Cerys recognized this sign. Lily was not great under pressure, especially time pressure. It brought out the worst in her constantly bubbling anxiety. "You get off," she said, shooing Lily away. "I'll take over. I've finished with the sheep for now."

"But he hasn't had breakfast…"

"I'll deal with it," she said firmly, before Lily locked into what Cerys now recognized as the girl's crisis mode, spiraling downward into thinking about what an unfit mother she was. "Off with you!"

Lily stared at her as she was shepherded to the door and handed her coat and bag. "I—"

"Have a lovely day, and we'll see you later," Cerys said as she shoved her gently out of the door.

"Phew!" she said to Sammy as Lily drove off, waving frantically back to Sammy who was seeing her off from the window. "Your mummy can be a worrywart sometimes." Sammy looked confused and Cerys laughed. "Never mind, let's go and get your toast."

Dilys was still sitting by the range with the dog. Cerys thought she brightened when the boy followed her in, but then she wasn't sure as the old woman's usual slightly sour expression returned. Dilys said nothing as Cerys made Sammy's breakfast and sat him down at the scratched pine table to eat it, but Cerys noticed how her eyes watched him as he ate. His first taste of the honey made his eyes widen in delight, and he licked his fingers enthusiastically. "Aye, that's the proper stuff from Welsh bees fed on good Welsh flowers," Dilys said with her sardonic chuckle. Sammy smiled politely, but his mouth was too full of toast to reply.

Cerys tidied up, giving the washing-up an extra good scrub in hot soapy water. None of the dishes were that clean, she found, and she suspected the old woman's eyesight wasn't what it was. She dried them with a fresh tea towel, and they made the satisfyingly clean squeak she expected from her pots.

When she'd finished, she realized Sammy and the old woman were regarding each other across the kitchen. Sammy was frowning slightly. "Why do you have a beard?" he asked suddenly.

Cerys opened her mouth in horror to cut in—oh, the awful candor only a four-year-old could muster—but Dilys's delighted peal of laughter stopped her.

"Because I'm an old woman," she replied with a grin that crinkled the skin around her eyes into corrugations. "And it happens to old women—they get whiskers. I should pull them out, but I can't see them so well now. Maybe I should shave them."

Sammy nodded. "My daddy shaves—"

And then he stopped dead and clapped his hand to his mouth.

Dilys gave Cerys a questioning look and she shrugged and shook her head slightly to tell her not to ask further.

It was the reaction more than the child's words. He'd been told not to talk about his father, that was pretty clear. But why?

She could press him but that would be wrong. She could ask Lily, but was that fair when she didn't want questions herself?

So many secrets.

She shook herself. There were chickens that needed tending to. And that's what women did—or women like her—when the problems were too big. They buried themselves in busyness, because if you couldn't solve it, you might as well be doing something practical.

She waited until Sammy finished his breakfast and then took him with her. He was, as she expected, delighted by the chickens. One of the hens was happy to be scooped up and cuddled by him and trotted round the pen after him when he laid a corn trail for her to eat. "Has she got a name?" he asked.

"I don't know. You can ask Dilys when we go back in."

There was a mist settled higher up on the hills, and the air felt damp, but the sun reached them dimly, and she took pleasure in the freshness of the outdoors and the light on her face.

Simple things. Things that used to matter to her before the darkness came and took the joy away.

It had stolen so much from her, that suctioning blackness, more than she'd realized.

For a second there she had a thought—as she watched Sammy laying the corn for the hen—that she was terrified it would come back. That stopped her in her tracks. For it was almost as if she'd forgotten everything, forgotten her *family*, forgotten how she'd got to this point where she'd decided the only punctuation point available to her now was a full stop.

Here she was, still alive, and surviving day to day. But, and this was the awful reality, she was less unhappy than she had been.

What a terrible thing to admit.

That today, right now, she didn't want to die. But at home, she had.

Her hands were shaking. In fact, her legs were shaking too.

She loved them. Didn't she? Then why did she feel this way?

Sammy came skipping back to her and took her hand. "Finished!"

A warm, sweaty, sticky little hand. The most precious kind there was. She pushed the emotions down and went back inside with him.

"What's up with you? You look like you've seen a ghost," Dilys asked her, narrow-eyed.

"Nothing," she replied.

"Ha!" said Dilys with a tone of contempt. "I might be old, but I'm not stupid."

Cerys sat down heavily at the table. "Sometimes I don't know who I am anymore," she said. "Do you ever feel like that?" She didn't really want to share that with this irascible old woman, but it came leaking out anyway. Maybe force of habit from a childhood surrounded by Dilys's type.

Dilys snorted. "I'm too old for all that business. When you get to my age, you're busy deciding if you're likely to wake up the next day. It stops you worrying about things like who you are. Alive is the only answer you need when you get past seventy."

Despite herself, Cerys laughed. And then Sammy announced he was hungry again, and she was off the hook while she had to go and deal with that.

She looked around once Sammy had been fed. This place was a mess. Rancid, in fact. It needed a good clean. She pulled out the cleaning products from under the sink. Well, it was going to get one. At least she could achieve that.

18

LILY PULLED A SLEEPY-EYED SAMMY into her bed with her when Cerys
went out to tend the sheep the following morning. Sammy's hair stood up in
little tousled spikes, and Lily smoothed them down with her hand. "You're
doing so well," she said. "Do you miss home?"

Sammy shook his head. "No," he replied with a force that both surprised
and relieved her.

"And are you managing okay? You know, with the toilet thing."

Sammy snuggled in under her arm. She loved it when he did that.
Something about it made her feel like a real mother, and like he believed in
her as one. And if Sammy really believed in her like that, did it matter what
anyone else thought. Did any of what Danny said count? Here, in this place,
far away from him and with a sleepy, content child cuddled up to her, it
really felt like it might not.

"I am four," he said. "I'm supposed to be able to do it myself. It's okay,
Mummy."

"I know, but even at four, you might need some help and it's so important you don't ask her. She mustn't know. Are you sure you can cope?"

He raised his head and looked at her with those big, solemn green eyes.
"Mummy, don't worry. It'll be okay."

She felt her eyes fill up slightly and squeezed them tight for a second,
because she didn't want him to think she was upset. It wasn't that. "Are you
happy, Sammy?"

His little arms tightened round her. "Yes. I love it here, Mummy."

Oh thank God, thank God. Because when she thought about what she was doing to him, sometimes it made her blood chill. She didn't know how this would end, but at least for now, it was all right.

19

"SHE CAN'T JUST HAVE DISAPPEARED!" Matt stared at his sister with incredulity. He'd gotten there as soon as possible, but he'd been on a uni friend's stag do in Croatia—some kind of fake-army-guns-and-tanks lads experience in some remote spot—so it had taken a few days to sort out flights and get back.

Katie had been so relieved when her big brother had appeared through the front door with the noisy, careless crash that always heralded his entry. Alex was the precise and sensible one; Matt was like a wrecking ball. But it was Matt she wanted in a crisis. Alex would flap and fuss whereas Matt would get something done.

"And Dad's not doing anything? He can't just do nothing!"

Katie threw up her hands in exasperation. "Oh, I don't know. I can't get any sense out of him. You try!"

Matt nodded and got up.

"I didn't mean now!" She hadn't even had the chance to off-load how worried she was.

"No time like the present," he called over his shoulder.

Their father was in the garden by the apple trees. Matt went to stand next to him, fastening his coat up. It was chilly out there. He stifled down the sense of impatience he felt at his father's silence, and they stood together, staring up at the skeleton branches of the trees.

"I think she's left me," his father said finally.

Matt estimated it had taken him a full twenty minutes to speak. It was one of the reasons he found his father so frustrating. He should have called Alex to come over. His brother dealt with Dad far better.

"What happened?" Matt bit down his rising frustration. Mum could be dead, and Dad didn't seem to have even considered that. He wasn't sure Katie had either, but she would crumble if he mentioned it, and he wasn't good with girls crying on him, even if it was his little sister.

"We had an argument the evening she left. I said some terrible, terrible things in the end. Things I don't think in the cold light of day she will ever forgive me for. I wish I could unsay them, but I can't. I was tired, and I knew inside I'd done enough damage and couldn't fix it, so I went to bed."

Matt just managed to stop himself from rolling his eyes. Wasn't that his father all over?

"In the morning the car had gone. I thought she might have nipped to the shop for milk or something, but the fridge was full of it when I checked. Bread in the bread bin too. I waited and waited but she didn't come back. Then I thought maybe she'd slept in the spare room and overslept, but she wasn't there. I checked all your rooms too. I called and called her phone but she didn't answer."

"Did you look for a note?"

"Everywhere, but there was nothing."

Matt sighed. He'd been hoping against hope that had been forgotten and they might still turn something up.

"So what did you do?"

His father shrugged. "I waited and waited and waited."

Matt rolled his eyes. Typical Dad—do nothing. He should have gone out looking for her, called her friends, anything but just sit there. At work, he was one of the most driven men Matt had ever encountered, but outside of that, he seldom seemed to shift out of first gear. It was as if he burnt away all of his energy on the business and there was nothing left for them.

Okay, how to progress this now. "Did you call any of her friends to see if they knew where she was?"

His father gave a deep sigh and closed his eyes. There was a long, long silence.

"I didn't really feel there was anyone I could call, Matthew."

Matt frowned in confusion. "What do you mean?"

"She hasn't been in touch with her old friends in a very long time. It was one of the things we argued about. She never speaks to them now, she never goes out. She just mopes around. And she's never happy."

"Why?"

"I don't know, Matthew." He held his hand up to his forehead as if in pain. "I don't know anything anymore." And he walked slowly back into the house, leaving Matt open-mouthed in shock because he hadn't known any of that. Not a thing. But they'd been fine, hadn't they? What Dad said seemed to indicate not, though. How had none of them known it had gotten this bad?

20

IT WAS BECOMING A HABIT—that waking in the middle of the night. That crushing sense of shame when she remembered just who she was and how far away that was from what Cerys believed her to be.

At least Danny had always known.

And look how that had turned out.

She was only just sixteen the first time she met him, walking back to the care home in her school uniform. She'd deviated off by the back of the tire factory to score. There was often a dealer there after school who'd have something for the kids for just a tenner. She knew it'd be cut with all kinds of rubbish for that price—she wasn't stupid. But getting her hands on a tenner was hard enough, so she didn't have much choice. The other girls in the home had less trouble getting money, but she knew what they did for it and something inside her balked at that. She wasn't ready to be like her mother, not yet. Though let's face it, that's where everyone thought she'd end up. She could see it in their faces: the staff at the home, the teachers, and definitely the other kids who didn't bother to hide it at all.

But when she got to the corner, the dealer wasn't there. Instead, there was a guy with a van parked and the hood popped open, and he had his head inside, fiddling with the engine. As she passed, he swore and jumped back, sucking his finger viciously.

He was a lot older than her, she realized immediately, but he was very good-looking. So much it made her blush when he noticed her and smiled.

"Cut my finger," he said, pulling it out of his mouth for a moment so he could speak. "You want to watch it down here on your own. There was some guy dealing here when I broke down." His eyes narrowed. "Or is that why you're here?"

She colored an even more fiery shade and shook her head.

"Good," he said. "That's a mug's game. Still, you shouldn't be walking round here on your own. I'll give you a lift home when I get this thing started again. Don't want you running into anyone dodgy. You need to be careful, you know." He paused and gave her a hard look. "Pretty girl like you," he said with a shake of his head, "all kinds of trouble you don't even know you can get into."

If only she didn't know. If only she was what he thought she was right now. He thought she was pretty, and that gave her a warm rush, like a smile on the inside.

She knew she shouldn't accept the lift. She didn't know him, and she was taking a big risk, but he was only offering to keep her safe, so that couldn't be a bad thing, right?

"Hop in the cab," he suggested. "Get out of the cold. It shouldn't take much longer."

She nodded and climbed into the front of the Transit. From here, she could see brief glimpses of him while he worked, and he was right, it was warmer out of the wind. He gave her a quick wave and a grin the next time he emerged from the engine, and her stomach did a funny kind of flip-flop of excitement.

After ten minutes he slammed the hood shut and dusted his hands off, then jumped back into the cab. "Here goes!" He turned the engine on and it caught with a splutter and then settled to a normal steady chug. "All right!" he yelled with a whoop. "Okay, let's get you home. Tell me the way."

She directed him back to the main road.

"So I'm Danny," he said. "What's your name?"

"Kayleigh."

"Nice name. This where I go left, yeah?" As they drove, he told her about the business he was starting up. She'd never met anyone with their own business before. He must've been really clever.

It wasn't far back to the home. A short block of council houses all knocked through into one long building. He looked at it as she directed him to pull up nearby, and then at her.

"I'm in care," she said with that flush of shame she always felt when someone found out. "But I'm sixteen so I leave soon."

"Where do you go then?"

"Don't know, but I'm not staying here. It's a dump."

He glanced down the road, and she followed his eyes to the next street corner, where a group of older teen boys and men were hanging around in cars, waiting for the girls at the home to come out. They didn't even bother to do it out of sight of the home, and there was nothing the staff could do about it. The police came occasionally, but not often enough, and the guys just moved on and returned when it was all clear.

Danny shook his head at her.

"I don't go with them," she said indignantly. Well, she didn't now. She'd tried it before she'd realized fully who and what they were. Since then, she stayed inside the home and kept her door shut when the other girls tried to get her to go too. It was horrible and she'd never felt so dirty in her life. And it made her think of her mum and cry.

"You were there to meet that dealer, weren't you?" he asked, and he completely knew, so there was no point lying. She nodded her head miserably.

He made an exasperated sound. "You're too pretty to waste your life on this," he said. And she was blown away that he'd still said she was pretty after what she'd just admitted. "I'll pick you up after school tomorrow and drive you home again. You need to get clear of this shit. See you tomorrow. I'll be by the gates."

She nodded and got out of the van with her heart singing, because he was gorgeous and older, and all the other girls would be totally jealous. She felt a warm curl of satisfaction as she kept replaying the scene in her mind that night. The way he had just told her, not given her any choice, because he wanted to take care of her. And nobody had ever done that for her before.

21

THE TOWN WAS BUZZING WITH Kayleigh's disappearance. The local paper had taken it up, and they were definitely on Danny's side. It was a sorry tale of a troubled young mother with her priorities all wrong and a father who desperately wanted his family back. Who could help?

So far there were no leads, and it looked like she'd got well away, but no news either of any local guy she could have absconded with. And that gave Danny some small ease. Maybe that policeman was wrong, and she hadn't hooked up with someone else after all.

He liked the headline: "Respected local businessman appeals for help on missing family." That eased his heart, and yeah, it gave him some pride. "Respected local businessman"—he'd worked hard for that.

Why couldn't she see what they had? Why did she have to do this to him?

The reporter was undoubtedly on his side. He was a middle-aged guy with a melancholy expression and sludgy skin that said he had a drinking problem. "I want some leads on where she's gone," Danny told him on their first meeting.

"I'll do my best," the guy replied grimly. "Women now just think they hold all the cards, and whatever they want, a judge agrees with in a custody case. You've got my sympathy, mate, you really have. I hope you find your kid."

Danny grimaced. "You got kids?"

"Yeah, once-a-month visitation and a couple of weeks in summer if I'm lucky. But she took me to the cleaners for child support. It's not right—the cards are stacked against us." He shook his head sourly.

"I want them back," Danny said. "She's not got the wherewithal to look after herself and a four-year-old on her own. I don't know what's got into her, but I want them back."

"Anything I can do to help, mate," the reporter said with a grim expression, "you just let me know."

So he had some people on his side, and that helped relieve the smart of the wound Kayleigh had dealt him.

By the time he'd finished, though, she'd be plastered all over the national news.

He'd get her home then all right. He'd get both of them back.

22

DILYS SHIFTED UNCOMFORTABLY IN THE chair by the potbellied stove, which sat at the far end of the farmhouse kitchen.

"Does your leg hurt?" Cerys asked as she fetched a glass of milk for Sammy. He was sitting at the old kitchen table, coloring. She'd managed to get him some pencil crayons and a book of dragons to color from the gift shop in Beaumaris. Lily had packed minimal toys for him, and he was starting to get bored after three days of teeming rain.

"The weather makes it ache more," Dilys admitted grudgingly. The farm collie shifted his head on her good foot and looked up at her like he understood.

Cerys snapped her fingers at him to come and get some scraps left over from lunch, and he trotted to her side. He was a good working dog, she'd found—happy enough to get out and do his job with her, though he clearly missed Dilys out there.

"He's taken to you," Dilys remarked.

"He'd rather be with you, but he's good with the sheep."

"So are you," Dilys said with a satisfied nod. "I've watched you through the window, up there on the hill."

Cerys smiled. "I was born to it."

"Been a long time though."

"Yes, but how did you know that?"

She snorted. "From the way you puffed up that hill the first day. And your face—that's not been out in all weathers for long years!"

Cerys laughed. "I'll take that as a compliment."

"You do that." She shifted again in her seat. "The damn thing itches too, as well as aching. They said I won't be able to do what I used to when it's healed, but I'll show them."

"Wanting to be rid of me already?" Cerys laughed.

Dilys fixed her with a gimlet stare. She had a habit of doing that. Lily found it disconcerting but Cerys didn't mind it. "No, surprisingly. The place has been looking nice since you got here. I'd gotten behind with it."

That was something of an understatement. The sheep were well kept, and the collie was in beautiful condition with a glossy coat Dilys brushed every day, religiously. But the farmhouse had been filthy. It had taken Lily and her a day between them to scrub downstairs clean, and then Cerys another day to sort out the upstairs when Lily had gone into work. Sammy had patiently sat with Dilys through all of it while she told him stories and fed him cookies. "He's never had that," Lily said softly when she came in to find them both dozing by the fire in an afternoon nap. "Someone like her. She's good for him, and he likes her."

Oddly, that was true. Cerys hadn't expected the old woman and the boy to bond, but they seemed to have done. Sammy loved sitting by the fire and listening to her tales while Cerys went out with the sheep. They made Welsh cakes together one afternoon, and Sammy fetched all the ingredients to the table for her. Dilys limped her way to the griddle to put them on to cook, and then the two of them sat together eating them with relish.

"It's funny," Cerys said to Lily after they'd put Sammy to bed. "I didn't think he'd be interested in sitting around with her like that, but he loves his time with her."

Lily nodded, biting her lip. "I know."

And she looked so sad that Cerys changed the subject and didn't pursue it any further. They'd been here two weeks now—the strangest two weeks of her life. It was as if this fortnight was a parenthesis in time. They existed inside here and not elsewhere.

She tried not to think about it. In fact, she tried not to think at all. That was her strategy, to exist in the moment and simply be. Anything more was too impossible to contemplate. There was no before and there was no after. There was only now, and here.

Up there on the farm, it was easy to pretend that there was nowhere else.

They were completely isolated unless they chose to leave, and Cerys avoided that. It was the best way to be.

She suspected Lily operated much the same way, although of course she went down into Beaumaris daily to work.

What would happen to them?

And even that thought caused a wave of panic so strong to rise up inside her that the room span and she had to sit down, dizzy and nauseous with it.

"Are you okay?" Lily asked, her face creasing with anxiety.

"I'm fine," she said, because she would be as soon as she stopped being stupid enough to step outside of their bracketed moments in time.

In here, now. That was safe. That was where they needed to be.

Let it go. Breathe out. Let everything go. There is only here, only now.

"Think I'm tired—this chasing up hills after sheep really takes it out of you when you're out of shape at my age."

"You are all right though? It's not too much?" The anxiety hadn't left Lily's face.

"Oh, I'll be fine! I'm just unfit. That old lady over there's been doing this for years and still would be if she hadn't broken her leg. I just need to get fit again. It'll do me good."

And doing kept her busy. Made the lack of thinking so much easier. Stretched the brackets out for another day, and then another.

The blackness hadn't returned yet.

This was the longest she'd been without it in a long, long time.

Brackets in time, keeping it away, keeping the world away.

That night in bed, she could hear the soft peace of the hillside, the hoots of the owl, and the quick, sharp bark of a fox under her window. The sounds of her childhood. And she could breathe again without choking.

If the blackness returned, she would know it was time to rethink, and that was so unbearable she didn't even want to go any further with those thoughts. For now, she listened to the night song of the quiet earth.

23

LILY WAS HAPPY, SHE REALIZED. One morning as she was trimming a customer's long hair to refresh dead ends back to healthy life, she discovered that she really was happy. For the first time she could remember, her heart felt light, and she didn't feel useless and stupid. She was doing her job, and she was doing it well enough for Angharad to tell her she wanted her to stay on, no question. Sammy had finally stopped flinching away if she moved too quickly or someone's voice was too sharp. And she herself didn't go back to the cottage with that sick feeling in her stomach that she used to associate with going home.

Was this how everyone else felt all the time?

Her inner voice told her it wouldn't last, but she couldn't help but treasure these moments. Where she got home from work to find Sammy skipping out to meet her. Where Cerys had something cooking that was wholesome and nutritious, proper food Lily didn't even know how to make. Where they'd go over to sit with Dilys around her TV, because it had better reception than the one at the cottage, and Dilys said there was no point burning two fires. Christmas was coming, the TV was full of festivity, and Sammy's excitement was growing.

Lily had never liked Christmas, but she wondered if this one might be different. Of course, it meant that the salon was growing extra busy and some days she was run off her feet, but oh, it was worth it when people left there happy and she got home to faces that were pleased to see her.

This was life, she told herself. If only she could have this forever.

She did worry about what to get Sammy for Christmas. And Cerys and Dilys? What on earth would she get them?

"Take a trip over to Bangor," Angharad suggested. "You can have a long lunch if you don't want to take the day off. You've worked hard—I'll cover while I still can."

But Bangor felt too risky. He'd be looking for her, she knew that, and she didn't know how far his search would spread. The local gift shops were safer. As she browsed around them over a few lunch breaks, she managed to track down something for everyone that she thought they would like, and the tourist shop had some toys at the back. And a bright-red scooter.

As soon as she saw it, she knew Sammy would love it. And also that watching him whizz around the yard would make Dilys laugh from her chair by the window. It was perfect. It even had a little horn.

Angharad laughed when she came back into the salon with it. "Well, he's going to love you on Christmas Day! Good choice! Do you want to hide it in the back until nearer the time?"

"That'd be great," Lily said in relief, wondering how she was going to hide it in the car when he ran out to meet her as soon as she was home. She could plan something with Cerys now if she knew in advance when she was bringing the scooter back.

Angharad grinned. "Put it in the storeroom. I wish I could see his face on Christmas Day. Mine don't get excited now." She rubbed her expanding stomach affectionately. "I can't wait for this little one to arrive and have all that over again. It's such a special time."

It had never felt like that for Lily, not until now. Was having this little, quiet life too much to ask for someone like her, or would Fate let her escape once and for all from who she was?

I'd like to be someone else. A proper mum, she thought as she stowed the scooter at the back of the storeroom.

She needed to color Sammy's hair again. His roots were beginning to show, so she stashed a dye mix in her bag while she was in there. It was getting harder to do this with Cerys about. Last time, she'd got him up early in the morning when Cerys went out to do the sheep, but getting rid of the smell of the dye had been difficult. She'd had to spray deodorant everywhere and then bury the evidence in the bottom of the wheelie bin before Cerys got back. Cerys wasn't stupid, and it was getting more difficult to keep their secret safe every day. She didn't know how much longer she'd be able to keep this up, but then she couldn't take that chance either.

He couldn't ever find out where they were, not ever. Not now she knew how good it could be without him.

24

SO, THE POLICE WERE TAKING this seriously, Danny thought, as he prepared to film a short section for the TV news. He'd managed to convince them—finally. His liaison officer, Mary, was setting up the table with a glass of water for him.

When he'd originally told them the money was gone and showed them the evidence, they'd relaxed, frustratingly, although at least it had stopped them digging around his whereabouts and suspecting him of having done something to Kayleigh and Drew. "I know it's worrying, sir, but it does look more like a marital dispute than that she's going to harm herself or the kiddie," one officer explained with a patience that just rankled Danny. Easy for him to say—it wasn't his wife and kid that'd gone missing. The guy might be right, but it still tore Danny apart not knowing where they were and what was going on. He wasn't sleeping; he was barely eating. He'd lost that contract he'd been bidding for, of course. And it hurt—it hurt so much that she'd done this.

"She was never good enough for you, Danny," his mother had told him on the phone. "I never wanted you to marry her, you know that."

He didn't give up easily though, and he pestered the liaison officer until they'd begun to listen in the end. And the longer it went on without any news, the easier it became to convince them that Kayleigh might be a risk and Drew might not, after all, be okay with her. They could see his concern and how it didn't abate and the more they dug into Kayleigh's past history, the more it supported his anxieties. It was all going on too long to point to a basic marital dispute. "It does look a bit more worrying now," that original officer acknowledged as they upgraded the status on the case. And finally they agreed to put something out on the TV, not nationwide as he'd wanted—not yet—but at least the regional news.

The police officer began the broadcast. "We are increasingly concerned for the safety of missing Kayleigh and Drew Harper, aged four, who disappeared in November. Mr. Harper will now give a brief statement to ask for your help in locating his missing family. As yet, there have been no reports of either of them being seen in the region, and we are appealing now to the wider public. You'll see some recent pictures of them in a moment. We would ask members of the public to contact us on the number at the bottom of the screen if you may have seen them." Danny took a deep breath. His palms were slick with sweat, and his shirt collar felt too tight, constricting his breath, and God, these lights were too hot.

"Kayleigh, if you're able to see this, please get in touch and let us know you're safe and that Drew is safe. I don't know why you needed to leave, but whatever it is, we can work it out." He swallowed hard. "And to anyone who sees them, please contact the police so they can check they are safe and well." He stared into the camera as if willing the faceless people on the other side to understand and help. "I just want my family home. I just want them back."

The police officer to the side of him put a hand on his shoulder as if to say well done, and after that, he zoned out while they finished the broadcast. Reinforcing how to report sightings, that kind of thing.

The house felt so empty without them, and he was going back there soon to be alone. He couldn't get that out of his head. As long as she wasn't with someone else, he could stand this until he got them back. But if she was?

He felt his anger boil his blood. There was no sign at all that she was with another man, but if she wasn't he couldn't understand how she was coping out there alone. He wouldn't have thought she had it in her.

25

LILY TRUDGED BACK INTO THE cottage after her busiest day in the salon yet. A good day, but her feet ached and her fingers were cramped from the scissors. That would pass as she got used to the work, and it was great to feel she was worth something again, but for now she wanted to flop in front of the TV and cuddle Sammy. It still felt strange to say that name in her head, but it was crucial they both thought that way—she'd told him that in the gas station when she'd dyed and cut his blond hair to disguise him better. "We need new names, both of us. And it's like the biggest game of pretend ever. I'm going to be Lily and you'll be Sammy. We have to pretend like we never had any other name. We have to even think of ourselves with our new names."

"So I can't call you Mummy?" he'd asked, puzzled.

"Of course! I'll always be Mummy! Just don't be surprised when other people think I'm Lily." She'd smiled as she'd dried his hair under a hand dryer in the deserted restroom. "I always liked that name. I'd like to be how it sounds—Lily. Sounds like someone who's got herself together." He couldn't really hear that last part with his head under the dryer, but it didn't matter because it wasn't really him she was trying to convince by that point.

As she entered the hall, Cerys stood in front of her, her face a mix of hesitancy and excitement. "I know this is a really bad time when you've just got in from doing this all day, but I need to ask now before I lose my nerve," she declared.

The very idea of Cerys losing her nerve made Lily smile. She had more nerve than Lily would ever have. "What is it?"

"I want you to cut my hair," she replied with a level of force that told Lily a lot.

Her feet and fingers protested but her head told them to shut up. If Cerys wanted a haircut, then it was the least she could do. "Okay, now?"

"I can't ask you to do it before dinner," Cerys said. "You've been working all day."

Lily's stomach growled, but she ignored it. She knew that look on Cerys's face. She'd seen it in the salon before on women when they reached a decision. For a woman, hair wasn't just something that grew out of your head; it was a life statement, and Cerys was about to make a big one.

"I'll give Sammy something quick for tea and then we'll do it," she said. Now, before Cerys changed her mind.

A quick frozen pizza later—she should always have those in for an emergency, Cerys had taught her, because food should never be stressful; as long as they were fed, it didn't matter what some woman on Instagram was doing, and she didn't need to feel guilty about that—Lily got her scissors out, and Cerys sat down on a kitchen chair with freshly washed hair.

"So any ideas? Any pictures?" Lily asked.

"Not a clue," Cerys replied with a nervous edge typical of a woman about to make this leap. "I've had the same haircut for over ten years, and I want something completely different. I *am* different now. I want something for the woman I am, not the woman I was."

"A new start," Lily said softly.

"Exactly," Cerys said, "but I've no idea what."

"Leave it to me?"

"Okay, make me a new woman!"

And Lily grinned and started playing with her hair a little, but not for long because she knew exactly what to do. Like an instinct, she knew what would work with Cerys's hair, her face shape, with the woman inside. So after a few moments, she began snipping. A small smile emerged on her face as she worked. Because this was going to be good. Twenty minutes later, she was nearly finished and rough-drying the hair so she could make those final and all-important finishing touches. Cerys wore the semi-terrified look of a woman who really hopes she's not going to regret her request. Lily ignored that with a bravery she felt a spark of pleasure at.

She mussed some light wax in her hands and gave a soft coating to Cerys's hair and then began to blast it into shape with the dryer. And soon Cerys was looking at a whole new her as promised. She'd lost some weight in the last few weeks, and the bones of her face were more defined, so Lily had worked with that to emphasize them with the soft pixie crop she'd chosen. Her existing highlights drew out the shape and texture of the new haircut, and she did indeed look a different woman.

"I look bolder," Cerys said wonderingly as she looked at her reflection.

"Do you like it?" Lily asked, and now was the time for fear, when the job was done and it was too late to go back.

"I love it," Cerys said with a trembling voice. She looked like a confident woman, one who trod her own path, one the blackness wouldn't catch. "It's perfect. Clever girl!"

And Cerys glowed, Lily realized, as she looked at her new self in the mirror. A seemingly small gift she had given in comparison to what Cerys had done and was doing for her, but a great one too. The framing of her new self, and Lily knew from the inside how much that was worth.

26

THE MEMORIES ALWAYS CAME AT night. Lily could keep them away in the day with the hustle and bustle of work, but they came for her in the dark. At least this one ended in some kind of happiness, unlike most.

She'd stared at the pregnancy test kit as the second blue line appeared. She wasn't ready for this, but Danny said she should be, and he'd insisted they try so she'd stopped taking the pill. Danny was always right, after all. They were settled, and he'd given her a lovely house to live in, but a baby meant the end of everything. He'd never let her go back to hairdressing now, and she had felt so good about passing her college course. As good as any A-level student felt going to university. It felt like she'd really achieved something. She'd graduated top of her class, and it turned out to be something she wasn't just good at; exceptional, her tutor had described her with pride.

She'd never been exceptional at anything in her life.

She definitely wouldn't be exceptional as a mother.

The thought of a baby terrified her. What did she know about bringing up a child? She wasn't the kind of girl who'd bothered much with babies when she was growing up. What if the baby cried every time she picked it up? What if it hated her?

She sat on the toilet, holding the hated and treacherous test kit in shaking hands. She wasn't ready for this.

And she was scared of telling Danny. She didn't know why.

No, that wasn't true—she did. She was scared of having a child with Danny. Of what he might do to her, and most of all whether he'd do the same to a child.

27

THE DAYS TOWARD CHRISTMAS SLIPPED by on the farm, so smoothly that Cerys found it easy not to mark time or think about how long she'd been there. It was just the blessed relief that the blackness wasn't with her. She still walked the tightrope of fearing its return, and it was impossible to believe it wouldn't. She had to get up before winter dawn to see to the sheep every day, her little shaggy friend at her heels, though he still abandoned her for Dilys, of course, as soon as they got back. But now he thumped his tail at her as she passed him in the farmhouse and wandered to her for the occasional lick of her hand.

"Need to order a turkey," Dilys remarked midmorning as the rain lashed horizontally outside and the lights were on to dispel the gloom. Cerys was glad of the cheer from the little woodstove at the armchair end of the long kitchen, which was where Dilys mostly sat during the day. Sammy played on the stairs with some of his toys. Cerys wasn't sure what the game was, but he was happy and occupied.

"Where from?"

"I'll find the phone book—Huw up the valley has them. I always get mine from him, and a good piece of Welsh Black beef too. I'll order bigger with you all here. You are here over Christmas?"

"Yes," Cerys replied cautiously because this felt like it was going somewhere and she wasn't sure where.

"Oh good, don't know how I'd manage without you at the moment,"

She rapped her cast in annoyance. "I thought you might have family to see, though."

Cerys didn't need to look at Dilys to know the old woman's eyes were boring into her. She might not see so well now but her instinct was sharp. "No, we're staying here."

A shiver ran down her neck like a December mountain stream. Her family. Christmas.

What would they be thinking now? She'd been gone a full month. Obviously they'd be looking for her. Would the car have been found? She knew it would be painful for them. She couldn't really understand anymore how she'd thought that there wouldn't be pain and it would all slip by easily for them. Of course they would be distraught at her disappearing, maybe being dead. But it was done now, and she couldn't make it better. Nor was she strong enough to fix it, especially when she still didn't know what to do. She needed longer; she needed her mind to become clearer.

How could she bear this? It wasn't supposed to be this way. She shouldn't still be here. This had never been part of her plan. It was an accident, this stolen time. But Christmas—no, she couldn't pretend through that. Perhaps it was time to go.

Go to what? And she knew somewhere in the back of her mind; she'd told herself she would one day finish the job she'd gone to start on that hillside. Because she couldn't ever go back. But she'd never intended to live without them either.

"Hope I haven't put ideas in your head," Dilys said in a dry voice. "I should have kept my big mouth shut, because I don't know what I'll do if you go."

She looked up. The old woman gave her a hard stare.

"I mean it—I need you. Kills me to say it, mark you, but I do."

Cerys ran a hand through her hair. Its short choppiness still felt strange after years of that old bob, but she loved it. "I don't think I can stay much longer," she said in a shaky voice.

"The girl needs you too," Dilys said. "For all, she's not your daughter."

Cerys frowned. "How did you know that?"

Dilys let out a shout of laughter. "She's never once called you 'Mum.' Not once. Never calls you anything, mind, but a girl wouldn't do that with her mother. And anyway, she's too careful around you, too polite. I don't know what the pair of you are up to, but you're helping me out, whatever it is, so maybe it's none of my business."

Cerys shook her head. "You pick up a lot for a woman used to living on her own!"

Dilys cackled, a proper evil old-lady sound that made Cerys laugh in return. "I didn't always live up here on my own, you know."

"No?"

"No, I was married once. A long time ago."

Cerys sat up. "Go on."

"He died. Far too young. Only forty. It was a heart attack. He had a weakness there, they said."

"Oh, I'm so sorry!"

Dilys shrugged. "It happens, doesn't it? We had a good life before I lost him, but no children. I wish there had been, so did he, but we weren't blessed."

"Did you not want to marry again?"

She shook her head. "No, no, never fancied it with anyone else. No, I've been content on my own."

Cerys felt the weight of the sadness in her comment about the lack of children, and she understood better now why Dilys loved having Sammy about. He came into the room now, and Dilys grinned at him. "Hey, mischief! I've had a good idea. Why don't we brighten this cast up a bit for Christmas?" She hauled her leg up onto the footstool. "Get your coloring pens out and let's get some Christmas cheer in here!"

Sammy danced over gleefully to look.

"See if you can do a big Christmas tree," said Dilys. She winked at Cerys. "If you can't act daft at my age, when can you?"

"I don't know," Cerys said, passing Sammy the felt tips.

"What I learned from Richard passing was to make the most of the time you have. Never to be worrying about what anyone thinks. To do the things you want to, because you never know if tomorrow will come or if you'll be dust in the churchyard."

"Can I draw a reindeer?" Sammy asked.

"You go ahead," Dilys told him.

Sammy picked up a purple marker, and Cerys started to pass him a brown one. Dilys waved at her to stop.

"Do you want the reindeer to be purple?" she asked him in that odd fierce way she sometimes used, which never seemed to faze him as if he perfectly understood her.

"Yes," Sammy replied with more firmness than Cerys had ever heard in his usually timid little voice.

"Then you color it purple, kid. You see, there are people who color reindeer brown and they color them very, very neatly and everyone says well done. And then there are people who color them purple. And if you're a purple reindeer kind of person, you be proud of that! And don't let anyone persuade you otherwise!"

Sammy nodded and quietly got on with drawing on her cast.

Cerys surveyed Dilys. "I think I wish someone had told me that at his age," she said quietly.

Dilys harrumphed. "Well, I'll keep saying it to you now, until it sinks in. Stop worrying about coloring inside the lines of your life."

"How did you know I did that?" she asked.

"It's written all over you." Dilys cocked her head to one side. "The thing with growing older is you can stop caring what people think and be yourself. Now on my own up here, I've been able to do that a lot longer."

"And I suspect you were always inclined that way," Cerys said with a dry laugh.

"I was," Dilys agreed. "And it's time you learned the benefits."

"What makes you think I haven't?" she asked with mock indignation.

Dilys rolled her eyes. "Like I said, it's written over you."

"Maybe you're right." Cerys drew a star shape on the cast for Sammy to color.

"Time to choose your own colors now," Dilys said, leaning back and watching them.

28

"I DON'T UNDERSTAND IT," HE said on the phone to his mother again. "She had everything."

"Ungrateful," she replied. "I did warn you, Danny. Bad blood outs. And look at her own mother. Girls like that, they can pretend, but in the end they can't run from who they are, and she's no good. Never has been. You focus on getting Drew back and then divorce her. I'll send you over some money for a lawyer if you need it, but you make sure she doesn't get a penny from you. Hire somebody good. I'll ask around over here and see if anyone can recommend somebody good for you. I hate to say this to you, but she probably had her eyes on your money all along. I bet she only had Drew to help her cause when it got to this stage. She's never loved that kiddie, really. I mean, what kind of mother would do this to their own child?"

And he could feel the anger boiling up inside him as she put into words all that he'd been thinking himself at those wakeful two a.m. moments that had haunted him ever since Kayleigh left.

Okay, so he'd put a stop to her games. If she didn't appreciate everything he'd done for her, pulling her out of that sewer she was in, then his mother was right. He'd get Drew back and then he was done with her.

He'd see when they found her what she was up to, and then, if his mother was right, the gloves were off. He'd take Drew from her forever.

That'd teach her.

29

TIME TO CHOOSE HER OWN colors, Dilys had said. And Cerys had felt a great pull of truth in that; but what did it mean for her now?

She'd been an intelligent woman once. Back at university, she'd been bright, sparkling, vigorous. Even when she had the children, she had still been that person. She'd used her intelligence and energy to give her children the best start in life they could have, and to give Gavin a peaceful home he could relax in after he'd spent all day working for them.

But Dilys was right. In all that effort she'd put into making everyone else happy, she'd fallen into a pattern she'd never really chosen. Nobody had made her discard her own interests. It was her who'd let it happen because, at the back of her mind, she must have thought that was the way looking after her family had to be done.

Cerys laughed as she leaned on the farm gate, one of her favorite places to think, looking out over the hill with the sheep dotted about. They weren't like the white clouds described in a poem, but rather some muddy gray splats in the distance all cannoning about because some of them had decided to have a burst of energy and gallop, spooking all the others.

Dilys would have had short words to say about how she'd let herself fall into her trap. And she hadn't even noticed until the blackness descended so far over her that it was a death shroud.

Gavin should have noticed, she thought, with a bitter sense of betrayal.

If he cared, he should have been watching out for her. He should have stepped in and helped.

But her mother's voice in her head answered her. "Don't expect him to be good at things he never was just because that's what you happened to need then."

She shook her head in frustration. But what was the good of a marriage if you couldn't lean on each other when you needed to?

That voice was right though. Gavin was useless at emotional support and always had been. That had been her job. So who was there to hold her up when she needed it? There had been no one.

The sudden rush of sadness she felt as she looked back now and saw the hurt and desperation descend on her through the lens of memory, as she saw the blackness coming, was overwhelming. She bent her head against the top bar of the gate and let some tears fall silently to the ground for a while.

But then, she lifted her head and brushed the remains of the tears away. And the blackness wasn't there, sucking her in. She had felt sadness and she'd let it out. Up on the hill, her little mud splats of wool were still frolicking about. The sun was out and was telling her to choose her own colors too.

She shook her head again, but in wonder this time because she didn't feel like giving up right now. She leaned her chin on her hands on the top of the gate and watched the sheep until Sammy came skipping out to see what she was doing.

30

LILY SLUMPED INTO THE CHAIR when she got home. "It's been so busy today. We've not even had time to breathe!"

Cerys put the kettle on as Sammy crawled on his mother's lap for a cuddle. "The postman told me today that they're having Santa's sleigh visit in Beaumaris on Saturday, and there's a little town celebration as he drives through. Should we go?" She wouldn't have suggested venturing further afield. Too risky for her, and for Lily too, or so she suspected. But Beaumaris would be safe.

Lily frowned, that odd nervous expression that Cerys saw far less of now, but it still returned sometimes. "I don't know."

"It'll be fun," Cerys told her firmly because Sammy deserved this. Lily needed to learn to enjoy her little boy. Maybe this was part of the problem. Lily didn't know how to have fun with him.

"Will it?" Lily asked in genuine confusion.

"Yes. Didn't you love that kind of thing when you were small?" It was a test really, to see if she was right in how she thought Lily would react. Heartbreakingly she was correct—Lily's face did that split-second crumple that she'd expected before she shuttered up again, just as Cerys knew she would.

And there finally Cerys knew she'd identified part of Lily's problem. For whatever reason, her own childhood just hadn't been right. She didn't need to say anything. It was written over her, as Dilys would say.

"So you'll learn to love it now," she said softly. "It's never too late. And you'll learn to see it through Sammy's eyes, and that's a special kind of magic." As soon as the words were out, she realized how much they applied to her too. She also needed to see that special kind of magic again. She missed that so much now her own were grown up and gone, as if there was no sparkle and spell left in life any longer.

They would go, and she'd teach Lily what someone should have taught her a long time ago. It was well overdue that this girl learned the value of that magic. If she was ever to leave here at all, she needed to make sure that was done so that Lily kept that with her. It was what sustained a mother through the long, hard days and the dark, tired nights; past sickness bugs and cleaning up vomit from child and floor, past tantrums and misunderstandings and scribble on the wall, past money worries and fear about pretty much everything. That light in the child's eyes at times like these blew it all away like winter cobwebs when the windows were opened for the spring.

Cerys planned carefully, using Dilys's local knowledge as her main informant. Dilys snorted in agreement at the plan. "That girl needs some fun," she said. They would go down to Beaumaris at two o'clock and get a late lunch at a café. It would be quieter then, and Sammy could take his time. Cerys would make brunch to keep him going until then. It meant Lily could still go into work in the morning and finish a few hours early. The whole town would come out for the afternoon events, so Angharad always closed the salon at lunchtime on the day of the Christmas Fair.

It felt good to be doing this. She had a purpose again.

Dilys chuckled. "You look pleased with yourself."

"I am," she replied as she cleaned round the kitchen. It sparkled these days. And she remembered how she'd grown too tired to clean her own like this over the past few years, how that heavy dragging in her body had translated to her mind and everything had been such an effort. That had gone, most of it. Where had it started first, in her limbs or her head? It was impossible to say. But she was glad to see the back of it. She almost felt like the woman she used to be again.

"She needs you," Dilys remarked.

"For now," Cerys said, "but then she'll learn and she won't, and that's how it's supposed to be." Wasn't it? That's what had happened with her kids, after all. Gone off and had no use for her now.

"Did you ever stop needing your mother?" Dilys scoffed. "Mine's been dead thirty years, and I still wish every day that I could see her, get her advice."

Cerys stopped cleaning and turned round to look at the old woman. "What would you ask her today?"

Dilys's eyes wandered from her to gaze out of the window. "I'd ask her how you're supposed to cope with this aging thing. How you're supposed to get closer to the grave every day and feel it in your bones and not give up when you know it's coming anyway. That's what I'd ask today." Then she waved her hand dismissively and turned back. "But tomorrow it might just be how did she get her fruitcake not to dry out in the oven because mine always does! And at eighty-eight, I think it might be too late for me to get it right now."

Cerys shrugged at her. "Well, we'll make one together and see. Maybe this time, at eighty-eight, it'll come good."

"Ha! Good try, but it's too late now. A cake needs weeks to season."

"Only if you ladle brandy into it, and Sammy won't be able to eat it then. It'll be just fine made now, and he can ice it with you."

"Ah yes, he'll like that," Dilys said with a smile.

"We'll do it on Sunday then. As long as it's iced for Christmas Day, that's all that matters."

"I hated Christmas cake as a child," Dilys said. "Let's hope he likes it. Now put the kettle on. It's time we had a talk."

"Is it?" Cerys asked, startled.

"Long past time," Dilys said firmly.

31

"I DON'T KNOW WHEN IT started, really," Cerys said, with Dilys listening intently. She found that reassuring about Dilys—when she listened, she really listened. Not many people truly did that. "But I know it got worse when my youngest left home. I just couldn't find a point to anything anymore. And it went from there into a downward spiral."

"So you have children? I thought so, seeing how you are with Sammy, and Lily for that matter. So yours would be about her age?"

"One younger and two older," Cerys said in agreement.

"And you missed them," Dilys said.

"Yes. I hadn't been feeling right for a while. Couldn't put my finger on it and thought maybe it was the idea they'd go sooner or later, but after they all left I got deader and deader. I used to call it the blackness, and it was eating me up. I really mean that. It was as if it consumed me until there was nothing left. I said I'd stopped seeing my friends so much, but by then I couldn't face them at all. I just didn't want to talk, to pretend I was okay, to do anything. Everything was too much effort. My body ached." She shuddered as she remembered. "I hurt everywhere, in my head, in my heart, and it spread into my joints, my muscles, and round my whole body. And the blackness just kept coming."

"Did you see a doctor?" Dilys said with a frown.

"No, because what could a doctor do? They couldn't give me back what I've lost."

"No, they couldn't, but did you ever think it was more than that?"

Cerys frowned. "What do you mean?"

"Did you never think a lot of how you were feeling could be due to the change?"

"What, with being alone? Yes, like I said—"

"No," Dilys said impatiently, "the change of life. The menopause."

Cerys looked at her blankly. "No, to be honest, that never occurred to me. And it had been coming on for ages. I mean, I got the menopause earlier this year, and it didn't seem much really. I just stopped, no hot flashes or anything like that. No, this has been building up a long time."

Dilys shook her head. "It's not all hot flushes. It can make some women feel like you've said. All kinds of funny feelings, it can cause. And they don't come on all at once. It can build for years before that. You mark my words, I bet a lot of it could be down to that."

"Oh!" Cerys was stunned. That had never occurred to her before. Of course she'd expected her cycle to go irregular and stop, and she knew about the hot flushes that had never really bothered her much. But what could the sense of impending doom, and panic, and that grinding sadness that spread through her very bones, have to do with it? That ceaseless sense of anxiety and otherness that made her feel like she wasn't herself any longer. When she could put that into some form of words, she asked Dilys that.

Dilys nodded. "Seen it before in other women. It goes eventually, but it gives some of us a lot of trouble before it does."

Cerys shook her head wonderingly. "How did you get to be so wise, stuck out here alone?"

Dilys gave her trademark snort of disgust. "I could drive before this leg, you know. I've not been stuck on this hill in isolation for decades!" She glared at Cerys. "I've lived here all my life. There's not a soul in these parts I don't know, and I know their stories. Now, where was I? Oh yes, pity you didn't see a doctor. I'm not saying a doctor can make it go away, though I know women who got that hormone therapy and swear by it, but I know others who don't. But sometimes just knowing what it is makes a thing a bit better."

Cerys thought about it. "You know, I think you're right there. I think it would have helped to know that, if it really is that. When you're that lost inside the mess in your head, it'd help to know why."

"Do you think I could be right about it?"

"Yes, you know I really think you might just have a point," she said wonderingly. "When I think now of when it started, how it crept up on me and I just had no idea, how it would come and go in waves at first until it settled in. You could just be right. It might have had something to do with it. Wow!" She stared at Dilys.

Dilys snorted. "That's the thing with living alone—it makes you better at listening to people. You'll find I'm right a lot."

And Cerys laughed at the wicked little twinkle in the old woman's eyes. "Yes, I know you are, and you love it." And on impulse, she got up and hugged her. "And you keep being you! Please don't ever stop."

32

SHE WAS TWELVE YEARS OLD when the social worker came into her bedroom to tell her that her mother was giving her up. And despite everything that had happened to her before and since, it was still Lily's worst memory.

"You need to pack now, Kayleigh."

"Why?" She pulled her headphones out of her ears.

"Your mum's not able to look after you right now, so she's agreed you should stay with a foster family for a while."

She put her headphones back in. "No." And she turned the music up to full blast.

The social worker bent down and tried to gently remove the headphones, and something inside her snapped. She slapped the woman's hand away. "Get the fuck off me!"

The woman stood up, shocked. Yes, whatever—she'd never done anything like that before. Well, she'd never been given away before. She used to fantasize when she was younger that another family would adopt her and take her to live with them, somewhere better and nicer. Then she'd wised up and realized that nobody was going to want her around, just like her mum had said. So her mother might suck, but she was a better option than the alternative.

Even if she was the kind of mum who'd give you away rather than give up the drugs.

Did this woman even know how that felt? She was standing over Kayleigh with a perplexed expression, wondering what to do next. All professional but zero understanding. They were all like that, this lot—said they cared, pretended they had an idea how you felt. But they only saw the pain from the outside. They didn't know what it was like to live with that etched into your bones, so they throbbed with it. So that every bit of you was dirty and unwanted, was human refuse.

Screw them—she wasn't going to go easily. She wasn't going to be a good girl. Not now.

33

COULD DILYS BE RIGHT? CERYS asked Lily to pick her up a magazine from the shop in Beaumaris, one of those health lifestyle ones for older women. She hadn't actually read one for years, but she'd seen the covers when browsing in the supermarkets, and there were always headlines about the menopause battle and supplements to survive it, that kind of thing.

Lily came home with a few. "Wasn't sure which you wanted, but I thought it's some reading for you anyway. No, don't give me the money back—these are on me."

Bless her, Cerys thought, because those things weren't cheap, and Lily didn't get paid a lot really. A wad of magazines would take a surprising chunk out of that. A matter Cerys had never had to worry about all her married life, of course, and no matter how angry she was at Gavin for how things had ended up, she had to remember how much of the gloss of those earlier years was down to him. When they all went to bed later, Cerys settled down to flick through the magazines. She'd been right—there were a few articles among them on menopause and managing it naturally, the benefits of HRT and what to do without it. Her eyes homed in on a text box to the side of a picture of a woman gazing meaningfully at a soy supplement. The headline "I thought I was losing my mind" grabbed her attention, and Cerys scanned through with growing interest. Some of it described exactly how she'd felt: the strange sense of anxiety when she'd never been an anxious person, how it came for no apparent reason at all, the joint aches, and fatigue that seemed to suck the life out of her at times. How that anxiety sometimes escalated to a sense of impending doom. One that had made Cerys often feel there was no point in going on. This woman had struggled at work and had ended up quitting her job before they sacked her.

It wasn't the same, Cerys thought, putting the magazine down on the bed. But there were a lot of similarities. Enough to make her think Dilys really might have a point. Maybe it wasn't all the kids skipping off to their shiny new lives and leaving her behind and useless with no purpose. Maybe it wasn't just Gavin's work obsession and failing to notice her existence at times. Maybe it was actually, at least partly, this.

Would it have made it easier if she'd known? She rather thought it might. It would have taken some of the guilt away.

She picked up another magazine and began to thumb through that with more interest. Knowledge was power, after all.

34

LILY DROVE DOWN INTO BEAUMARIS. The visitors' car park was closed for the event, so they parked up along the coast road on the way out and walked back in. A couple of volunteer marshals were present along the road to help people park most effectively and bump up onto the shoulder to keep the road clear. There was a bucket out, raising money for the Lifeboat charity. A boat ran out of Beaumaris and Cerys dropped a couple of pounds into the tub. This little town was very proud of its crew.

There was that sense of excitement in the air that Cerys remembered from her own childhood and countless trips with her children to see Christmas lights. Sammy felt it too and began to skip as they walked down the coast road toward the main street. It made Cerys smile to see that, but Lily bit her lip and looked round to check for traffic. She really couldn't relax with him. Would today be the breakthrough that Cerys wanted to see? She wasn't sure, but they had to try.

They strolled down toward the car park, which was filled with market stalls for the afternoon event. The local craftspeople were out in force with local honey for sale, Welsh cheeses, traditional wooden carvings, and textiles. Predictably, Sammy showed little interest in any of those, and as it was part of Cerys's mission that they all had a relaxing time, she didn't expect him to trail round patiently with them while they looked. She had a little cash saved from what she earned for looking after the sheep for Dilys, and she planned to make sure they had fun with it. She spotted a sweets stall and headed them toward that.

Lily only had the filter on what he should eat when someone else made her nervous, Cerys had noticed, so she had no concern at all when Cerys suggested to Sammy that he choose one of those beautifully wrapped cellophane cones of sweets, tied up with long trails of swirly red and green ribbon. His eyes glowed as he held his choice in his little and soon-to-be sticky hands.

"You choose something," Cerys told Lily.

"Me?" she said, shocked.

"Yes, you. Look, they've got handmade chocolates there."

"Are you getting some for yourself?" She wore a slightly anxious expression, as if she thought she might have committed some kind of faux pas without really being sure what that was.

"No, because I've spotted the hot chestnut stall over there so I'm going to get some of those, but they're an acquired taste, so I don't know if you'll like them." She sniffed the air as the scent of roasting chestnuts drifted over to them. "But nothing says Christmas to me more than chestnuts. I love them."

"Oh, could I try too?" Lily asked, in the manner of a very polite child, Cerys thought.

Sometimes Lily wasn't really far away from that stage. At times like this, Cerys could see her regress, and any adult certainty that she had managed to acquire disappeared like mist. But that was part of the plan, to let her experience what Cerys was by now certain she'd missed out on. You couldn't give that to your child unless you knew that fun from the inside, Cerys had determined. She'd never consciously known that before until the puzzle that was Lily presented itself for her to solve. She bought three cones of the chocolates to take home with them and popped them in her bag.

"Can he open his now?" she asked Lily as she bent to unwrap the sweets for Sammy.

"Yes…but he might drop them," Lily said with that edge of nerves Cerys hated to hear, because she didn't like to think about what might have put it there. Sometimes the not knowing for sure was the worst, she thought.

"He might, but I expect he'll be extra careful because they're so very beautiful," Cerys said, smiling at him as she bent down to untie the ribbons. She whispered to Lily as she straightened up. "Don't worry if he does. I've got enough to get some more if we do have an accident. Little hands do drop things sometimes, but they have to learn."

"Is it okay to do that?" Lily whispered back as Sammy stuffed a flying saucer–shaped sweet into his mouth, with big eyes. "It's not spoiling?" She wore an apologetic expression for questioning Cerys at all, because she really didn't understand if even that was acceptable.

"Oh, I imagine some people might say that, but I don't agree with them. I've always found it's rare they make a mistake like that anyway. It does happen sometimes but not so much when they're not worrying about it. It's important they learn to make judgment calls, and I don't think you can do that effectively unless you feel secure. And you can't feel secure if you're constantly worried about making a mistake and the consequences. I know some parents would say if he dropped them, he'd learn to be careful, but actually I don't think that's true. That's what we'd like to think, but that assumes he was being careless in the first place. Usually, they're just being little! What they do learn is to trust you to put things right, and that's much more important in my eyes."

Lily nodded thoughtfully.

And really, without intending to, I've just described what I'm trying to do with you too, Cerys thought.

She led them over to the chestnut stall and bought two bags and then, on impulse, spotting they sold hot drinks too, a couple of cups of mulled wine and a hot chocolate for Sammy.

"Now what I have learned myself," she said with a laugh as she stuffed the bags of chestnuts in her coat pocket and shared the load of the cups with Lily, "is never to try to balance too much with a small child in a crowded place, so let's grab a seat for a minute while we enjoy these."

They headed toward some café-style tables set off to the side of the stalls. Sammy sipped his hot chocolate eagerly with his hands cupped around it to warm them. Cerys watched Lily's face as she sipped the mulled wine.

"Oh!" she said in surprise. "Oh, I didn't expect it to taste like that." And then a moment later, "Ooh, it gets right down to your toes!"

Cerys laughed. "That's such a good description. Try a chestnut and see what you think."

She showed Lily how to peel the shell away, and Lily nibbled cautiously.

"They're not nutty at all!" she exclaimed. "But nice, yes, I like them."

"These are Christmas to me," Cerys said. "My mother and I used to make the chestnuts together when I was a child. She loved them as much as I do."

"What was she like, your mum?" Lily asked.

"She was a farmer's wife, no nonsense and no fuss. A very practical woman. She had no time to be anything else. She wasn't much of a reader, but she loved to settle down in the evening for an hour with a favorite TV program. She'd have loved the on-demand TV we have now." Cerys could feel her eyes sting as they sometimes still did when she saw her mother through the eyes of her memory. "She was a wonderful mother, always there for us, and such a strong woman, right up until she died. Even after we lost my dad, she picked herself up and carried on. I miss her more than I can possibly say. Every single day."

"You were very lucky," Lily said softly. There was no jealousy in her voice but a sort of quiet sadness that Cerys noticed she often wore around her like a coat.

"I know." She almost didn't ask her next question because she didn't want to ruin the day, but maybe it needed to be asked, and perhaps it was indeed the right time to do so. "What was your mother like?"

Lily gave a quick glance at Sammy, who was reassuringly occupied prying a sweet from the cone. "Oh, nothing like yours," she replied. "And I went into care when I was twelve. I never saw her after that."

"Oh, Lily!"

"It wasn't nice," she said, looking off into the distance. "I think that's why I'm no good at this. I just wish I was better. Every child should have a mum like yours. And like you."

Cerys found her voice choked up inside her. She reached out and put her hand over Lily's. "It is *never* too late to be who you want to be. It is never too late to create that life."

"I don't know how. Or I didn't." She smiled and it reached her eyes and dispelled some of that gentle melancholy that resided there too much. "I think I'm learning a little. You know, I honestly don't know what I would have done if you hadn't come along."

Cerys didn't know either quite what would have happened to her if Lily hadn't happened along.

As she looked at Lily, she was reminded of how very much she missed

Katie. And her boys. They might not seem to need her much now, but life put everyone through its twists and turns, and she knew how much she'd needed her own mother so many times. Wasn't it strange how the blackness had stolen that knowledge from her and twisted everything out of shape and pattern?

"Could you help me make this a special Christmas for him?" Lily asked. "I was hoping you could show me how to do it, and then I might get it right for him. I might be a better mother."

Cerys got up and dusted her hands off. She collected their rubbish and put it in the nearby bin. Then she held her arm out to Lily to link through hers, as she would have done with Katie.

"One day, you need to tell me why you're so convinced you're not. But not now. Now we're going to enjoy ourselves. And yes, we're going to have a wonderful Christmas."

The only way she could stand being alive and yet not being with her own children at Christmas was to make this great for Lily and Sammy and Dilys. She didn't know what the new year would bring, but it looked like she would be here to see it in after all. And that was somewhat incredible.

She had a job to do with these two.

If only she knew who she was when she wasn't here.

꩜

Sammy loved the stalls. There were so many for children. Little fairground games with a Christmas theme to keep the little ones happy while the parents shopped the crafts. Cerys stopped at a stall with handmade Christmas decorations. Just looking at them made Lily feel like she'd taken another sip of that mulled wine. She glowed with Christmas and she'd never felt this way before.

"They're so lovely," she said to Cerys. "Just looking at them makes me feel happy."

Cerys smiled. "Favorite colors?"

"Oh, it's so hard to choose! I love the red and green, but those silver and white glittery ones are so pretty, and the ice blue."

"I know. I had three boxes of different color schemes that I'd built up over the years. I used to rotate them round because I could never just have one. We're going to pick a decoration each for the tree, to make some memories. Sammy, come here and choose."

He grinned and held up the little wooden rocking horse he was playing with at the side of the stall, painted in Nutcracker colors of gold and red and green.

"I guess he's picked the colors for all of us," Lily said with a laugh, and she realized she didn't feel nervous that he'd chosen for them. There would be no consequences; Cerys would think that was absolutely fine, and actually it had saved her from making a difficult decision.

And it was…nice. Sammy had picked, and that made him happy, and the contentment on his face made her happy too.

It really did and it was all okay.

Lily felt a rush of happiness, warmer than that mulled wine glow.

This was it—this was really living. This kind of feeling was what she'd been waiting for her whole life.

The people milling round them would think she was crazy if they could see inside her head. She was twenty-two years old, and she was supposed to love adventure and nightlife and wild excitement.

But no, what made her happy was contentment on her child's face and a woman who made her feel like she was worth something.

Like my mum should have done.

Like Danny had never done, though she'd thought he would when she met him. She'd believed all that stuff he'd told her.

Suddenly she knew she wanted to tell Cerys about it, wanted her advice. Did she dare? Not now, of course. But she thought she might, one day soon when they were on their own. She might tell her. It might help.

Cerys was showing Sammy the ornament she'd chosen—a fat, jolly Santa that her child appreciated with a squeal and a clap of his hands.

She might need to tell Cerys that other thing too, about Sammy, before it went on for too long. How they'd get round that with Dilys, she didn't know, and it wasn't safe to change things yet—it had helped keep them safe up to now, but it couldn't go on forever and she knew that. Also, she worried about the effect it could have on Sammy. She glanced around nervously like a reflex.

And in the crowd, some twenty people between them, she spotted a man with hair just like Danny's.

Fear isn't always cold. Sometimes it's a hot flash of heat, warming you, preparing your muscles to run. Preparing you to grab your child and flee to safety.

The heat swept through her. Her stomach lurched in response as he moved through the crowd in the opposite direction.

Had he followed her here? Had he somehow found her location? She had to know.

She edged through the crowd after him, her nails clenched into her palms. A quick look back showed Cerys was busy with Sammy and not looking. She had a few moments.

He stopped suddenly and waved at someone further ahead. Lily ducked back in case whoever it was saw her.

A burly man dressed in farmer's gear and carrying a crate grinned and shouted out in return, "Huw! Well, give us a hand then!"

And then as the man pushed through again, she saw his face and it wasn't Danny.

It wasn't Danny. It took a while for her rapid heartbeat to subside.

She turned around to go back before she was missed. As she did, she caught sight of a newspaper in a man's hand as he waited at a hot dog stall. The headline said "Missing Nantwich Mum—another appeal to get her home for Christmas," and her heart jolted again, and she looked more closely. It wasn't a local paper, and it wasn't her picture under the tagline.

It was Cerys.

She sucked her breath in and tried to see more, but the man had moved away.

Nantwich. She had no idea where that was, but it didn't sound Welsh.

People came from all over for this event, Cerys said, and the hotel still had holidaymakers staying even at this time of year. Most likely the man was one of them.

Or was he looking for Cerys? She watched him carefully to see if he stopped and showed the picture to anyone, asked questions, or seemed to be searching.

But no, he was just wandering from stall to stall.

"Okay?" said Cerys's voice behind her, and she turned quickly to find Sammy holding up glittery foil paper chains for her to look at. "We couldn't resist them," Cerys said with a laugh as she helped him keep them from trailing on the ground.

And Lily was reminded of what she'd been thinking about before she saw the man in the crowd. About the secret she was still keeping.

After Christmas—she'd talk to Cerys then.

She picked a candy cane in red and green stripes, dusted with golden glitter. The kind of treat she would have loved to find in a stocking on Christmas morning. The kind Cerys's kids probably did find.

"It's never too late to learn to love Christmas either," Cerys whispered in her ear with a soft laugh. "Never too late to understand its magic."

So this was happiness, and it was a gentle and a beautiful thing. Lily had had enough in her life of hoping and being disappointed, of the roller coasters. This quiet joy was all she'd ever wanted, though she hadn't known what she was looking for.

Please don't let it be taken away, she prayed silently, though she wasn't the praying kind. *Please let me have this.* She kept thinking of that man in the crowd and how Danny would not give up, would never give up, until he'd found her. Please, couldn't she just be free of him—somehow, anyhow?

And Cerys—her family was looking for her. That much was clear. And they were spending Christmas without her. But if they got her back, a little voice said inside her, then Lily would lose her. And that thought paralyzed her with fear. She should help them.

But she wouldn't. She already knew she was a bad person, so what difference would one more bad, selfish deed make? And this was for Sammy as much as herself.

She looked at her happy, smiling child, beaming up at Cerys. She would do anything to keep this life they were building safe for Sammy. Anything. Whatever it took. She had no guts, no courage, no sense. Danny had told her that so many times. But if he tried to take this life from her child, he'd find out that he was wrong about her.

She remembered him slapping her down onto the bed, choking her. But this time she imagined grabbing the bedside lamp and clubbing his head with it until he stopped hurting her.

Her face twisted into an expression of triumph until she caught Cerys looking at her oddly. And then she smiled and hugged Cerys. "Thank you for today. You have no idea what it's done for me."

35

CERYS STOOD ON THE HILL as the sun rose brighter in the sky and the dog moved the sheep together to shift them to the next pasture. They were changing, Lily and her, she realized. While they were here together, Lily was becoming a mother—or the one she wanted to be. Cerys herself, well, she was becoming an un-mother. That was the phase of life she was in, and she had to get over that if she was ever to move forward. Probably for the first time, she understood what Dilys meant about the change of life. She could no longer have children. Of course, she hadn't thought of having more for years. She remembered back to that decision that they would stop at three.

She had just finished wrestling Matt into bed. Alex was sitting up in his bed with a small lamp, reading, and she gave him the signal for lights-out. He responded with a nod, and she crept in so the floorboards didn't creak and wake Matt again, who had only just, finally, dozed off. Katie was asleep in her cot and had been for the last hour. Fortunately, once she was well away, she didn't tend to wake, but it took a good while to achieve that. Katie seemed to have a second sense for her standing up to leave, so Cerys resorted to a comedic crawl on all fours to the door. Then she'd close the door softly and sit outside for at least ten minutes to let her get into a deeper sleep before going to get the boys into bed. There was always much shushing and "don't wake the baby."

They were all so different, her three, and all so special in their own ways. She kissed Alex good night, and he put his book down carefully on the bedside table. Such a precise, serious little boy. Always hard working in school, always the sensible one. As she went past Matt's room again, she could hear him turn over restlessly. The total opposite of his brother, a constantly moving ball of noise and chaos who greeted everyone with a big grin that disarmed them completely. And she snuck back into Katie's room, still a nursery, to give her a last kiss now she was far enough into sleep not to be woken. Her baby, and such a mummy's girl. Oh, she loved her daddy, but it was Mummy she always wanted to be with. She breathed in the soft little girl scent of her as she leaned over the cot to place a last kiss for the day on that warm baby hair.

Then she made her way quietly downstairs and flopped on the sofa, exhausted. She flicked through some TV but there was nothing much on and she had a vague nagging building inside her. Katie was one now, and Cerys had that broodiness building in her again that she'd had with all her babies when they reached this age. She knew what it was, and knew it passed. They'd deliberately left gaps between the children after watching her sister's kids who got on far better where there was an age gap than the two who were only a year apart.

But still, she got up and went through to the home office where Gavin was punching numbers into a spreadsheet and frowning. "Can I disturb you for a minute?"

He looked round, as though a fly had buzzed in his ear. "What?"

She pressed on; otherwise, she'd never get to say what she needed to. He'd probably be in here all night if left to his own devices. "Can I disturb you?"

He sighed. "I'm just in the middle of something... What is it?"

Gavin was always in the middle of something, so she ignored this. "I wanted to talk to you about having another baby."

"No," he said firmly. "Three is enough."

She was taken aback. She'd expected more discussion on this, rather than this bald refusal. "Aren't we going to actually talk about this? Is that it?" she asked indignantly.

He pushed his mouse away and turned to her. His eyes were red with fatigue from too long at the screen. "No," he said. "Every single time before, I've gone along with it because it was what you wanted."

"Gone along with it? These are our children!"

He waved his hand in exasperation. "I used the wrong words, I didn't mean it like that! Look, we're both working our fingers to the bone for our kids, and we don't get time as it is to enjoy life. You're shattered by the time they go to bed, and another one is just too much. I have to keep the business going and that means long hours. I recognize that, and it's the sacrifice I was prepared to make for this family. But I don't want you to struggle like that. I want to know you can relax in the evenings or go out and see your friends when they're in bed. I want you to enjoy life. That's why I'm doing all this."

He didn't seem to understand they *were* her life, and, shattered though she often was, she cherished her time with them.

"Another one would stretch us too thin, and I don't want you put under that pressure. I think three is enough." He turned back to the computer as if the discussion was over.

In her heart, she knew that was because he was uncomfortable and hated conflict with her, but the seeming dismissal still made her mad as all hell with him. However, she left and went back to the sitting room. After flicking through the channels aimlessly again, she realized that if he really didn't want another baby now, then he would probably never change his mind about that. And actually, another baby wasn't something to be talked into. She decided to call her mum for a chat.

"You've got the three of them, and there's women who would give anything for just one. And you can give them all the time and attention they want, *cariad*. Sometimes you just have to be grateful for what you have instead of wishing for more. And there's a point where you always have to stop. It's the one-year-old broodiness! And it'll go."

She knew her mum was right. She still prickled with resentment that Gavin wouldn't give the whole idea the time it deserved.

"That man works hard for all of you, just like your dad did for us," her mother told her when she complained something of this to her. "And like your dad, he's not a talker. Sometimes you have to accept their differences, love."

So that was that, and there were no more babies, and there were times when all of them were little and the broodiness had passed off as predicted that she didn't regret at all not having another one. When she was worn out from chasing round after all of them, and making sure they'd been collected from their various clubs, and homework was done, and their bags were packed and uniform ironed. And just the mental burden of remembering it all. Yes, there were times she was glad Gavin had put his foot down. She had her share of heartbroken moments though where she sobbed that there would be no more babies for her. Where she got up in the quiet of the night and curled up in an armchair in what was the nursery bedroom and rocked with the pain of it.

೦~

Now on the hill, she understood that she had been in that place again. Her body was telling her she could no longer be a mother, and her heart was once again broken by that. And, at the same time, her children were leaving, and there really was no use for her at all.

Maybe if she'd had them later, these times wouldn't have collided, and it wouldn't all have been such a mess in her head. Or younger, and they would already have gone before she had to go through this.

"But no," she said slowly, talking to the wind, "I lost my babies at the same time as I lost my ability to be a mother. That's why it hit so damned hard. That's why."

Understanding that felt like a blow back at the blackness. Like knowing what made it work took away some of its power.

She nodded in satisfaction. That felt good. And she walked down the hill, whistling the dog to drive the sheep forward, both of them reveling in the freedom of doing their job out there in the chill wind on a sparse hillside that had a beauty all of its own.

36

LIKE ALL CHILDREN, SAMMY WAS up just after first light on Christmas morning and running to his stocking. Lily held him back from ripping open the presents with difficulty.

"Santa's been! Santa's been!" he shouted as he bounced around the cottage.

"Yes, and we're going to open them with Dilys," Lily said, seeing Cerys coming back through the yard with relief. There were no days off for sheep farmers, and Cerys had made sure to go out extra early this morning, knowing Sammy would be desperate to get started on his presents. "Come on," Lily said. "Let's get you washed and dressed, and then we'll go over for breakfast with your presents."

It had been Cerys's idea to do it this way. "Dilys will love it," she'd said, and that was all the convincing Lily needed. She didn't understand Dilys the way Cerys seemed to, and at times she was still a bit scared of her, but she saw how she was with Sammy, and that was all she needed to see.

Dilys was hobbling about making breakfast for them all when they got there. "Sausages!" she told Sammy with a grin that he returned in full, and she'd got some Welsh cakes on the griddle for anyone who didn't care for such a heavy breakfast ahead of a turkey lunch. She looked like it cost her a lot physically to be doing this, and Lily felt immediately guilty, but seeing her face, Cerys drew her back and whispered, "Let her, it's important to her. We'll make her sit down later."

Sammy loved the scooter, and the three women loved his face when he opened it. As Lily glanced round them, she was glad they were together. Dilys opened the yard door and sat beside it, despite the cold, to watch him zooming around the yard on it. She touched Lily's arm as she passed. "He's a blessing," she said, and Lily's eyes stung at the words, which were so far removed from the old woman's normal brisk way.

⌒

Cerys stole away for ten minutes to herself after the turkey was safely in the oven, basting in butter. There was a hole in her heart today. She'd done a good job of stoppering it day after day, but this was too much. This was a day when they might all have been home together.

And then they might not, and it might have been like last year where it was just her and Gavin stepping around each other, not knowing what to do with the silence in the house and between them. All the kids off doing their own things: Katie staying over with a new boyfriend whose family had booked some big parties in over the festive period, and Matt off skiing, and Alex spending the day with his new wife's parents. But God, she missed them today. No matter how much she told herself that this was still stolen time, not real, that wouldn't wash today.

She couldn't let the tears out because if she did they wouldn't stop, and then what would happen?

There was no way back. After a week, she might have gone back and been excused. But now, nearly two months had passed, and what could she say to them?

I love you. That's what she wanted to say, but those words would seem empty now, and she couldn't bear to see the disappointment on their faces that she wasn't the woman they'd always thought her to be.

Better this—her bracketed time. And not to think.

She pulled herself up straight and went back to where she had a job to do.

⌒

Danny sat in front of the TV, surfing the channels to ignore the happy family crap. He didn't need to see that today. His mother had wanted him to go out to Spain and spend Christmas with her, but he'd refused. In some way, he'd thought Kayleigh might come back.

She hadn't.

And now here he was. No wife. No kid.

He'd got some oven-ready stuff in the fridge ready to heat up. He'd even bought extra in case she did turn up.

To think of it made him hot with anger and shame that she'd made a dupe of him this way. Bloody little bitch! Leaving him sitting here like this, alone, waiting for her to come back. She was probably laughing about it.

Straight after Christmas, he was going back to the police. Enough was enough now with their fooling around. His child still hadn't been found, and it was time they stopped messing around and got this on national news.

For today, the best way to deal with it was to get smashed. He cracked open a can of beer and found a war film that was nothing to do with Christmas or kids or families.

⁓

It was their worst fear, Katie thought as she looked round the silent lunch table. She and Alex had tried to cobble something together between them. Matt was useless with cooking, so they hadn't even asked him. He'd been delegated to sit with Dad and try to keep him company, though that had been hard going as Dad was in one of those slumps where it was difficult to get anything at all out of him.

Their worst fear—she hadn't come home for Christmas. And that meant something to all of them. Mum made Christmas and she loved it. If she hadn't come back now, it was because she couldn't. It was what they were all thinking as they sat around that table. It was the end of hope. Something must have happened to her.

And what Katie wanted more than anything was to put her cutlery down with a clatter and run upstairs and sob it all out on her bed. But there was no Mum to come after her and comfort her.

She realized for the first time, as she sat there, how many times her mother might have felt that way herself and put those feelings aside and carried on as if it was all okay because that's what the family needed.

Katie had never thought of that before, not until she had to sit there now and try to do what her mum would have. And it was so hard.

She wanted to tell her that. She wanted to hug her and say sorry and she'd never known how tough it was to be a grown-up with all that weight to bear.

But she'd lost her chance.

@~

"Thank you for your gift," Dilys said quietly to Cerys as they left that evening to go back to the cottage.

"Well, I hope you like the scent," Cerys replied with a smile.

"I wasn't talking about the toiletries," Dilys said. "Thank you for your gift."

And Cerys understood and nodded.

37

LILY ARRIVED BACK FROM WORK after a ridiculously busy day dealing with the "January Sale" at the salon, which was Angharad's way of offsetting the post-Christmas slump by offering half price on hair color for the first two weeks after the New Year. Angharad had been to a maternity appointment and felt drained afterward, so Lily had run the place on her own, which would have been fine, but Angharad had clients booked in for half the day, and she'd had to juggle them all to fit. As it was, she'd run over by an hour. She pulled into the farmyard and turned the engine off in relief. She was starving too as she'd skipped lunch to try to keep up and it was now past six o'clock.

Cerys came out of the cottage but there was no sign of Sammy. Lily frowned, pulling herself out of her fatigue to realize he hadn't run out to see her as he usually did. Cerys opened the car door.

"I am so glad you're back. I'm wavering over calling a doctor."

"Sammy?"

"Yes, he's running a temperature."

Lily shot out of the car and ran into the house. Sammy was lying on the sofa, pale and clammy.

"He's been struggling all afternoon," Cerys said behind her. "He's had Calpol but it's not bringing the temperature down."

Lily bent down and scooped him up. His forehead burned against her, and he whimpered in discomfort.

"What do I do?" she asked Cerys.

For the first time since she'd met Cerys, the older woman looked unsure. "We're not registered at the doctor, and it'll be shut now anyway." She bit her lip. "I think I'd take him to A&E."

Lily stared at her in horror. Cerys never panicked so her words filled Lily with dread. My God, was she going to lose Sammy? After everything?

She buried her face in his neck to hide her fear from him.

He craned his neck and whispered in her ear so Cerys couldn't hear.

When Lily heard what he said, she stiffened and her head shot up. "I'll take him now," she said, and she scooped him up in her arms to carry him to the car.

"I'll come with you," Cerys said, following her to open the door for her.

"No, no! You stay here!"

Cerys stopped. "Lily, are you angry with me for not taking him sooner?"

Lily couldn't look at her. She couldn't afford to give anything away, and she thought furiously while pretending to concentrate on maneuvering him through the front door.

"Of course not! But you can't leave Dilys alone at night when we don't know how long I'll be. It could be ages."

"You don't even know where you're going, though," Cerys protested.

And Lily knew how oddly she was behaving. Any other time she'd have been desperate for Cerys to come, but she didn't want Cerys to find out the truth, not like this. "Don't worry, I'll find it," she replied with a brightness that sounded false even to herself.

"I'm sorry," Cerys said as she helped Lily get Sammy into his car seat. "It's probably just a bug, but it's best to get him checked when Calpol hasn't worked."

"Of course, no problem. We'll be fine, honestly," she said, forcing a smile.

"Hang on, I won't be a minute," Cerys said. "Don't go just yet." She rushed off to the farmhouse.

Lily strapped Sammy in and whispered, even though there was nobody to hear. "It's okay, we'll get some medicine and you'll feel better soon, then it won't hurt." He shifted uncomfortably in the seat, and that pierced her like a spear—this was all her fault.

She hovered for a moment, wondering where Cerys was, and then went to open the gate. Cerys ran out as she was returning to the car and pushed a piece of paper into her hand. "Directions to the hospital in Bangor," she said. "Go down toward the bridge and look out for the signs to the university. If there're no signs for the hospital, there's some instructions from Dilys here on how to find it. Be careful, and pull over if you get lost and read these. Oh, I wish you had a phone!"

"I know," Lily replied mournfully. "It's my fault, I should have sorted something long before now. Thanks, Cerys—thanks for looking after him so well."

"I'll have something ready for you to heat up when you get back," Cerys said, going to the gate so Lily didn't have to get out of the car again to close it. Lily could see her waving through her mirror as she trundled down the track, with poor Sammy wincing at every jolt.

They drove off the island and into Bangor. It seemed to take forever to get there, and Sammy was so quiet. She kept reaching back to touch the only part of him she could reach, which was his little foot. He slipped his shoe off so she could hold his toes, her hand cuddling them as she drove. He'd always loved that.

She had a brief moment of panic until she saw the signs for the university, and then, soon after that, the hospital was signed too. She slowed right down and took her time through the unfamiliar streets. Slow and steady, and she realized she'd learned that from Cerys. For all this mess was completely her fault, she had a moment of pride then that she'd been able to learn something about being a proper grown-up mother.

"Nearly there, Sammy, soon be feeling better," she crooned, and again she realized that was what Cerys had taught her. She smiled a little, despite everything. She was getting better at this. At least until now.

The car park was pretty quiet, as the hospital was mostly empty now and any evening rush to A&E hadn't started. Lily eased Sammy out of the car seat, and after a moment of watching him try to limp toward the doors, she scooped him up again and carried him.

The double doors parted automatically as they approached, and she left the darkness of the car park to enter a too-bright reception area with plastic seats in rows attached to metal frames. Scattered among the seats were a few people already waiting, or perhaps still waiting after several hours. She hoped not.

"Name?" the woman on reception asked, barely looking up.

"Mine or his?"

She did look up at that. "Which of you is ill?" And then she saw Sammy's pale, pained face. "What's his name?"

"Sammy."

She typed that into her computer. "Surname?"

Lily paused. "White," she said uncertainly. The woman didn't seem to notice.

"Date of birth?"

Lily swallowed. And added a day and a month on to her reply.

"Address?"

She gave Dilys's.

The receptionist frowned. "Your GP?"

"We haven't got one yet. Only moved up here a few months ago, and I've been so busy with my new job, I've not had the chance to register us yet."

The woman looked up at her as if she was completely stupid. "You need to register, especially with a child that age. We're not a replacement for your family doctor, you know." And there was an unpleasant edge to her voice. "Who was your old GP?"

Lily shifted Sammy in her arms and he moaned. His weight was starting to drag on her arms. "I can't remember the details," she said snappily. Let the woman have as good back as she was giving. "Can we see a doctor, please? He's four years old, and he's had a temperature for hours. My mother told me to bring him, and she knows what she's doing. If she said he needs to come to hospital, then he does."

Wow, she was proud of herself for that!

The woman looked at her like she was an unpleasant smell. "Sit over there. He'll be seen as soon as someone is free."

Lily found a quiet spot where she could arrange Sammy on a seat and he could put his head on her lap and lie down. The knot of fear in her stomach tightened again. They were taking a terrible risk here, but he was so sick, and it was all her fault that Cerys hadn't recognized what this was earlier.

She wished she'd had that conversation with Cerys now, the one that she'd decided to have while they were at the Christmas fair. She'd been intending to do it this week but kept putting it off because she was scared to, and now this had happened, and it was too late. Cerys would have sailed in here and dealt with that receptionist far better, but Lily couldn't afford for her to come tonight and find out like this. She'd hate to see Cerys's face if she found out that way. Lily would tell her, she would, but not like this. Cerys had done so much for her. She deserved a proper explanation.

She might understand, Lily told herself. If she explained properly, Cerys might just understand why she'd done it and forgive her. But Lily needed the right time and the right place to do it, because there was no coming back and she wasn't ready for all those questions.

She really hoped they would be quick here. From the faces of some of the people in this waiting area, she wasn't convinced, though they were all adults, so she could only hope a young child would be seen soon.

She stroked Sammy's hair softly as he lay with his head in her lap. It wasn't at all like him to be so quiet. He must feel rotten as well as being in pain. They needed to hurry up before he got worse. She knew—even stupid her knew this—that he needed antibiotics for this, and the faster he got them, the better he'd recover.

She sat still, with her stomach growling and protesting the longer it went on and poor Sammy shifting in the seat, trying to find some kind of comfort.

It felt like an age before a nurse called them through to a cubicle. "Does he see a doctor now?" she asked.

"No, I'm triage. I'll look at him, and then he'll be put in a queue to see the doctor depending on the severity of his symptoms."

Lily could have screamed but she bit her tongue for Sammy's sake. The nurse took his temperature and grimaced. "No wonder he feels rotten. When did this come on?"

"Just this afternoon. My mother was looking after him while I was at work. He was fine when I left this morning."

The nurse frowned. "That's pretty quick, and you said he's complaining it hurts when he goes to the toilet? Okay, I'll get a doctor to look at him." She smiled and ruffled Sammy's hair. "Shouldn't be too long, young man, and then we'll have you feeling yourself again." She looked Lily over and nodded. "I'll try to make it quick for you, okay?"

They got to wait in the cubicle, which was a huge relief as Sammy could lie down more comfortably. Lily sat on the chair by Sammy's bed, stroking his hand while he tried to doze. He wasn't even hungry, poor lamb.

It took around half an hour before the curtain moved again and a man entered, wearing a stethoscope. "Hello, I'm Dr. Jones," he said with a smile. "Dr. Rhys Jones, because there's about four Dr. Joneses working here at the moment. Perils of having a common name in Gwynedd, eh?" He had a lilting accent that reminded Lily of Dilys and Cerys combined, and he had the dark hair and eyes she now knew were often a Welsh feature. She estimated he was only a few years older than her.

"So who's this?" He went to the other side of the bed and grinned down at Sammy. "Let's get you better. What's your name?"

"Sammy—" Lily started to answer for him but Dr. Jones held his hand up to stop her.

"We like them to answer if they can," he said in a perfectly nonthreatening voice, but Lily wasn't convinced. Maybe it was her paranoia, but she didn't think this doctor was as inoffensively benign as he seemed at the moment. "So what's your name?" he said again, perching on the edge of the bed.

"Sammy."

Lily could hear how unwell he was in his reply, but the doctor didn't seem as concerned.

"Sammy what?"

Her child looked at her quickly and she knew he couldn't remember. The doctor caught the look but didn't comment.

"And what's your birthday?" he asked, ignoring the lack of answer to his previous question.

She winced as Sammy told him the unedited version. She'd known it was a risk coming here, but what alternative did she have when he was so sick? She couldn't have registered him with a local doctor either because they would still have been found out.

The doctor wrote something on his clipboard and turned to her. "Shall we have a quick word outside?" he said. "I'll get a nurse to sit with him." Underneath the apparently friendly exterior, she could now see something else. Something that didn't bode well.

She stood up and drew herself up to her full height. "I'd prefer it if we did that after he's been treated. He's really not well, and I brought him here to get better. Isn't that the most important thing? The rest can wait." She glared at him. It probably wasn't very impressive, but she saw a grudging acknowledgment. No, he was on to her, and he didn't trust her one bit, but that was less important now than Sammy getting better.

He sighed thoughtfully. "Okay, Sammy, tell me how you're feeling? Try to give me as much detail as you can, eh, so I can help you?"

He didn't have a bad manner with a four-year-old, but Lily was ready to bet he didn't have kids of his own yet. But of course, that was to be expected at his age and with a career like this. Little ones didn't fit well around that.

"It hurts," Sammy said, looking fearfully toward Lily. She nodded to him—it was okay; he needed to tell the doctor.

Again, she saw Dr. Jones assessing their silent communication.

"And where does it hurt?"

Sammy pointed at his pants. "When I go for a wee?"

The doctor nodded. "And when did it start hurting?"

"Before today," Sammy replied, his face creasing as he tried to think.

"Before yesterday?"

"Yes."

"Before this week?"

Sammy frowned. "I don't think so."

"He can't remember," Lily cut in. "He's only four and not at school yet so he gets muddled with days."

The doctor nodded curtly. "That's okay. I'm just trying to get a sense of when it may have started. It doesn't need to be strictly accurate. When did he tell you about it?"

"He didn't until I got home today," she said miserably. She knew why he hadn't told Cerys, but why hadn't he told her?

He turned back to Sammy. "Can you remember when you last went for a wee? Was it today?"

Sammy shook his head. "Hurts too much."

"Okay." The doctor stood up decisively. "I'm going to examine him. It sounds very much like a UTI—a urinary tract infection. Is he toilet trained?"

"Yes, since two. He's very independent and goes on his own, and dry at night now."

He looked surprised, as if he hadn't expected she would have got him toilet trained to that level. She supposed that told her something about what he was thinking of her as a mother. "Well done—boys normally take longer, not that I'm an expert. But these infections are more common after toilet training. Now I do need to do an exam so I'll get a nurse to step in with us."

"Do you have to examine him?" she asked. She'd thought they could just give him some antibiotics. And she'd been in such a rush that she hadn't really thought through the consequences. Her whole focus had been on keeping their identity hidden. She'd tried so hard to get them to this point, and it was all about to crumble. She had to have one last try to keep them both safe.

He gave her a hard stare. "Yes, I do. UTIs are very treatable, but we need to make sure."

She nodded and sat down again. Suddenly she had no energy left. The fight, such as she'd ever had, drained from her, and she desperately wished Cerys was there or that she could at least call her.

"I'll be back in a minute."

She sat and held Sammy's hand while he was gone. Her heart was pounding, and she felt sick and cold.

He was gone longer than she'd expected, but when he returned he was alone. "We've had an emergency come in, a road traffic accident," he said, "and everyone's tied up. If I wait for a nurse, it's going to be a while. Do you mind if I examine him with just yourself present?"

"No, I just want to get him better so get on with it," she said in an exhausted voice. "Why do you need a nurse anyway if I'm here?"

"It's for my professional benefit," he said dryly, "but this child needs treatment, and I think he's waited long enough for that. Can you pop his clothes down, please? Sammy, I just need to examine you to make sure I give you the right medicine, and your mummy is going to help you do a little wee if you can in this container. I know it might hurt a bit, mate, but I really want you to try for me, okay? And then I can get you all fixed up."

She hated the way Sammy looked up at her with big, frightened eyes as she pulled down his joggers. What had she done to her baby? She'd tried to protect him, but she hadn't thought about the long term. Typical, stupid her. She should have told Cerys. She should have asked Cerys for help getting out of this mess. Oh God, what was she going to do now?

The doctor walked toward the bed, looked at Sammy, and then stopped dead in his tracks. "What the—?"

He turned his head to look at Lily and his face was thunderous.

"Yes, she's a girl!" Lily snapped at him. "We have our reasons, and it's none of your business!"

Dr. Jones stared at them both. "I'm afraid it's very much my business," he said in a low voice, but Lily felt the menace. No, he did not like her at all, and he was sure now that she was a danger to her child.

Lily lifted her chin in what little defiance she still had left. And her poor child started to cry softly. "Sorry, Mummy. Sorry, I couldn't keep the secret."

"It's okay, sweetheart," she said, sitting on the bed and cuddling her daughter to her. "The doctor is just going to have a look at you and check what medicine you need and then we can go home." If only she'd thought this through and realized that he'd need to examine her daughter. But she'd thought keeping as close to their story as possible was the safest way to hide their identity. She knew Danny would be looking for them. He'd have gone to the police, she had no doubt about that.

Dr. Jones shook his head, as if waking himself up to what he needed to do here in the face of a distressed child. "Yes, of course I am. And then by tomorrow you'll start to feel much more like your old self." He looked meaningfully at Lily, and she could see anger behind the now carefully placid professional expression. "And then your mummy and I will just pop out for a little chat about future appointments for a checkup. Okay, little lady! I just need to have a quick look and I promise I'll be superfast and it won't hurt."

As he promised, he didn't take long. "If we can get a urine sample to confirm, that would be good, but if she can't manage it, don't worry. I'm sure this is a UTI. Often in girls it's caused by wiping the wrong way and bacteria spreading forward from her bottom. You said she goes to the toilet by herself?"

Of course she did, and that was all Lily's fault for this charade she'd put her through. "Yes, she's been going on her own for a while." And all the time since she'd left her with Cerys, to be exact.

He nodded. "That may well be it then. Can you try to get a urine sample, please?"

But it didn't work. She was just too uncomfortable to do more than a trickle. "It might be enough, don't worry," Dr. Jones said. "I'm going to give her antibiotics anyway, as I'm sure this is what it is, and also an anti-inflammatory to help with the pain and calm things down so she's more comfortable."

Lily got her dressed again while he got an anti-inflammatory shot.

"Be super brave!" he said. "Over in a minute!"

She squeezed her eyes extra tight but didn't make a sound.

"Superstar!" he said. "I'm just going to pop outside with your mummy and get you a sticker. Back in a tick!" He motioned to Lily with his head to come outside the cubicle.

As soon as they were inside the neighboring cubicle, his face changed. "And just what is going on?" he demanded and his dark eyes flashed with fury.

Well, to hell with him! She was doing the right thing. She might be doing it badly but it was still better than having done nothing. "I'm keeping her safe, that's what!" she snapped back, and her anger at him and all men like him who had no idea, absolutely no bloody idea, rose up inside her, overcoming everything. And she lifted her top up. Right up to her bra and revealed her skin beneath. "See! See that!"

Comically, from his face, he obviously thought she was about to flash her breasts at him and he reached out a hand to block her…

And then his hand fell and he stared at her stomach, appalled.

"Not pretty, is it?" she asked. "And it never will be now." She looked down herself at the red welts and the circular shiny scars. "Only where it doesn't show, where no one will see. Would you want the man who did that around a child? Well, I didn't, not any longer. That's my little girl in there, and I need to protect her from living with somebody who'll do this to her mother. And the rest of it."

"Are those cigarette lighter burns?" he asked, pointing to a scattering of the disc-shaped scars. His face had turned ashen.

"Yes." Her anger was fast burning away at the sight of his revulsion, to leave in its place the kind of shame and disgust she was more used to.

He swallowed. "I'm really sorry." He looked up at her face. "I'm so sorry I spoke to you like that."

She couldn't stand kindness, not now. "I had to keep her safe."

"Yes, you did. I believe you." He held his hands out in an apology. "I believe you."

Such a simple thing. Three words. But they broke her. They absolutely broke her. Her eyes filled with tears, and she felt her whole body begin to shake with the shock of it.

"Is her name really Sammy?"

"Drew." It was out before she had time to think, and for all she was terrified about what was going to happen next, it was such a relief to say her daughter's name again. To stop the lying.

He ferreted in a plastic tub on the shelf behind them and passed her a sticker. "Give this to her. I'll be back in a few minutes with the antibiotics."

He whisked off out of sight. Lily rubbed her eyes dry and went back to Drew. She didn't know what she was going to say to Cerys now. This guy was going to blow her cover to social services—that was inevitable. And she couldn't pull Cerys into her mess, so she'd have to leave before it all blew up. If only she'd told her earlier and not kept putting it off. Cerys might have been able to stop it from getting to this point—she was so much smarter than her. Now it was too late, and they'd have to run again, but Drew was too ill. How could she do that to her? And, right now at this moment, Lily was out of plans and out of fight.

Drew was sleepy now. The painkiller was taking effect, and now that she was more comfortable, she wanted to sleep. She smiled as Lily put her "Bravery" sticker on. "Have I got us in trouble, Mummy?"

"No, sweetheart, it's all okay. You just have a little snooze while the doctor gets the rest of your medicine. We'll be home soon."

Drew's eyes shot open in alarm for a second, then she smiled and relaxed again. "Oh, you mean the farm," she said sleepily and closed her eyes.

She was well away by the time Dr. Jones returned and Lily was gently stroking a strand of her dyed hair.

"What are you going to do? Call social services?" she asked him as he gave her the medication wordlessly.

He grimaced. "So I searched you up. Or rather I searched Drew."

She swallowed hard. "And what did you find?"

"You don't know?"

"I haven't looked."

"There's a nationwide alert just gone out for you and for her. The police are looking for you both."

As she'd expected. Danny was that vindictive. "Why? Because I'm an unfit mother."

"It said she could be at risk with you and they need to find her to ensure her safety."

"Yeah, I bet it did," she said bitterly. "So what are you going to do? Call them?"

He bit his lip. His brown hair was tousled as if he'd had his hands in it, clutching it in thought. "No," he said, "You have my word that I'm going to lose the paperwork as soon as you leave. So you should probably get off home with her now. She needs a checkup in a week."

"And how will I do that? I can't register with a GP. You can see why."

He gave her a card. "Clinic appointment. I'll see her then."

Lily took the card in shock. This couldn't really be happening. Any minute he was going to change his mind and call security.

"Good luck, and take care of yourself," he said quietly and then disappeared back into the bowels of the department, leaving her staring after him in utter surprise.

38

HE HADN'T MADE ANY PROGRESS in finding her. Bitch! She had his money and his kid. He'd had to go to his mother for a loan to get his creditors paid. All the time he'd taken off work to deal with this, along with the money she'd cleared out of his account, had left him short of funds. He'd finally figured out how she'd been able to get several thousand out of his account without him knowing. She'd worked out that he used his usual password of his mother's maiden name for his online banking and Drew's birthday as the PIN. Yes, he knew he was supposed to change them and not use the same for everything, but who on earth had time to do that? She'd shifted funds out of his business account into the joint one he had her named on. They only used it for the shopping and day-to-day expenses, so there was never much in it, but because there were regular transfers in, it hadn't pinged his phone as an unusual transaction. She'd then been into the branch to withdraw the money, and of course, as she was on the account, it had let her. She'd acted quickly too—done the transfer and the withdrawal all the day before she went. She must have been planning it for a while, probably checked that she could get into the account online first, then plotted her escape.

He'd not been chasing up the customers who owed him, his eye off the ball while he sorted all this out, and now he was the one left struggling. But he was back in business now and he was going to work every hour of the day and fight back on this. He wasn't going to take this.

She'd be dragged back by the courts with her tail between her legs. He was going for full custody. She wasn't fit to look after a child on her own. He'd get custody and she'd have to come crawling back to him because she wouldn't have any other way of seeing her child if she didn't.

Time she learned she couldn't mess around with a man like him after he'd given her everything. She'd be nowhere without him. Probably half dead in some drug den, pimped out to get a fix. That's where she'd been headed when he met her. And look what he'd given her! A proper family life, a good home, a child, and a husband who brought the money home and never cheated on her.

And that hadn't been enough for her.

His mother was furious when he told her.

"I told you she was trash! Don't you let her get away with this, Danny!"

"Oh, she won't, Mum. Just as soon as I'm on my feet again, I'll deal with her, don't you worry."

"Can't you let her go and find a better woman? You'd have your pick. Why does it have to be her? Let her go, Danny, and find someone worthy of you. A girl from a proper background who knows how to behave."

But she didn't understand. Kayleigh was his, and no other man was having her. The bitch wasn't going to have her own way either. She didn't just walk out on him after everything he'd done for her and get away with it. Never going to happen. And she knew it; that's why she covered her tracks so well. But Kayleigh was forgetting how stupid she was, and she didn't have a hope of escaping him for long. She could barely look after herself—actually, he didn't believe she could even do that—let alone a child—on her own with no support.

Only a month before she left, he'd come down the stairs after his morning shower to find her standing over the dishwasher that *he'd* bought her to help her out, and she was crying.

༄

A plate lay smashed on the floor in front of her.

"I dropped it," she said, sobbing, cringing away from him as he came toward her.

He felt his anger rise in response. Why was she behaving like that? He hadn't done anything. "Well, can't you pick it up?" he snapped, stepping over the shards and reaching for a bowl from the cupboard. "It's not difficult."

She scrabbled around on the floor, picking up the pieces, while he got breakfast. Just cold cereal, as she clearly wasn't ready to make him anything. And he had a long day ahead of him too. This just wasn't good enough.

When he looked round, she had gone, the dishwasher half-hanging open. Jesus, couldn't she even close it? No wonder things got broken.

He sat down to eat his breakfast. When she came back some minutes later, he noticed a blood-soaked plaster on her finger. He supposed she'd cut herself, and he rolled his eyes. Typical. Always had to create some drama for sympathy. He ignored her finger and her tearstained face and carried on eating his breakfast. He had a meeting in half an hour and no time to waste on her nonsense. His mother would have made him a cooked breakfast. She'd have remembered he had a big meeting and set him up for the day. Kayleigh probably hadn't even registered it. It wasn't about her, so she'd be oblivious.

He left his bowl on the table, pointedly, when he went out, but she was still fussing with her finger in an attention-seeking way.

She'd phoned him later that morning in the middle of his meeting. He'd ignored her until they finished. It hadn't gone as well as he'd hoped, and he was frustrated. Her disturbing him hadn't helped his concentration, and they wouldn't give way on the rates they were prepared to pay for the contract, so he was getting much less than he'd needed to make a decent profit.

"I'm in the supermarket," she said. He could hear her crying again. "The card's been stopped, so I rang the bank and they said there's no money in the joint account."

"You didn't tell me you were going shopping today—that's why!"

"I always go on Wednesdays."

"You must have spent more than usual last week! There was plenty in then. I need to check your receipts."

"Please, Danny, can you just transfer some money over? I'm here in the supermarket waiting, and they've put the trolley in the walk-in cooler until I could get in touch with you."

"I need to check how much you've been spending first. You'll have to wait. I'll call you back." He could hear her pleading as he hung up. This was ridiculous and typical of her lack of organization. She knew how much money went in each month, and she should be keeping an eye on how much was being used and dealing with it in advance, not having a crisis in the shop. What would people think of them? People around here knew she was his wife—he had a local reputation to maintain, and it was bad for business if his wife was known to not be able to pay her bills in the shops. If that got round, it'd seem like his business could be in trouble, and then that really would cause him problems. Like he didn't have enough already!

He accessed the account details on his phone. Blast! He'd forgotten that payment was due to go out yesterday—the annual insurance cover. But she'd been edging the food shopping bills up, he could see, higher than last month. He'd follow through and check the receipts when he got home. He transferred some money over and called her back. "It should clear now," he said.

She was still crying. For God's sake. At this rate she'd still be at it when he got home. Okay, so he wouldn't tell her what had happened as she was being so silly. Give her something real to worry about. "I'll see you later," he said and rang off.

When he did get back, she was red-eyed and sullen. Was it too much to ask to be greeted with a smile, as if he was welcome home? This was just typical of the rubbish he had to put up with. She didn't have the pressure of work. All she had to do was look after him and one kid. A woman should be able to take that in her stride. He was too soft with her, had given in to her too much and spoiled her.

※

Danny sighed. He could see how true that was now, and where had it got him? Skint and made a fool of. He clenched and unclenched his fists. Oh yes, she'd regret this when he got her back, all right.

39

LILY BOUGHT A PHONE AS soon as it was safe to leave Drew with Cerys again. She still couldn't quite believe that doctor hadn't turned her in, but it was time to face whatever was going on out there and what danger she was facing as a result of what Danny was saying about her. On her lunch break, she drove over to Bangor and got herself a basic pay-as-you-go smartphone, nothing fancy. The reception was pretty awful up at Dilys's, but when she was in bed that night, she sat and waited for the pages to load while she searched for evidence of what Dr. Jones had said in the hospital. It didn't take long to find it.

Her hands trembled, and that familiar panic surge of adrenaline coursed through her veins as she read the results of her search.

FATHER'S DESPERATE SEARCH FOR MISSING CHILD

POLICE CONCERNED FOR SAFETY OF MISSING GIRL AFTER SHE VANISHES WITH MOTHER

FATHER BEGS FOR HELP IN SEARCH FOR MISSING WIFE AND DAUGHTER

PUBLIC ASKED TO INFORM POLICE AFTER FEARS FOR MISSING GIRL AND MOTHER GROW

Drew's name, and hers, was all over the internet. Danny had gotten lawyered up and the media were on his side. In some of those papers, she was an irresponsible, unfit mother who'd taken off with his daughter and Drew wasn't safe. In others, Danny was a distraught husband who just wanted his wife and child back home. Oh, he'd been clever. There wasn't one quote from him that said anything negative about her, but he'd managed to swing everything in his favor so it was her who sounded like the risk. She knew he'd do that. And nobody knew better than her how convincing he could be when he turned the charm on.

She threw the phone down on the bed, bile rising in her throat. She was never going to get away from him. She'd never be safe anywhere. She ran to the bathroom and heaved into the toilet until there was nothing left in her stomach, then collapsed onto the cold floor, her whole body in tremors.

How long was she safe here? How long would it be before somebody recognized them and phoned the police? She couldn't keep pretending Drew was a boy forever, and she was terrified that, even at this level, it was doing something awful to her little girl.

But she couldn't go back either. She wouldn't survive this time. Either he'd finish her or she'd do it to herself. And Drew would be left with him and that was unbearable.

She remembered his hands on her, pushing her down onto the bed, and the hate on his face as he did it.

She couldn't go back. And she couldn't stay either.

She didn't hear the bathroom door open. She didn't even know Cerys was there until she felt hands on her, cleaning her face and helping her back to bed. Cerys sat beside her as she lay unmoving and barely there. Cerys stroked her hair as if she was Drew. Like a mum. Lily couldn't speak; she couldn't even move.

"You know, someday you're going to have to trust me enough to let me help you," Cerys said softly. "You're stronger than you know, but we all need someone."

She closed her eyes because that was true, but Cerys was wrong—she wasn't strong at all. Eventually, Cerys must have thought she'd fallen asleep, and she left silently.

She wasn't asleep. She was locked in the torture of her own head, in the fear, in the dark place he'd put her.

40

AFTER LILY HAD FALLEN INTO a troubled sleep, Cerys went to the kitchen to make coffee. She wouldn't be able to sleep now, not after seeing Lily in that state. Something had happened, but she had no idea what or how to get Lily to trust her enough to tell her.

She did wonder sometimes, because she wasn't stupid, whether she was wrong to entirely trust Lily. She knew nothing about Lily, and that was a risk. These things happened—people were conned and taken in. And the people that happened to believed they couldn't possibly be mistaken about the person they had placed so much faith in, just like she felt about Lily.

So was she wrong? She felt right down deep inside that she wasn't. That Lily was a lost, damaged child who wouldn't have been that way had she had her as a mother. But she was no fool, and damaged people could be dangerous. And she wasn't stupid enough to think that damage could just be loved away. You couldn't love a scar better. All you could do was show them they were still beautiful even with it.

For some people though, that would never be enough.

Was Lily what Cerys believed she was?

Or was she not?

That was the thing with unconditional love. It was what children needed. It was what Lily should have had. And if Cerys set conditions on it now, then it wasn't what it needed to be at all, was it? So she had to have that leap of faith that all her maternal instincts were right and that she could believe in this girl.

Because if she didn't, then she was just another one in a long line letting Lily down.

She was acutely aware that right now at this time, she was letting her own children down. The pain that caused when she allowed herself to let those thoughts intrude was so unbearable that she tried to shut them down as much as possible. Back in what was now the last depths of the blackness, she had thought everyone would be happier without her, but now she knew that was wrong. And what it meant was that she was causing them pain. It was too unbearable to consider, and the only way she could cope was to block it out and keep pretending that this time wasn't real.

She wasn't ready to face reality yet. Or the consequences of what she'd done.

It might come back, you see, she told herself. *It's only been such a short time that it's been gone and what if it comes back? I can't trust myself to be safe, not yet. I need more time. I need to know for sure.*

They'd be hurting. She couldn't hurt them more by making another mistake.

41

CERYS OPENED THE DOOR OF the farmhouse, startled at the authoritative knock on the door. There was a youngish man standing there, somewhere between her Matt and Alex in age, she estimated. He had the traditional Welsh dark eyes and hair but was too smartly dressed to be local, in business trousers, an open-necked dress shirt, and polished brogues. Neither good nor ill-looking but somewhere in the middle. His dress looked out of place in the farmyard, but somehow he didn't.

"*P'nawn da*," he said in a local accent. "I'm looking for Lily and Sammy."

Cerys went from curious to alert mode in a flash. "And who exactly are you?" she demanded.

"Dr. Jones, from the hospital. Here about a follow-up appointment." He showed his hospital badge.

"Oh!" Relief flooded through her. "Oh, I am sorry, I didn't know you were due to visit."

"Sorry," he said with a smile, "I'm not sure who you are?"

"I look after Sammy while Lily is at work," she replied. She wasn't sure what Lily had said so best to play safe and not claim any relationship.

"She missed an appointment at the clinic for a checkup yesterday, so I thought I'd call and check everything was all right."

"Oh yes, Sammy's much better, thanks. Come in and see, if you like."

"Thanks." He followed her through into the kitchen.

"Hi, Sammy," he said and Sammy looked up, startled. The doctor grinned at him. "Well, you look much better. How are you feeling?"

"I'm fine now," said Sammy. He gave her an odd look, Cerys thought, but she couldn't see any reason why.

Dr. Jones crouched down on the floor beside him. "Are those dragons?"

"Yes, Mummy bought them for me for Christmas," Sammy said, showing the doctor the small plastic figures he was playing with, bought from a tub in the gift shop in Beaumaris.

"A proper Welsh dragon," Dr. Jones pointed out, holding a red one up.

"Of course," said Dilys, hobbling into the kitchen. She seemed short of breath, and Cerys wondered if she was in more pain than she was letting on. "And who are you, young man?"

He straightened up, laughing, immediately completely at ease with Dilys in a way that told Cerys he really was a local boy. "I'm not that young," he protested. "Dr. Jones, here to check up on Sammy after last week."

She snorted. "You're all young to me. Sammy's fine now, so I suppose you must know what you're doing. You seem to have fixed him." She sat down heavily in her chair and winced. "Pity the one who was supposed to fix this wasn't as good," she said, nodding at her leg.

He grimaced. "Being difficult, is it?"

"At my age, you don't heal well," she replied. "Don't suppose it's their fault. Still, I'm supposed to be getting the cast off next week, and I can't wait."

He nodded sympathetically and turned to Cerys. "I could do with getting a urine sample to test the infection's cleared up, but I'll need to get his mother's consent if she's not here."

"She's at work," said Cerys. "I could call and you could speak to her?"

"Where does she work?"

"Beaumaris—the hair salon."

He shook his head. "I'm going past on my way back. I'll call in and ask her and leave a sample bottle with her. It's not much trouble to pick it up again tomorrow. I'll be over this way for another appointment."

"Will you now?" Dilys muttered from the corner with a chuckle in her voice.

Cerys pretended she hadn't heard her.

"Okay, well, thanks for coming," she said to him.

"No problem at all. Glad to see Sammy recovered and thanks for your time." He bade his goodbyes to Dilys and Sammy and left.

Dilys crooked an eyebrow at Cerys when he'd gone. "That's interesting," she said.

Cerys raised an eyebrow back. "Do you think you're reading too much into it?"

"No," said Dilys with a laugh. "And a nice, local boy is just what she needs."

Cerys was about to contradict her but then stopped. Maybe Dilys was right. Cerys had been about to tell her what Lily needed was to find her own well of strength, to become her own person, to learn to love herself. And all of that was true, but Dilys might have a point. Perhaps a decent local lad would help her do all of that. Whether this doctor was that or not, perhaps what Lily needed was just good, plain, old-fashioned love from someone honest and reliable.

Don't we all need that? she told herself. And if Cerys still had that, would she be here now?

⁓

The door of the salon jingled, and Lily glanced up from sweeping up the hair from her last customer. Her three p.m. had canceled this morning, so she had a rare afternoon break. Angharad was taking advantage of the January lull to put her feet up upstairs and take a power nap.

Lily froze, sweeping brush in hand, dangling a few inches above the floor, when she saw who it was.

"What are you doing here?" she said, and she hated the tone of panic she could hear in her voice.

"You had a clinic appointment for a checkup yesterday. You didn't show. I was worried," the doctor said, coming over to the counter.

"She's fine. She's much better." Lily could feel her heart pounding fearfully.

"I know. I've just been up to your place and she looked fine."

"You've been up there?" The brush fell from her hands to the floor with a clatter.

He pushed away from the counter and stooped to pick the broom up. "Don't worry, I didn't give the game away. They think she's a boy, don't they?"

Lily nodded miserably. "I can't tell them. I don't know how, and I went and bought a phone and looked us up, after what you said. It's everywhere, all over the news. I don't know what to do."

He propped the broom against the wall. "Who are they to you? Can't you trust them?"

She shrugged. "The stupid thing is I don't even know. Cerys is…she's the best thing that's ever happened to me. And I've lied to her and let her down. I'm so scared she'll hate me."

Lily looked down at her hands, and they were trembling, and she could feel the panic begin to take over, and suddenly she couldn't breathe. She grabbed her chest but the air wouldn't come in. Her mouth opened as she tried to suck it in, but it wasn't reaching her lungs.

She didn't resist the hands propelling her into a chair. She was past resisting. She wasn't even sure they were real. Her vision was going and there were bells ringing in her ears. Unceremoniously she felt her head shoved down between her knees.

"You're okay, don't move, just rest like that," a distant voice said. "Rest easy and listen to me: breathe in, in, in, in, and now out, out, out, out. Now slowly follow me: breathe in, two, three, four, and out two, three, four, and in…"

The voice murmured on, softly and slowly above her, and she could feel a hand resting heavily but gently on her shoulder, a firm pressure. She tried to focus on the voice and the ringing started to recede a little. Eventually, the hands straightened her up, but she kept her eyes shut as the voice carried on encouraging her to breathe slowly, and that pressure on her shoulder resumed.

She didn't want to open her eyes and have the world come back.

In the end, the voice stopped and she had to.

He was on a chair beside her. "You had a panic attack," he said very quietly. "Have you had them before?"

"Yes, occasionally," she said in a croaky voice. "Not for a while though."

"Not since you left?"

She nodded, her eyes welling up. No, she was not going to cry and shame herself in front of him, she was not. She already felt so dirty that he'd seen what had been done to her, so ashamed.

"Are you okay?" It was the kind of voice she could imagine him using on a very small and frightened child. So soft and so gentle, it nearly made the tears start again. Kindness hurt very badly sometimes.

"I can't go back." She ground the words out like she was being dragged over glass.

"You should never go back to someone like that," he said, and she couldn't look at him because she could hear his disgust and she felt so humiliated.

"You know I'm an unfit mother. I didn't bring Drew back to see you. That's why you're here."

He tutted dismissively. "Rubbish! I came because I was worried about both of you, actually. And Drew is absolutely fine and well looked after. Believe me, I see neglected children, and she's not one of them." He hesitated for so long that Lily did glance up at him. "I shouldn't say this because you're not my patient, but it was you I was more worried about. That's why I came. When you didn't come to the clinic, I was concerned for you. I thought you'd…oh, I don't know what I thought…that you were scared, maybe?"

"Yeah, well I was."

"I'm supposed to report it."

"I know."

"I haven't, and I'm not going to. I told you the file is lost and it is." He paused again. "Yes, I could get in trouble for that, but if I know Drew is okay, then nobody can say I put her at risk."

"And that matters to you?"

"Of course. And the alternative is putting you at risk, and I'm not doing that."

She was surprised by the sudden tone of ferocity. She wanted to cringe even though it wasn't directed at her, but she resisted the urge. Adrenaline was still coursing, and she focused on his face, which strangely wasn't fierce at all.

"Why haven't you told anyone about what he did to you? Or have you?"

She shook her head. "Because they'd believe him. Everyone always believes him, and they'd only need to look at my records, where I grew up, to know that I wouldn't be a good mother."

"Did he tell you that?"

"Yes."

"He lied, Lily. That's not how we work. Not at all. We wouldn't believe him that easily, and nor would the police and social services, not if you spoke out. I've seen the articles, and I understand why you think we would. But we are trained to recognize people like him and to look past the front."

She really couldn't stop the tears then. Explosive, messy tears with sobs that racked her body. She buried her face in her arms so he couldn't see her. She had no dignity. She'd never had any. Her mother had stripped her of that, the system had put the boot in harder, and then Danny had finished the job. She would never be anything at all, never.

"Oh shit, I'm sorry," she heard him say. "I didn't mean to do that. I don't know what to do now, I'm not supposed to…"

She couldn't process what he was talking about, and his earlier words were going round and round in her head.

"Oh, to hell with it," he muttered, and she felt herself being scooped against him, buried against warm solidity, and cocooned as his arms wrapped her tightly. She waited for the panic of being trapped to come but it didn't—it didn't come at all.

"You're safe," he said. "You're safe."

And it was ludicrously untrue. She wasn't safe at all. According to the press, half the country was on the lookout for her and Drew, and she could be dragged back to face the consequences and Danny's fury at any moment. She was even less safe now than when she'd been back there trapped with him.

But for a few seconds here, now, she did feel safe. It could be deceptive, that. She thought she was safe with Danny once, way back when she met him, and look how that turned out.

She heard the doctor sigh and then the gentle touch of his hand stroking her hair, much as Cerys had done that night in the bathroom. He didn't hold her as Cerys had, though, but like he was a wall that could keep trouble away. She wished that was true, that a person could do that for her, but she'd seen too much in her life to believe that could be possible. Still, it was a nice sensation even if it was fake comfort.

The floor creaked above them, and she realized Angharad was up and moving about. She wriggled and he let go of her immediately. He looked more shocked than her, she realized, when she sat up and wiped her face dry with tissues from the counter.

"I'm sorry," he said. "I shouldn't have done that. I could get in a lot of trouble for that."

She shook her head. "You didn't do anything wrong."

"I did. I crossed a boundary. I'm sorry."

He did actually look worried, really worried. She shook her head again. "It helped," she said simply. And that was true. It had.

The creak on the stairs stopped the rest of what he was about to say, and he reached into his pocket and handed her a sample bottle. "I think she's absolutely fine, but those infections can linger and flare again, so I'd really like you to get a urine sample, and I'll get it tested to make sure she's completely clear. I could pick it up tomorrow?"

"Okay, thanks. I'll do that."

"When do you finish so I don't disturb you?"

"Half five, but that's not fair," she protested. "I can't inconvenience you."

"Oh yes, you can," he said quietly and turned and left without another word, leaving her staring after him once again.

42

"WE'VE FOUND THE CAR," THE policeman told Gavin. "What remains of it, at least."

Katie gasped.

And the policeman went on quickly. "There was no sign of your wife, sir. None at all. We are now scouring the area more closely, but early examination of the vehicle shows it was empty when it was set alight."

"Set alight?" Gavin asked.

"Yes, sir. Looks initially as if it was deliberately set on fire to destroy it."

"Where did you find it?"

"North Wales, sir. In the hills in a remote spot called, er…" He reached for his notebook.

"Pengwyllen," Gavin said, and it wasn't even a question, Katie noted.

"Yes, sir, that's it."

Her dad looked over to her. "She went home," he said.

Later, Katie persuaded him to go out for a walk with her. Because she needed him to do something other than just sit and look lost. She'd not only lost her mum, she realized, but her dad too, because this shell of a man wasn't him.

"Do you think she's dead?" Katie asked him. Maybe it wasn't the right thing to ask somebody in his state, but she couldn't get it out of her head and he was still her dad, and she still needed him, even more so with Mum gone.

"Yes," he said. "That's why she went there. Pengwyllen is where she'd want to be if she was going to do something like that."

"You think she's killed herself?"

"Yes."

And after that she couldn't get a word out of him. She knew he'd be remembering their row and blaming himself.

But there was no sign of a body. That's what the policeman said. So there was still hope.

Mum was good at that—hoping and having faith in all of them. Maybe Katie needed to do that now for her.

"I think we need to assume she's alive until we hear otherwise," she told her dad.

He looked at her. "You do that," he said. "Try to do it for both of us."

Katie could have cried for him but that would do no good. He was still in there, her dad, but she couldn't find a way through to him.

"I only ever wanted what was best for all of you," he said. "But I was never as good as your mother at knowing what that was. She said all I cared about was work, that last night. But it wasn't. I worked for all of you, to give you all everything I never had, and your mother too. I just wanted to see her enjoy it and she wasn't. And I couldn't make that right."

She patted his arm. "You did fine."

"Not for her," he said as he walked ahead. "Not for her, and I wanted to so much. I wanted to be the best husband I could be, and I let her down. The worst is, I didn't even know it."

43

LILY HALF-EXPECTED DR. JONES NOT to turn up that evening as the salon was closing. She sent Angharad off to rest as soon as the last customer was gone and made a start on clearing up. When she looked up from putting the fresh towels back on the shelf, she saw him hovering at the door and beckoned him in. She had an odd feeling in the pit of her stomach at the sight of him. It could have been fear, or not—she no longer trusted her feelings. They always let her down badly.

Only what she felt for Drew; that was the only real thing.

"I've got the sample for you," she said and retrieved it.

"Thanks," he said, stashing it in a small bag packed with various kits that she didn't understand; the tools of his trade, she guessed, as the scissors were hers. "She's still fine?"

"Yes, thanks. No signs of any pain. I keep asking her, and I'm getting on her nerves now with it." Lily gave a laugh but knew it sounded nervous. No surprise there as she was a wreck of fear these days, constantly watching over her shoulder.

"Can I get your phone number and I can give you a call with the results?" He didn't quite meet her eyes when he asked her, and, suddenly suspicious, she wondered if he was going to give it to the police.

But that was silly. Why would he? He could just tell them where she was.

"It's okay if you don't want to," he said hastily, making toward the door.

"No, hang on—wait! Of course I want to know she's okay." She got her phone out. "I just can't remember the number. It's a new phone."

"Oh!"

"I got rid of my old one when I left."

He came back toward her. "Of course. Sorry, I didn't think." He smiled, and she thought he looked nervous, but she couldn't see any reason for that.

She read out the number to him as he put it into his phone.

"I'll text you," he said. "Then you'll have my number in case anything happens. You know, if she seems unwell or anything."

Now actually that was a relief. She hadn't thought about that, because honestly, she hadn't thought anyone would want to help her once they heard what Danny had to say. But Dr. Jones didn't seem to believe any of it.

Of course he didn't—he'd seen the state of her. She flushed with humiliation.

But still, Danny could be very convincing, so even that was no assurance. No matter what Dr. Jones said, she still couldn't quite believe that she'd convince anyone over Danny in full manipulative mode.

Her phone pinged with a text—"from Rhys Jones," it said, "in case you need me."

"I'll go now," he said, shuffling his feet. He looked much less at ease here than he had in the hospital. "I'll be in touch as soon as I get the results."

"Thank you…so much." She remembered to call after him this time as he left. And this time he gave her a quick, startled smile before the door closed behind him.

She found that smile strangely comforting every time she thought of it.

⁓

"Results completely clear," said the text that came through to Lily's phone the following evening. She heaved a sigh of relief. She had been lying in bed unable to drift off to sleep. They went for early nights in the cottage, and Drew was in bed, of course, and Cerys had to get up so early to tend the sheep. She leaned up on her elbow to reply.

"Thank you," she texted back. "So pleased!"

There was a delay, and then, "Good. Hope you are okay too?"

"Fine, thank you," and then after she hit send, she bit her lip and added,

"But worried." She didn't know why she sent that. It was really nothing to do with him, and why should she tell him that except that she so desperately wanted to speak to someone? She could have talked to Cerys, but it was her own stupid fault she couldn't. She couldn't stand to see Cerys disappointed in her for lying. She might forgive her eventually, but Lily wasn't brave enough to get past that first wave of disillusionment. Lily knew what it felt like to be disappointed in people, to be rocked to your core. It would kill her if Cerys felt like that because of her.

He didn't answer for a while, and she thought how stupid she had been to send that message. She was just considering how much she bitterly regretted it when a message pinged back.

"Not surprised," it said. "If you need to talk, I'm here."

She stared at her phone in surprise. Really? Did he mean that? Of course as a doctor, he must realize the effect that this kind of stress had, so he was being helpful. She wasn't quite sure what to say back, although she was suddenly quite sure that she really did want to talk to him.

So that was unexpected. She never usually wanted to talk to anyone about the important things, Cerys excepted of course. In fact, she wasn't much of a talker at all. Angharad said she was the quietest hairdresser she'd ever known. "We're usually all so chatty," she said, though of course Lily did make the expected small talk with the clients, but some of them told her they liked it that she didn't go on and on like some stylists did.

"Yes, please," she texted back, holding her breath because she wasn't quite sure what would happen next.

"I can call you now?" was the reply.

She switched her ringtone to silent and messaged back, "Okay, thanks."

A second later it rang. "Rhys Jones" lit up on the display, and it gave her an odd sense of warmth to see his name there, even though, of course, she knew who it was.

"Hi, Lily," he said in that quiet voice she was beginning to associate with him.

"Hi, thank you," she replied, not really knowing what to say but very grateful he had called all the same.

"Tell me," he said, "just tell me whatever you want and I'll listen."

She felt a lump in her throat, and she thought to herself that he was perhaps the kindest man she'd ever met. Could a man this kind be real?

Experience taught her no, but she wasn't sure her instinct agreed. It had been wrong before though—or had it? Maybe she'd always secretly known about the others and just not listened to it in the past. Heard what she wanted to hear.

"I'm scared," she said, her voice catching on the words. "I'm scared he'll find us and they'll make me go back. And I'll have to because I can't let him take Drew. I'll have to go back to him." She swallowed a sob. "And he'll make me pay, he really will."

"It's not going to happen," he said in that same quiet voice. So soothing she could almost believe in it. "You're not going back, and he's not going to get custody of Drew."

"I wish I could believe that," she said, "but you don't know him. People always believe him, and nobody will listen to me."

"Why do you say that?"

"All they have to do is look at my background. I might as well walk round with 'Rubbish Mother' stamped on my forehead."

"Do you want to tell me about it?"

"I-I don't know."

"Okay, not now then, but whenever you're ready." He let out an exasperated sigh. "I'm sorry, I have to go. My pager's gone off."

"It's okay. Thanks for calling." Oddly she felt better although nothing had really been said to make her feel that way, nothing logical.

"Can I call you tomorrow? Same time?"

Something warm flooded her veins. Maybe relief that there was someone to talk to, after all. She wasn't entirely sure. "Yes, thanks."

"Okay, I'll speak to you tomorrow. Hope you sleep well."

The sense of peace she got when she lay back and could hear the echoes of his soft voice, even after he'd long since gone, allowed her to finally close her eyes and sleep.

44

LILY'S PHONE RANG AT THE same time as the previous evening, right on cue. "Hi," Rhys said when she answered. "Is this a good time?"

"It's fine," she replied. The warmth in his voice enveloped her straight away, like a blanket.

"Everything all right at your end?"

"Yes, thanks." And then because she realized this was always one way, she asked him, "And yours?"

"Busy, busy day. Ridiculous. But it's always like this in January."

"Oh!" She'd never really thought of that. "I guess a lot more people get sick in the winter."

"Yup, always run off our feet, and into February too."

She felt guilty now for taking his time up.

"So I was thinking," he added, "I'll never get time to go and queue at the barber at this time of year. Is there any chance you could book me in with you? It's getting a bit scruffy."

Honestly, she hadn't noticed his hair looking scruffy at all, but it was the least she could do. "Oh, of course. When are you free? Or I can slot you in after the salon closes if that's easier?"

They agreed he'd try the day after tomorrow, but she told him not to worry if he had to cancel because of work—she'd fit in around him.

"Thanks for taking time to call when you're so busy," she said.

"It's good to speak to someone who isn't a doctor or nurse, so thank you." And she could hear the smile in his voice. It sounded genuine.

She found that Rhys Jones was strangely on her mind until the appointment arrived. Despite a busy day in the salon, her mind kept returning to the prospect of seeing him. She was starved of friends, she told herself, and had been for years, so when somebody showed even the mildest interest in her company, it mushroomed out of all proportion in terms of how pleased she felt about it. Still, when he came in through the salon door and hadn't had to cancel, it really did make her day. Especially when he smiled at the sight of her.

"I'm a bit early," he said. "I'll just wait over here."

The client she was finishing up with showed far too much interest in the situation, so Lily tried to downplay it. The last thing she needed was a nosy customer. Nosy customers remembered things, and everything about Lily was best left unnoticed right now. As the woman paid and booked her next appointment in to get her roots done, she cast an amused glance between Rhys and Lily, both of whom ignored it.

He seemed nervous again as she washed his hair. Maybe he thought she might scalp him or send him out with that stupid cut all the farm lads were having at the moment. To relax him, she spent extra time on his scalp massage, and eventually, she felt him soothe under her fingers. "The barber doesn't do that," he said contentedly. "That's so good after today."

"Difficult?"

"Yeah." He sighed heavily. "Lost a patient today that I really thought might make it. Knocked me back a bit. It happens, and you learn to deal with it, but it's still a bummer when you think you've nearly pulled them through, and then they don't survive."

"I can't imagine having the guts to deal with it," she said. "I'd be useless."

He opened his eyes for a moment and looked up at her. "You've got more guts than most people I know," he said, and then he closed them again and smiled as her fingers moved to another spot on his scalp. "You're very good at this. I've obviously been missing out at the barber."

It gave her an odd feeling in the pit of her stomach, looking down at his face, relaxed and unaware of her scrutiny, enjoying her touch. She had to catch her breath for a moment and remind herself that he was just looking out for Drew, that he needed to know she was safe if he wasn't going to hand them over, or he'd breached his professional code. Well, actually he'd breached it anyway, but morally if Drew was safe, then he didn't feel he had. She examined the lines of his face. They were starting to become more familiar to her.

She would never have realized when she met him in the hospital, glowering down at her suspiciously, what a kind man he was. It came as a shock to her that a man could just be nice to her. Even when Danny had been trying hard in the early days to leave the kind of impression that it suited him to make—to get what he wanted from her, of course—there'd always been a different edge. Not like this man. She felt that he just had kindness right down in his bones. Maybe that was why he'd become a doctor.

She rinsed his hair off and he smiled sleepily. "I was kind of hoping that would never end," he said. "It was so nice."

She dried his hair and took him back to the cutting chair. "So just a trim to get it back into shape? Anything specific you want?"

He waved his hands. "Do whatever you think with it."

She screwed up her face in thought. "Okay, but I won't quite get it there this time, so you'll have to let me cut it again to get the final result."

His face lit up. There was no other way that she could think of to describe it. "Okay, sure."

A man like him had no interest in someone like her though, so she wasn't the reason. He could do so much better than her, and he would inevitably know that. He was so far out of her league.

She got to work on his hair, and he watched her in the mirror, no chatter, just watching her work. He was remarkably easy to be around, and he really shouldn't be—they were from such different worlds.

Her finger brushed his cheek as she moved her hand to a different angle, and he jumped a mile, then laughed at himself sheepishly. "Sorry!"

"No, my fault, don't worry."

He touched her elbow. "It really wasn't."

And she had to smile, just because the way he was looking at her made her feel happy inside. He looked at her like she mattered, like she was worth something. Like he enjoyed being around her, which was fundamentally pretty incredible as he was...*him*, and she was her.

"Why do you have such a low opinion of yourself?" he asked wonderingly as she trimmed the front of his hair, tongue caught between her teeth as she concentrated. "You're smart, you're funny, you have more courage than any woman I've ever met, and—"

She looked down at him in astonishment. "And what? And I am not smart…or the rest."

"You are," he said, and she thought his cheeks had flushed a little. "So why don't you believe it? Is it him?"

"Him, yes, and a lot more than him," she said, and suddenly it began to slip out like she'd planned to say it all, like it was easy, and that was because of Rhys and who he was and his dark eyes watching her, filled with kindness. "I grew up in care after my mother dumped me. I didn't have a very nice time before that, and she wasn't anything like any mother you'd imagine, but I think she was better than what came next. Anyway, she didn't want me because I got in the way of getting her next fix, so she dumped me and I went into foster care."

He watched her silently, but she saw understanding, not condemnation, on his face.

"I didn't deal with it very well, and I ran away a lot, and I did a lot of things I shouldn't have done." She swallowed hard because it was hard to admit this to him. She was terrified that when he knew, that look in his eyes would change, become distant. "With a lot of people I shouldn't have done them with."

"It happens," he said in that quiet voice that always undid her. "It happens a lot. Don't look like that about it, because kids react like that for a reason when they're dumped and everyone lets them down. You didn't do anything wrong."

She paused, the scissors motionless in her hand. "You don't know what I did."

"You didn't do anything wrong," he repeated more firmly. "They did, not you."

Danny had never said that to her. No, he'd make her feel like he was magnanimous for forgiving her for it, like she should be grateful to him for overlooking it all and giving her another chance.

She got the hair dryer and gave his hair a blast dry before getting the styling wax and rubbing just a little in to give it texture. She didn't want to talk about it any longer because then she'd have to talk about Danny and she didn't want to this evening.

"I wish she had wanted me," she said. "I wish I could have stayed with her, because she was the only mum I had, and something died in me the day she got rid of me."

He reached up and held her hand. "Don't blame yourself because other people in your life weren't enough. You deserve better even if you haven't had it yet."

She stared at him, with no words to express how that made her feel.

He squeezed her hand. "But you will—you will have that one day. You just have to believe in yourself."

"Sometimes that's very hard," she said.

"I know. But I believe in you." He laughed suddenly and unexpectedly as something struck him. "And you should trust me—I'm a doctor!" It was as if he knew the tension was too much for her now and he broke off to look in the mirror. "Oh! Okay, so I look a lot better. What did you do to me?"

"Just changed the length through here," she said, running her hand through the front part of his hair. "It still has a little way to grow to look absolutely right."

"I look way less of a geek though," he said, looking at his hair and tilting his head to see a different angle.

She laughed and shook her head. She'd never thought he looked geeky anyway but was too embarrassed to say, too aware that she'd had an opinion of his appearance that she had no right to have.

"Can I buy you lunch tomorrow to say thanks?" he asked. "I'm not on call so I've actually got a proper day off."

She chewed her lip. "Oh, I don't get a lunch break now because Angharad's so far along. I just scoff down a sandwich between clients."

She could tell he was trying to judge if she regretted having to say no or not. "Dinner?" he asked tentatively. "Or will that mess your time up with Drew?"

"It will, but she won't mind for once as long as I'm back for bedtime."

"How about half five and we'll go to the diner then?" he said with a laugh. "That's the fastest service we'll get round here."

"Oh good," she said with obvious relief. "The restaurants round here scare me—they're so posh." And then she colored up at revealing how limp she was about things like that. He must think she was an idiot.

"There's nothing posh about me," he said, grinning. "Diner suits me."

"You're a doctor," she protested.

"But my family is not posh, believe me. I grew up in a little terrace in a hill village. There's nothing upmarket about us Joneses."

⚬

Again, she spent all of the next day with that sense of nervous anticipation. She told herself it was because it was so long since she'd had a friend. It wasn't any more than that because she knew fine well that a man like him wasn't interested in her and never would be, so she wasn't stupid enough to think of him as anything other than an amazingly kind friend. Or perhaps that's how normal friends always were; she'd just never had one. Friends had always been people who used her for something.

But Rhys didn't ask her for anything.

He waited outside the salon for her to finish. It was a dry evening for once, although there would be a sharp frost that night. She could already feel it in the air. "Good day?" he asked, and his breath blew clouds.

"Busy again, but okay." She felt less tired already at the sight of him.

"Do you enjoy it?" he asked as he began to stroll slowly in the direction of the diner.

The smile lit her from the inside out. "I do, I really do. I trained to do it but then he never let me. But I actually do love it. I feel good when I see how happy it makes people to get a good haircut. I send them out feeling good about themselves, and that's a great feeling." She paused. "Of course it's nothing compared to what you do, where you make people better when they're sick, but still, it feels nice."

He shook his head determinedly. "Not nothing at all. It's just different."

"It's not an important job though," she protested.

"Well, you made a doctor feel better today, so I'd say it is." He quirked an eyebrow at her, and she couldn't help but laugh.

In the diner, he found them a seat and checked what Lily wanted, then went to the counter to order. The restaurant area was still quiet although the takeaway was starting to get busier. They wouldn't have to wait long, but the food was being cooked fresh.

"You know something?" he said while they were waiting and there was nobody at the surrounding tables to hear them. "That evening in the hospital when I was being an arse, and you got mad at me and showed me your scars to save Drew, I thought that was the bravest thing I'd ever seen."

She snorted but blushed too. "You thought I was going to flash you!"

He gave a rueful grin. "I have had that happen, actually."

"No way!"

"Yup, people can be weird, especially drunks in A&E. Anyway it *was* the bravest thing I've seen, and now I know you a little better I know how hard it would have been."

She took a long breath out to prepare herself. "He did that, you know, to make sure nobody else would ever go near me. He told me that. Every single time he did it, that's what he said."

"He's a psycho." Rhys's face was tight and angry. "And he's wrong as well. No man worth anything would be put off by them."

She couldn't find any words to answer him, so she just stared back.

"I'm absolutely serious about that and I'm right," he said with that quiet firmness that she'd come to associate with him. "You need to believe me."

She nodded, swallowing, not sure what he was really saying to her. She was relieved when the waitress brought their food over and saved her from having to respond. He lightened up then, making her laugh over funny stories of patients in the hospital.

He walked her back to her car, though he was parked at the other end of town. "Thanks for hanging out with me," he said after she got in and rolled the window down to say goodbye. "And thank Drew for letting me borrow you for a little while at least." He grinned and gave an awkward wave and turned and jogged off.

She shook her head. *He does the oddest goodbyes*, she thought as she wound the window up and drove off.

All the way home, she remembered the absolute sincerity on his face when he'd told her Danny was wrong, staring at her as if his eyes could expunge the scars from her body. She didn't doubt he meant it, but she had no idea what the maelstrom of emotions she was feeling in response was.

45

DILYS WAS STILL GRUMBLING ABOUT Cerys interfering when the doctor arrived. "I don't care," Cerys told her. "You're not well, and sometimes you need to stop being so stubborn and admit it." Dilys had used the excuse that it was a January chill for too long now and they were into February with no sign of her self-diagnosed cold improving. She was still frustrated that after the cast had come off, her leg was nothing like it used to be, and she didn't want any more fuss about her chest, but it seemed less of a cold and more like breathing difficulty to Cerys—something she thought was getting worse, not better.

Dilys griped a bit more about interference and meddling and then packed Cerys off out of the farmhouse so she could speak to the doctor herself. Cerys smiled and busied herself sweeping the yard until he left. He was in there a good long time, and Dilys was subdued when she went back in.

"Everything all right?" she asked as she put the kettle on.

"Just gave me some tablets to help my chest," she replied. "Told me I'm old and I'll have to get on with it."

Cerys rolled her eyes. "Pretty sure that's your interpretation."

"It's what he meant," Dilys said with a sardonic quirk of her eyebrows. "Anyway he said I have to rest, so I'm doing as I'm told and off to do that. And minding my own business."

She called the last comment over her shoulder in a deliberate barb as she went, Kip trotting after her at her heels.

Cerys ignored the irascibility and got on with cleaning the kitchen. The older woman never liked to accept help, and Cerys could sense her frustration at being trapped in a body stopping her from having the independence she'd so fiercely guarded throughout her life.

She was gone a long time. She must have needed the sleep, Cerys thought, which wasn't like her and did show she'd been right to call the GP. Dilys perked up when Sammy came round, but Cerys still kept catching her with an unusually pensive expression in quieter moments. She knew better than to ask her what the doctor had said, especially after it was her fault he'd been called in the first place.

She'd have to get it out of her by more covert means and wait until she had her guard down. No chance of that now for a few days at the very least. She'd have to play the long game.

46

LILY HAD FLIPPED THE SIGN on the salon door to CLOSED but had not got round to locking it yet as she tended to prop it open to help dry the floor after mopping. She was just filling the bucket with detergent when the doorbell jingled and Rhys came in. He looked agitated somehow, but she couldn't put her finger on what made her think that. It had been a few weeks since they'd gone to the chip shop together that first time, and they'd seen each other a few times a week since, even if only for a quick walk by the sea after work before she headed home. Rhys had been covering extra shifts this week though, as the hospital had been short-staffed, so this was the first time he'd been able to get here.

"Hi," she said, surprised. "I didn't know you were coming over."

He cast his hands up in the air, an expression of frustration—or was it confusion?—on his face. "I missed you," he said.

She felt herself flush from head to toe and hoped her face wasn't burning enough to be obvious. "Oh, um, thanks…" She honestly wasn't sure how to take this, but he didn't look like he was just being friendly.

But he had to be, right?

"Um, have you had a bad day?" Maybe he needed a friend to talk to.

"Yes," he said determinedly, almost forcefully actually. "I missed you."

"Yes, you said," she replied faintly while she tried to process what on earth he was on about. Was he on drugs? No, she didn't think that seriously, but he was acting so out of character.

"I'm shit at this," he said with a groan as he tried to read her face.

"At what?" She had a horrible thought that he might be trying to tell her he'd called the police or social services, but that was just her go-to fear. She didn't believe he would.

"Talking to you," he said, waving his hands again despairingly.

She screwed up her face in confusion. "Well, you're not usually, or I don't think you are."

"I am. I've been trying to tell you this for ages and I can't."

"Can't tell me what?" No, it couldn't be that he'd called the police. It couldn't, could it?

"Arrgghhh!" he growled, grabbing his hair in his hands in frustration.

She flinched back. She couldn't help herself. And he saw it and his face fell, crumpled, his defenses down.

Suddenly she understood what he was trying to say. She saw it there in his eyes. She shook her head in confusion.

"Men like you aren't interested in someone like me," she said slowly, like she was drugged and waking from it.

"Yes, we are," he replied, as if he could get her to understand that with the quiet force of how he said it. "Yes, *I* am."

She could feel how her face twisted to betray every emotion she was now feeling. Her confusion, her sudden, brief surge of hope, her disbelief because this still couldn't be.

But his face was telling her it was. And did she dare believe it, believe in this, believe in him? Because men always let her down.

He looked back at her, thinking frantically, trying not to mess this up and to get her to understand.

In the end, he just held his hands out to her.

She wanted him to come to her but then she understood why he couldn't. That this had to be her choice, her free will. No coercion or control. He understood that.

And when she realized that, she pushed all her confusion and doubts aside and walked toward him.

The second she leaned against him and put her arms round him, his wrapped round her in return.

He brought her into safety, brought her home. A protective force around her, not a trap.

She could feel his warm breath on her hair as he buried his face in it. "The most fantastic and bravest person I know," he whispered.

She looked up at him, searching to see if he looked as happy as he suddenly sounded, and was alarmed for a moment to see that he actually looked worried. Then she worked out from his frown that he was trying to decide if he should kiss her or not. She knew why—he still didn't want to push her. Her choice. And she found it was an easy one to make. She reached up and pulled his head down and kissed him. In fact, all it took was that brief pressure of her hand on his neck and he did the rest, as if he'd just been waiting for her signal.

It felt as if he'd been waiting a long time to do this, though they hadn't known each other that long at all. As his arms wrapped tighter round her when their kiss deepened, she realized she'd been waiting for it too. She'd just never believed it could happen.

She looked up. "How is this going to work?"

He laughed, a relieved sound. "I have no idea," he confessed, "but it is."

Hope, she discovered, felt like a spring tree greening itself with fresh leaves. It felt good.

47

CERYS WATCHED LILY AND RHYS from the farmhouse kitchen window as they ran through the heavy March rain from the car into the cottage, laughing as the downpour soaked them both. They shook themselves off under the porch and went inside.

She smiled to herself. The pair of them were just glowing. They looked like something from an afternoon feel-good film. Lily didn't quite understand what a decent relationship was supposed to look like, so she often appeared fairly startled by it all. But Cerys loved seeing how she was gradually slipping into understanding what real romantic love was. It was sweet to see her surprised glow as she made that journey.

Cerys looked out at the rain as she continued the washing-up. Dilys napped by the fire. She'd seemed tired today and was still troubled by an annoying cough that hadn't cleared since her first illness after Christmas. Probably coming down with another cold, but Cerys was a little concerned, and if she wasn't better tomorrow, she'd call the doctor for a visit. When she'd suggested this to Dilys, she'd shook her head furiously. "No need to trouble them because I'm old," she'd said. "Anyway, I've got business to do tomorrow and a visitor."

"Oh, who's that?" she'd asked.

"Never you mind!" Dilys had snapped and hobbled off.

Cerys had stared after her, affronted, and then shrugged and gone back to polishing the kitchen table. Probably Dilys really did feel grotty and didn't want to admit it. She was never usually that crotchety. Maybe a couple of acetaminophen would help if she had a bad cold coming on. She'd suggest that with a cup of tea when the old woman had come out of her grumps.

The rain continued falling relentlessly, bouncing off the cobbles.

If things worked out with Lily and Rhys, then Lily would no longer need her. That was the way with daughters. They grew away from you and left.

"Or do we?" she whispered to her own mother as if she was there. "Do we ever really leave? Did I get it wrong when I thought mine had, when I thought they didn't need me? Did the blackness tell me lies?"

The weight seemed overwhelming, crushing her down as if she couldn't breathe under it. The weight of truth, or lies? She didn't know any longer.

"What's up with you?" Dilys's gruff voice asked behind her, hoarse with coughing.

"I don't know what I've done anymore," Cerys said, and she found that standing was too difficult, so she staggered to a kitchen chair and slumped into it.

"What do you mean?" Dilys asked her. "Or are you finally going to tell me what you're doing here?"

Cerys just stared at her.

Dilys gave a harsh laugh that turned into a cough. "It's obvious something went wrong for you. You don't show up here with that girl and her child in tow and live stuck out here for no reason. No contact from friends, no family. You're running from something, so what is it?"

"Myself," Cerys said. And then she looked up. "But if you thought that all along, why haven't you asked me until now?"

Dilys stopped herself from cackling again to avoid setting off another coughing fit. "It's your own business, and I thought you'd tell me once you were ready. Also, I decided you were harmless, and there's always the shotgun in the cupboard under the stairs if I needed it." She winked at Cerys.

Cerys had noticed the rusty old gun cupboard under there but never thought much of it. It was common enough in farming. Her own dad had had one.

"You've the blackest humor I've ever known," she said, smiling faintly no matter how rough she felt inside. Because it was just so Dilys.

"So, come on then, spit it out. You might not have long before I cark it at this rate."

Cerys shook her head. "There's not much to tell. I'm running from myself, from the ideas in my own head."

Dilys eyed her, with that sharpness that saw past failing eyesight like it could get right into your soul—that's how Cerys always thought of that particular look she was getting now. "Tell me who you were then, before you were this woman now."

"I'm not really anything now," Cerys said. "This isn't real. It's not me. It's a place carved out in time." She paused. "My happy place, but I can't stay. I don't belong here."

"Go on. And tell me about your children."

Cerys shrugged. "So what do you want to know?"

Dilys shifted in the old chair to make herself more comfortable. "Start at the beginning."

"I grew up on a hill farm in Gwynedd, a little like this one must have been when you were running it fully. My dad was a true farmer and didn't have much interest in anything else. My mum and I were close, but I couldn't wait to leave and experience the city as soon as I was eighteen, so off I went to university. I did a degree in English literature, but then I met my husband, Gavin…" She paused for a moment. It was hard to say his name. It stuck on her tongue with disuse and something else.

Resentment, she realized with wonder, because she'd never understood that lived within her until just now.

"So I never used my degree, really. I got married and had children and I kept the home going."

Like a dusty ornament on the mantelpiece, it had sat there within her, all that knowledge and old passion, doing nothing, largely ignored from year to year.

Resentment brewing all that time and she'd never even known.

"I was a full-time mother. And I loved my children, loved being their mum, loved everything about it." She smiled because honestly, she could say their infant days had been the happiest of her life. "I focused everything on being the best mum I could be. And I think I did a good job. They're all off and happy and doing well now."

Dilys gave her a hard stare. "So why are you here and not there?"

She shook her head. "I don't understand it myself. Somewhere in all of it, Gavin and I grew apart, but that happens to lots of couples. We didn't fight, but we just spent more and more time away from each other."

"Your choice or his?"

"His. He's always working; that's the whole focus of his life. I don't think he really cared whether I was there or not sometimes."

Dilys nodded. "Did you ever ask him?"

"I tried to talk to him about it, but he said he was doing his best for the family and that's what doing his best looked like. I don't think I believed him, and the longer we were together, the worse I felt about it. But I put up with it. We had a good life in other ways. We didn't often quarrel and the kids were happy and we were comfortably off. More than most people get, isn't it? My dad would have given anything for what we had. He had to fight all his life to make enough to put food on the table—no family holidays abroad three times a year for him."

She paused to think and Dilys waved her hand at her to go on.

"You already know it started to go really wrong when the kids started to leave home. You know, they've been my whole life. I never had a career, just little jobs that didn't amount to much as they got older. And Gavin's business was so full-on that I barely had time to think about a career for me. I'm not sure I missed out, really, because I had the kids and they were all that mattered—they were my career. But when they left, I started to think about what I am and what was left for me. It wasn't too bad when Katie was still at home because, although I could feel this brewing sense of dread building that eventually she'd go too, we were still so close and we did so much together that I kind of pushed the fear to one side. And I ignored the fact that Gavin was just never there."

She could see in her mind's eye, those moments when Katie had gone out with friends and Gavin was in the home office with the door shut and she'd open it to ask him if he wanted a cup of tea. He'd say yes without even looking up from the computer screen. And when she brought him his tea, he'd receive it in the same way. Not even a glance. He'd say thank you but he didn't see her. His staff at the company would get more civility than that. He'd never treat them that way, but she didn't seem to matter at all. Every single time, it was another tiny cut. But you could bleed out from a thousand cuts just as much from one large wound. And that's how their marriage had been—a death of a thousand cuts.

"My mother died. That's when I really began to struggle. A friend once told me that she never felt she grew up until both her parents were dead.

'Then there's nobody for you,' she said, 'and you really are on your own.' When Mum died, I felt it hard. I missed her, being able to pick up the phone and chat. Having her come over and stay, though she hadn't been able to do that for a few years, so I'd go and stay with her every couple of months for a few days. I'd usually pick the school holidays and Katie would come with me. We sold the farm a long time ago, and she lived in a little bungalow where she could still see our old hills." Her voice caught painfully. "And then when she was gone, part of me seemed to go with her. I felt cut adrift and the world started to feel hostile, alien. But I distracted myself with looking after Katie and plowing everything into my time with her and supporting her through her A-levels."

"What's she like?" Dilys asked.

"She's a very caring girl." Cerys swallowed hard. "Or she was; at least she still is to her friends. I just bore her now. She's got a whole new life ahead of her. She doesn't want her dreary mother whinging and holding her back. Of course she doesn't, and at her age, I did the same thing and flew the coop too." A tear rolled down her cheek. "I hope I didn't make my mother feel like this. Oh God, I really do hope that." She dashed the tear away with her hand before more came and overwhelmed her. "Katie gets quite stressed about doing well, so she needed me a lot through her A-levels. She's a bright girl but not top-of-the-class clever, and she wanted to make sure she got into the university she wanted. She put a lot of pressure on herself and I had to be there for her. So I put everything into that. I had less time for my friends and we sort of drifted a bit."

She stopped again, remembering that day they'd taken Katie to university. Gavin had taken the day off work.

＊

He was tetchy and irritable and checking his phone the whole morning they were packing up the car. He didn't let Katie see it thankfully, but he didn't bother to hide it from Cerys, and she could feel herself getting more and more anxious. She already wanted to cry before they left. She'd been awake all night, trying not to weep and failing, and at three a.m. her pillow was wet with regret at losing the last of her babies. So she started the morning red-eyed and exhausted. His inability to forget about work for this one day, which to Cerys felt like the end of her existence, made her want to just lie down and give up. Because what was this all for now?

They drove Katie to university, a good couple of hours away even in excellent traffic. Cerys felt like she was being driven to her own execution. She couldn't speak. Gavin had the radio on and was chatting to Katie sitting in the back among a pile of her belongings that Cerys had lovingly packed for her. Every single object placed in those cases had felt like a stab in the heart, but she'd insisted on doing it herself.

Cerys stared out of the window and watched the miles go by and wished that she could drift off into the clouds so she no longer had to face this, the third time, the last time, the worst time.

When they got to the university halls of residence, she knew the drill. Knew they weren't to stay too long. Knew not to cry all over her daughter. She'd done this before with the boys, and she'd done well then. She hadn't embarrassed them, or even Gavin, and had kept her tears to the privacy of her own room at home where nobody could see.

They helped Katie carry her suitcases in and Gavin set up her TV for her, while Cerys fussed round by the wardrobe, unpacking her clothes. Katie was looking out of the window and watching who was going past while pretending to organize her desk, but Cerys could see she was far too excited to really do anything of any practical use. She could hear through the wall that other students were arriving in the corridor too. Gavin popped out to the drive-through nearby to get them all some food, and Cerys's heart began to pound faster and faster because the time was coming when they'd have to leave. Dread rose up inside her like floodwater.

The burger and fries were like cardboard. Normally she enjoyed a good old bit of junk food—a definite guilty pleasure now and again that her hips couldn't take anymore. When she'd turned forty, the weight had piled on too easily like it had for her mother and she needed to take care, and it got worse again when she hit fifty. Didn't mean she didn't enjoy a treat usually though, just had to be careful there weren't too many.

This wasn't a treat. This was like the condemned man's last meal on death row. She'd raised these children, and her success as a mother was how well she prepared them to fly, to soar on their own wings. But what happened to her when they were gone?

All too soon, the food was finished by everyone except her, and she stuffed hers back into the bag to take to the bin on the way out. It just wouldn't go down her throat. Katie was almost bouncing on the spot to get them gone now as she could see other students saying goodbye to their own parents and faux-casually making their way to the communal areas to begin making new friends. She was dying to get started herself.

Cerys was no longer needed. Gavin nodded at her, signaling as he had with the other two before her. "Well, time to be on our way. Let you get settled in."

Katie faltered for a split second and then rallied again. She hugged her father. "Bye, Dad, thanks for driving me down. Love you." He hugged her back as if letting her go was the most normal thing in the world and, in that moment, Cerys hated him for it.

Katie turned to her mum and again her resolve faltered for a moment. She wrapped her arms round Cerys, who hugged her back with a ferocity she hadn't known she would let loose, but neither could she keep it in check. Nor could she stop the tears from coming. It wasn't like with the boys. That had been hard but this was far worse—her little girl, and her baby. Her last chick. "Mum, don't—I love you and I'll see you soon. I'll be fine," Katie said.

Her daughter wanted her not to do this, but she couldn't stop herself, not for anything. All she'd learned with the boys. and she still couldn't hold it together for Katie. It was as if all that pain had lingered and concentrated into this final loss. It wasn't that she loved Katie any more than the boys, but they were closer, had always spent more time together.

Gavin patted her on the shoulder. "Come on, Cerys, let's go. Don't worry, Katie. Your mum will be fine."

Oh, famous last words, Gavin. Look how that had worked out.

But she'd gone along with it and hidden her face on the way out so that she didn't shame Katie by being led weeping to the car. Gavin had told Katie to get along to the kitchen, where the others were gathering to mingle, and not to worry about coming and waving them off.

He hadn't known what to say to Cerys as they got into the car. A half-lifetime of never bothering to say anything of importance to her meant that, when he needed to, he didn't have a clue how to make it right. He glanced over at her a few times as they drove off and awkwardly patted her knee when they stopped at a set of traffic lights. "She'll be fine. Don't be upsetting yourself."

He was so stupid. But what did he know? His life hadn't just ended. He still had a purpose, things that made him important. Whereas she was a nothing now, a no-matter to anyone.

She stared out of the window into the gathering dusk as they traveled home and the silent tears continued to fall down her cheeks. How could the emptiness inside her brew up such a river? The tears wouldn't stop coming.

⁓

"When I got home, I left him to it and just locked myself in the bedroom and howled," she told Dilys. "An awful state I was in. I'm surprised the neighbors didn't hear, to be honest. I think he knocked on the door a couple of times and tried to get me to open it, but I could barely hear him and I didn't care anyway."

"Men are sometimes very stupid," Dilys said in a very Dilys way.

Cerys nodded. "You know what hurt most though? She hardly came home. I could tell when she called that she couldn't wait to be off again with her friends. And she'd go off to stay at their parents' houses at weekends, not bring them home to us. After that day, she really did leave, both physically and in her heart. I think it was that that killed me—the woman I was, I mean."

"So then what?"

"That's when the blackness came, like I told you before. I just carried on. And on. Until one day, I made Gavin speak to me, and the things he said… I hated him. I hated me, and being like that, but then I really hated him. I even think I hated Katie and Alex and Matt for leaving me like this right then. And I hated life—it just hurt too much to stand anymore. So I got into the car that night and I drove up to the hills where my dad's old farm was. It's all been broken up and sold off now. I ran the car right out into the hills and I torched it. Then I sat out on the hills and waited to die. That's where I wanted to do it, in the home I'd happily run from all those years ago."

"But you didn't die obviously," Dilys said, quirking an eyebrow.

"No, I didn't. The weather turned that night, and something shifted inside me too, so I got up and walked out of there. I don't know why. I walked until I got to a village, then a bus to the coast. I saw the sea, and it was as cold and gray and dead as me, so I thought I'd maybe walk into it and let it take me. That was the only thing I could think of when I was left in that state. Not dead but just not wanting to live anymore and face all the mess behind me. I was all over the place. I was supposed to be dead and I wasn't but I couldn't go back. It would hurt too much. You know, Dilys, I never thought I'd say this to you because it's not my business to and one woman's pain can't compare to another's, but there's a blessing in never having a child. You don't have to suffer when they go and they no longer want you in their life. When you don't matter anymore. When they've bled you dry and left you with nothing and you're alone."

Dilys shrugged. "What you never have, you never miss? Maybe, but the longing hurts something terrible too. You're right—women shouldn't compete over their pain. It's enough that we hurt. Anyway, you are about to tell me that you aren't drowned."

Cerys smiled despite it all, just at the Dilysness of Dilys. "I'm not. I was walking down the road, deciding where to do it, just where to walk into the sea and let it carry me off until I just went under. They say drowning is painless, and I didn't want more pain. I just wanted it all to stop. So I was trying to see a quiet point where I could do it and whether the tide was right, whether it really would work this time because I didn't want to get it wrong again. I couldn't afford to. And then as I walked along the seafront, thinking about how and where to make it happen, I passed a food van. There was a young woman sitting there with her child and he dropped all his food on the ground, and she just burst into tears, so I stopped to help."

"Lily."

"Yes. And she needed help. I was only supposed to get her somewhere to stay, and we were headed to Beaumaris and I thought there's plenty of sea there for me to do it. Another day wouldn't hurt."

"But then she still needed you." Dilys nodded in understanding. "Or maybe you needed her. But anyway, here you are. You have a family back there though. What do they think has happened to you?"

"I don't know. I imagine the car was found. I didn't leave a note, and I haven't been in touch with them since." She looked away from Dilys's sharp gaze. "I can't. I don't know what to say to them."

"Part of you wants to punish them," said Dilys. "Don't deny it, either to me or yourself. It's true. Accept that as part of you. It's part of your pain."

"Is it?"

"Bit like an animal in a snare. You'll bite out of pain. It's not something to feel guilty about—it just is. They hurt you, you lash out back."

"But I love my children."

"And that's why they could hurt you so much. Doesn't mean you can't be angry with them too. Even if you don't admit it to yourself and let it fester inside." She sniffed, and shifted again in her chair, trying to find an easier position. "Now you have a phone call to make. Use the landline in there. Shut the door if you don't want me to hear, but you need to do it."

She shook her head. "Later, when I know what to say. I'll do it later, I promise. I'm just not ready yet."

"You mind you do! And you can stay here, you know. You can always stay here, for as long or as short as you need. For good if that suits. If it's this life you want."

She was choked up by the offer and nodded her thanks. That was okay—Dilys understood.

But later, she still couldn't find the words for that phone call. By the time Dilys mumbled and grumbled her way off to bed, Cerys was still brooding over it. It had to be done. It had been months now and it was never supposed to be that way. It wasn't fair to anyone. She didn't want to punish them, not now—even if Dilys was right about that. She simply didn't know what she wanted now or who she was, and she wasn't ready yet to face any of that. The blackness was still too close, as if it squatted on the edge, waiting to overwhelm her if she made a wrong move. It would laugh as it pulled her back into itself.

Lily didn't need her over there. Rhys was staying over, and she'd only be in the way. So she sat by the fire after Dilys had gone to bed and watched the flames for answers. It was long past midnight when the last of them died down, and she noticed the chill growing in her limbs, forcing her up.

She went to the phone in the hall and, with cold fingers, entered the code to hide her own number and dialed. It would go to voicemail. He always had his phone on silent after nine p.m. It had that setting that if you called a couple of times in quick succession, you could override that, but she had no intention of calling more than once.

To her utter shock, after four rings, the phone was answered.

"Hello," the groggy voice said, and then sharper, "Hello?"

She couldn't speak. She hadn't heard Gavin's voice for months, and the last time she had, he'd been telling her what a failure she was as a human being. Bitter words, vitriol dropping from every syllable.

All those years of marriage, and now she had no idea what to say to him.

"Cerys?" he asked with a crack in his voice. "Cerys, is that you? If it is, please speak to me. I'm sorry, I'm so sorry." The words tumbled out fast, so fast she could hardly make out what he was saying and she couldn't process them. "Please tell me you're all right. Please come home. We all miss you. Please? Cerys?"

She couldn't stand it any longer and she put the phone down quickly, her heart pounding in her chest so hard that it made her feel sick. She'd thought it would be safe at this time of night and he wouldn't answer and she could just leave a message. She hadn't planned that he'd have taken night mode off and actually picked up.

She went back into the cold kitchen and sat with her head in her hands. What on earth was she going to do now?

48

CERYS WAS STRANGELY QUIET AND distracted the next morning as Lily got ready for work. "You're not cross that Rhys is staying for a couple of days, are you?" Lily asked her anxiously as he was in the shower. "Because I can tell him to go."

She shook her head tiredly. "Not at all. No, it's nice he's here spending some time with you. The more the merrier, after all, and he's a good man. I'm just tired."

The age-old excuse for everything when you're too weary to talk, or too heartsore. Lily wasn't convinced and eyed her suspiciously. She'd used that excuse too many times herself to believe it at face value. But Cerys smiled at Rhys when he emerged and didn't seem cross with him at all, so perhaps it wasn't that.

He wasn't in work that day or on call, which is why he'd chosen to spend a few days up here getting some fresh air and exercise but, first of all, she was getting pampered by being driven to work and dropped off. He popped in ten minutes later with a deli sandwich in a bag for her from the shop up the road. "In case you don't get a chance," he said and blew her a kiss as he left.

She was a little jittery that day. Since she'd had the phone, she'd started obsessing about the police hunt for her and Drew, and she tracked it on her phone when she had breaks. She hadn't looked last night because Rhys was there, but when she got a short break between clients today, she searched up the latest on the missing persons case.

When she read it, she wished she hadn't. Maybe it was better to know, but it certainly didn't feel that way when she saw how he was twisting the truth. Anyone who saw her or Drew was urged to contact the police as soon as possible. Danny was starting court proceedings to get custody because he was so worried about them.

She knew what Rhys would say, that it was all bluff, but it didn't feel that way when you were seeing his lying face plastered all over the media. *You don't tell them how you burned me to punish me, how you raped me, how you completely controlled every aspect of my life until I felt like nothing*, she snarled inside. *Tell them that, Danny. Tell the truth for once.* But the danger was that Rhys was wrong. After all, he hadn't met Danny, so he didn't know how plausible he was.

She did. She'd fallen for it all, after all, so nobody knew better than her how he could lie and make you believe every word of it. He was clever like that, maybe not so much in other ways, but he was cunning at getting people to trust him and believe what he chose to make them believe.

It was only now with Cerys and Rhys teaching her that she understood how wrong her relationship with Danny had been. *That wasn't love, Danny. Love doesn't treat people like that. I know that now*, she thought as she glared at his apparently worried face on the screen. "You go to hell!" And she turned her phone off.

She was agitated today anyway without this. She and Rhys had talked last night after Drew was in bed.

"You're going to have to tell them soon," he'd said. "You can't keep up this deception about Drew being a boy for much longer. The longer it goes on, the harder it will be for Cerys to understand why you didn't tell her before."

"I just can't bear for her to hate me."

"She won't hate you. She'll understand when you explain, but I think you need to tell her about Danny too, or maybe it won't make so much sense."

Lily curled her knees up to her chest on the sofa. "I don't want her to know what he did to me. It makes me feel so dirty."

He shook his head in amazement. "Why? The last thing you should feel about that is dirty. He's the scumbag. He's the one who should feel like filth, not you."

But he'd humiliated her so much. What she remembered was how he made her feel like she was nothing, like she was never going to be worth anything and this was all she deserved. He'd called her a whore often enough when he hurt her that the feeling was burned into her like that lighter had been.

How could she tell Cerys all that? She'd not told Rhys all of it—he'd worked out most and it was better that he didn't know the rest. The part he knew made him mad enough. She'd learned to block out thoughts of Danny when she was with Rhys, and that helped her be "normal" around him, or as normal as she could get right now. He was patient though, was Rhys, and he understood that sometimes she acted strangely, and she needed time to learn a new way to be. Miraculously, or so she still thought of it, he didn't seem to mind any of that. He just seemed happy with her the way she was, however that was.

He was right though about Cerys and about Drew. And it was for Drew's sake that she needed to find the courage. She didn't think she could have done it for any other reason, but she would walk through fire for her daughter, and so tonight she'd find some bravery and do it.

"Oh, Cerys, please don't hate me," she whispered, and then another client came in, and she could put her fears to one side until later and focus on her work instead.

They ate at the farmhouse that night, all of them. Cerys had made a huge bowl of stew. Rhys was starving as he'd been out walking that day, and she'd picked up fresh bread from the bakery on the way home. His eyes lit up at the sight of it. "That smells so good," he groaned, as he fidgeted around by the table while Cerys finished thickening the stew.

"You'll need to feed him soon or he'll be starting on the chair leg," Dilys cackled. She looked much brighter than she had in days. It was the company, perhaps, Lily thought. She looked like she enjoyed the kitchen being full of noise and life. Like a family, Lily thought with a smile. An odd motley family who shouldn't fit at all but who had found each other somehow. A better family than any pretense of one she'd ever had. And one where she was learning what family really meant. That mattered so much to her, both for herself, because it made her feel safe and happy, and for Drew because she deserved that kind of childhood, the kind Lily had never had.

She looked around as they all sat down over the meal, Dilys laughing as Drew screwed her face up at proper stew and Cerys splodged some ketchup in to encourage her. "It's disgusting," she said, "but it works and it's not the worst thing for them." Yes, they were a little family together and it made her feel snug and safe like the stew inside. Whatever happened, she would always have these memories and a new knowledge of how life could be.

Should be.

She volunteered to help Cerys wash up after dinner and plucked up the courage to shepherd Dilys off into the sitting room in front of the TV with the promise of something called a hot toddy. She had no idea what that was but Cerys did and, as usual, saved the day.

"I've got something to tell you," she confessed as she put the stewpot in to soak before she gave it a good scrub.

"What's that?" Cerys asked, drying a plate and smiling encouragingly.

Lily took a deep breath. "Sammy isn't really Sammy," she said.

"Oh, I guessed that," Cerys replied. "I thought you might have changed your names. I don't know why—just an instinct. Like why you dye his hair brown."

"You know about that?"

"Not at first," she said with a laugh. "But you can't spend as much time with him as I do without noticing the roots occasionally and then see them disappear. And it's easy for you, in your trade. I must say you do a very good job on him. It took me quite a while to realize. I did wonder if you'd changed yours too?"

"Yeah, it used to be much longer, to my waist, and highlighted—balayage—and it was beautiful—but I lopped half of it off and covered the highlights up," Lily said miserably because she knew, though Cerys didn't, that there was much worse than some hair dye to come. "And what did you think about me dyeing Sammy's hair?"

"I thought you had your reasons, *cariad*. I don't know what those are but I do know you love that boy, and that's the most important thing for me to know."

"He's not a boy," Lily blurted out.

Cerys stopped as she reached to put a plate in the rack above the draining board. "What?"

"Sammy's a girl," Lily said, staring at her feet because she couldn't bear to meet Cerys's eyes. "Her name's Drew."

Cerys put down the tea towel. "Well! Okay, I didn't guess that!" She sounded every bit as shocked as Lily had expected. Of course she did—how else could she feel? "Wow! Drew!"

"I'm sorry," Lily said in a small voice. "Are you mad?"

"No, no," Cerys replied, but she did sound disappointed. "I just don't quite know how to get my head round that."

"I wanted to tell you but I didn't know how."

"No, I can see that. It is awkward. I'm struggling to process it a bit." She gave a strained laugh, and there was no humor in it.

"Do you hate me now?" Lily asked.

"No, of course not, I just wish you'd told me before. What made you decide to tell me now?"

"Rhys said I needed to before it went on any longer and I made it worse. I wanted to tell you, but there was never a right time, and then it had gone on too long." She found the courage to raise her eyes to Cerys's. "What I dreaded the most was telling you and you hating me or being disappointed. You've done so much for me, and I couldn't stand to let you down. And that's why I haven't told you, which is stupid because that just made it worse and more likely you'd be disappointed." She held her hands up in despair. "But I'm not very bright, you know, and I'm often too scared of everything to see a way out, so I avoid and make it all worse. You've helped me see that I do that, but I haven't found a way to stop doing it yet."

Cerys gave a rueful smile. "You'll get there! You're not doing half as badly as you think you are, but I know why that is and you're right, it'll take a long time to relearn those patterns. But you will! I'm glad you felt you could tell Rhys though, even if you couldn't tell me."

Lily scratched her nose with her arm, hands still covered in suds from the washing-up. "Well, I didn't. Not really. He's always known."

Light dawned on Cerys's face. "Of course! The hospital. He would have examined her. Good grief, didn't you get some trouble over that?"

"Nearly," she admitted. "He was about to call the police and social services, and he knew we'd given fake names. So I had to tell him why. I didn't have a choice." She sighed heavily. "He says I should tell you and then you'll understand how I got into this mess and why I kept it a secret for so long."

"And do you want to tell me?"

"Yes and no. I know you will understand but—" Her face crumpled. "I hate talking about it. It makes me feel disgusting and dirty and—"

Cerys dropped the tea towel and went and put her arms around Lily's shoulders. "You know what? We'll finish this later. I'll check on Dilys and make sure she's okay, and then I want you to tell me everything. It might feel horrible to start with but, I promise you, you'll feel better afterward to have it all out in the open."

49

"AFTER DREW WAS BORN, HE got much worse," Lily said. She could see Cerys flinch as if what had gone before wasn't bad enough, so she stopped.

"No, go on," Cerys said grimly. "I've only got to listen to it; you had to live it, so don't spare my sensibilities."

Lily felt that swift barb of shame she always felt when having to admit to what her life was. Even if others were to blame for some of it, she'd still let them.

"The first time he really hit me was after Drew was born. He wanted sex and I didn't feel like it. I was still sore, and it just didn't feel right. So he slapped me and I was so shocked, I let him do it then. After that, he made it clear I didn't have a choice and I should never have dared say no to him. He was careful not to leave marks where anyone would see, but you don't have to leave marks to hurt someone. And I had a baby—I had no choice anymore. I had to stay."

"I understand," Cerys said.

"I should have known before. I did really but he was more careful at first. It was only really after Drew that it got very bad, when he knew I was stuck. And even then, while I was still getting checkups, he didn't go too far. The worst part was when his mother visited from Spain, because she wanted to see Drew, and she hated me. I couldn't do anything right around her, and he got worse after that too. Like he was more ashamed of me and who I am. He said he didn't tell her anything about me, but that she could spot it a mile off. I think that might have been true and I felt so dirty. It was after she left that this started happening." She showed Cerys the scars on her stomach.

Cerys's hand flew to her mouth. "Oh dear God! Why?"

"He looked at me differently after his mother came. Started saying mean things about me wanting to be with other men because that's what I was like and he'd put a stop to it. So he did this so they wouldn't want me. Not all at once. Over time, whenever I annoyed him."

"And does Rhys know this?" Cerys asked.

She nodded. "He says the scars don't matter to him."

"Of course they don't," Cerys said with feeling. "Only a twisted mind like your ex's would think they would."

"I feel dirty," Lily said. "I always feel dirty. Not just because of what I did when I was a lot younger. Mostly because of him."

She was not going to cry, Lily told herself. She would not cry over Danny. Not anymore.

What she needed to focus on was what he was up to right now. With a nationwide hunt on for her and her face blasted all over the media, it was just a question of time before somebody spotted her and called the police. Especially as she couldn't keep Drew hidden as a boy much longer. It wasn't fair to her. Up until now the little girl had treated it much as an elaborate game, but it couldn't carry on. But what would she do then? He was trying to get a judge to rule in her absence that she had to return Drew.

She might have to run again and leave everything she'd found here behind because she would not let that happen. If Danny got his way and they did rule without her there, then as soon as she was found, Drew would be taken from her. Her time was nearly up—she'd have to do something soon.

50

CERYS WAS SICK TO HER stomach at the thought of what Lily had been through. And honestly, if that man had been in the room now, she'd have smacked him in the face as she might have done had it been Katie in Lily's position. Actually no, scratch that—if a man treated Katie that way, she would tear him limb from limb with her bare hands. She was mad enough for Lily though, and the girl had been through so much already. But that was the point, wasn't it? Men like him preyed on girls like her because they were vulnerable and could be conned into thinking they needed them and that this was how things had to be. They hadn't had that sense of self-worth to let them walk away at the first sign of this coercive hell.

It was the casual cruelty that most sickened her, the violence, which he clearly enjoyed as so much of it wasn't done in temper or loss of control. He liked what he was doing.

Bastard!

She hoped to God she'd given Katie enough self-confidence and security and a strong enough self-worth that she'd never let a man like Danny near her. And to think she'd complained about Gavin and his neglect. As infuriating and destructive as his indifference had been, he looked like an angel next to a man like this.

"You have nothing to feel dirty about," she told Lily. "Not one thing, do you hear me? I am telling you as a mother. Now I might not be yours but—"

"You're the closest I've got," Lily said, red-eyed. "And better than the real one ever was."

Her words packed a punch into the remains of the lingering blackness that lived inside of Cerys.

"Do you understand, Lily? You never accept a man treating you like that ever again."

"I do," she said falteringly, "because I have Drew and that's what I want for her."

"Good, then you don't accept from any man what you wouldn't want for Drew."

"That's how I found the courage to go in the end," she said falteringly. "I was too scared to do it for myself, but I didn't want Drew growing up seeing that, her being poisoned by it like I was. Her turning into me."

The overwhelming sense of emotion that rocked Cerys at those words could only be described as pride. That her "adopted" daughter had found the strength to do that. That she had protected her own child to the best of her ability. Any lingering feelings of bruised ego she felt that Lily hadn't told her about Drew earlier vanished like mist in the morning sun. She understood completely that visceral, primitive need to protect your children at all costs.

And when she thought back to that girl she'd found sobbing on the picnic bench because her child had dropped their food on the ground, dear God, no wonder she had wept after everything she'd been through.

You were meant to find her, a voice inside said. *You were meant to not walk into that sea. You were meant to be there that day at that time.*

And there was no logic to that at all. There was only a mother's instinct, and if Cerys had one thing left in her wretched life, in the wreckage of that world she'd inhabited, it was that. She was still a mother, and she could still give this girl what she so badly needed, even if her own children had moved on.

"You're going to come out of this stronger," she told Lily. "You're going to be that mother you want to be and that Drew needs. Look how far you've come already. You listen to me, I know how hard it must have been for you to leave. I don't understand how it feels because I've never been you, but I know you and how scared you must have been. You did a tremendous thing there for Drew. I am so proud of you! I don't think I can find the words to tell you how proud of you I am. And you've kept going, keeping your secret to protect her. So, *cariad*, I am not disappointed or mad at you. Not in the slightest. I'm devastated that you've been so hurt, I'm mad as all hellfire at that man for doing that to you, but most of all I'm prouder than I've ever been of anyone in my life that you did what you did for your little girl—you are a fantastic mother!"

And she stopped, totally out of words and choked up by how strongly she felt. It overwhelmed her, and what lifted it beyond the effect of her words on herself, of that outpouring of emotion that she hadn't understood before she said it, was the look on Lily's face. She looked as if she'd been waiting for her whole life to hear someone say that, but only in a dream—as she'd never believed it could actually happen in real life.

It was a heady thing to realize you'd made somebody's dream come true. Cerys didn't quite know what to say anymore, so instead, she followed that well-honed mother's instinct and flung herself over to Lily to hug her as tight as she should have been hugged by the mother who had never been there for her. And it was as if she could put all of the love that Lily should have had but didn't into one embrace. Cerys wanted her to remember the feel of that hug whenever trouble came and she needed a mother's love. As she remembered her own mother's arms every single time she'd needed her.

To lose a mother like Cerys's was a dreadful thing. It could tear you in two, and you could never be the same again once they'd gone. But she understood that far worse was never to have had a mother like that in the first place.

Lily hung onto her too like she could receive everything she'd missed. Like it was making her whole.

"I do feel better," Lily said finally when they let go of each other and weren't quite sure what to do next. She said it wonderingly. "You were right. I really do feel better."

Cerys's eyes were brimming as she said, "You always do when you talk to your mum and get the world put right."

And Lily nodded, because she understood who they were talking about and also that Cerys had just made her a promise.

"Can you sit with Dilys now for a minute?" Cerys asked her. "I need to make a phone call. I need to call my daughter."

Lily's eyes widened, but she just nodded in response and went through to see the old woman.

Cerys went into the hall and picked up the phone. She dialed the no caller ID code and then the number. It did go to voicemail, and she was relieved she didn't have to run the whole gamut of emotions she'd had when she'd called Gavin. It was hard enough hearing Katie's voice on the recorded message.

"Hi, this is Katie. Sorry I can't answer but leave a message and I'll get back to you."

"Hi, sweetheart, it's Mum. I'm okay and I love you—I need you to know that. Bye, love."

She couldn't have said any more and not lost control. Besides, it was enough. She didn't know what she was going to do next, so it was best not to be drawn into more.

She closed her eyes and leaned against the wall. She could feel her daughter on her lap as a child, feel those little toddler-chubby arms round her neck as they cuddled, feel the soft weight of her and the scent of the strawberry shampoo on her hair.

"I want to go home," she whispered, "but I don't know where home is anymore, Katie. Please forgive me."

51

DILYS WAS STILL COUGHING BADLY when Cerys left to see to the sheep. Dawn was coming faster now at the beginning of spring, but it still wasn't light when she left. Kip was behaving strangely. He wouldn't get off Dilys's bed. Cerys went to give his collar a quick tug, and he growled at her.

She pulled back startled, and Kip whined and laid his head on the old woman. His tail wagged in appeasement. Cerys eyed him, thinking. She didn't like the look of this. Whether Dilys wanted it or not, she was calling the doctor back again when she returned. It was only a week since she'd had him out but that time had been at Dilys's request and she'd not improved any since then.

"You stay there and look after her then," she told Kip as Dilys still dozed. "I'll see you later." The cup of tea Cerys had brought Dilys before she got dressed was still untouched on the side table. That wasn't like her—she was normally awake in time to tend the sheep, even though she couldn't do it anymore. Years of habit still woke her though. Kip wagged appreciatively back at Cerys for understanding that he needed to do this, and he settled himself in closer to his mistress.

Cerys set out on her own. Without Kip, the work took three times as long, and there was a pale sun well up in the sky by the time she returned back down the hill. At least she didn't have to worry about getting back to care for Drew as Rhys was there and didn't have to go into the hospital until late afternoon. On the way back, she noticed a lame sheep struggling to get up the hill and stopped to check on her. She was a hard catch without the dog there, despite her lame foot, and then Cerys had to administer some first aid and a spot of spray to the sheep's fleece to make her easy to locate again for daily checking to make sure the cut was healing. It looked like she'd torn it, probably on barbed wire, and there was some inflammation but no infection yet. Cerys suspected it might turn nasty though, so definitely one to check tomorrow before bacteria took hold and she had a big job on her hands.

She trudged down the hill slowly. The ground was soaked after days of rain and it made for tough going in places. It gave her time to think about what she was going to do next, what she really wanted.

It was probably time to talk to Dilys again about what she wanted. The old woman wasn't getting better at all at the moment, and it was clear Cerys couldn't leave without some form of plan. Dilys would need a nurse and someone to look after the farm for her if Cerys did go.

If Cerys even wanted to.

Did she?

Dilys's offer turned over and over in her head, slow graceful cartwheels of promise.

She could stay. She could have a life here. A completely different one to what had gone before, but there was peace here. Her heart was at rest. The blackness was held at bay.

The trouble was, she didn't know if that was a temporary thing, or if Dilys was right and it was her time of life and she'd be released from its claws as she moved through that. Up here in the hills, what she understood was that life moved with seasons and the slow turn of the earth from day to night. The rhythm of the country still lay deep in her bones, for all she'd rejected that for years. But in times of trouble, her soul turned toward it again gratefully, like a compass needle to the north. Her heart aligned with relief.

She would stay, she thought. She would contact her children and explain and that would be a hard conversation. Maybe they would drive over and go out for lunch somewhere and she could talk to them about it.

Gavin would move on with his life; he had the business. He'd been weary of her for years anyway. Perhaps he'd be glad to be cut loose. She rather thought he would.

And she would have peace. After the last few years, that was really all she wanted now. That quiet stillness that brought a gentle joy, and an escape from the blackness. That was enough for her.

She went into the farmhouse and pulled off her raincoat. The dog didn't come to greet her, but after his behavior this morning she wasn't surprised. She filled the kettle and turned it on and went to see if Dilys was ready for a cup of tea and some breakfast.

When she padded into the bedroom in her thick welly boot socks, she heard the sound immediately and she froze. The dog lifted a quick sorrowful head and whined softly.

Dilys lay motionless under the quilt. Her chest rising and falling and that dreadful, cracking wheeze that Cerys knew.

The death rattle.

She'd heard it before from her own parents and as a child from her grandmother when she was taken to say goodbye for the last time. Her mother had told her what it was then.

Dilys stirred slightly, and Cerys hurried over to the bed to take her hand. "Don't bother the doctor," she croaked. "It's time, I know that; I've felt it coming for a while and he told me last week I was right. I wouldn't let him tell you—didn't want you worrying before you had to."

This was how her dad had been. A last generation of farming folk who understood tides and rhythms well enough that they accepted their own with an equanimity that was lost in the rest of society. It didn't surprise her. These folk didn't make a fuss when their time came. They let it happen like the wild things did, and they went with a grace that escaped those battling and out of place in hospital beds.

Cerys knew what Dilys wanted now and it was her duty to provide that, as it had been for her own parents.

"Give me a few minutes and I'll be back," she said.

Dilys nodded, the horrible rattle adding impetus to Cerys's movements. She sped over to the cottage, leaving Kip on the bed with Dilys to keep her company, and indeed nothing would have moved that dog from her side.

Rhys was playing Snap with Drew at the table.

"Hi, what's up?" he said when she burst in.

"Dilys," she said, nodding at Drew to indicate she couldn't say more.

Rhys, with a few years of hospital experience under his belt, understood immediately. "Drew, let's move this over to the farmhouse, and Cerys will help you set up while I just go and do a doctor-type thing, then I'll come back and play."

Drew still lived in that inhibited world where she didn't pout or argue with grown-ups in case of repercussions, but Cerys had a minor moment of pleasure to see that she allowed a faint expression of disappointment to gleam through. Cerys helped her collect everything and when they got over to the farmhouse, she drew Rhys aside.

"I think she's passing." She marveled for a second that her mother's old term for it was the one she found on her lips, and then continued, "and she doesn't want a doctor again, but I need to know it really is her time and there's no more we could do."

He nodded. "Leave it with me," and he headed off to Dilys's room.

Cerys helped Drew arrange the cards into the correct piles again, and by the time that was achieved to Drew's satisfaction, Rhys was back at the door. "I'm just going to hand over to Cerys and then I'll be back—let me steal her for a moment."

"Why don't you get a biscuit from the tin?" Cerys suggested over her shoulder as she followed him out, closing the door behind her.

Rhys cut to the chase. "She has a DNR notice in her bedside drawer. She pointed me to it."

Cerys knew what this was from her own father's death—a Do Not Resuscitate plan, agreed by the patient following a conversation with their doctor. "Did she do that last week when he was here?"

Rhys nodded. "She kept it there for when it was needed. She didn't want to tell you too soon in case you tried to talk her out of it."

"She's going, isn't she?" The reality of it hit Cerys like a cold wave from the Irish Sea.

"I'm sorry, yes, she is. I'll call the GP and notify them, and I'll also call a friend and get swapped off shift so I can stay here. There's not much I can do, but you'll probably feel better having a doctor around, and at least I can look after Drew. I'll let Lily know in a minute."

"I will, yes. I'm going to sit with her, so it would be a big help having you here for Drew too."

He hesitated. "Not my specialist area, this, but for what it's worth, I don't think she's got long. I'll pull out all the stops to stay for as long as needed."

"Thanks," Cerys said, "I don't think she has either."

"I'll bring you a cup of tea as soon as I've finished this game with Drew. And I'll help you if she's able to swallow any water. Don't be surprised if she can't or won't though."

Cerys nodded and went back to the bedroom. She pulled the bedroom chair up to sit beside Dilys. She took the old woman's hand in hers. Dilys stirred and opened her eyes for a moment. She smiled faintly. "It doesn't hurt," she whispered and closed her eyes again and drifted back into sleep. The dog whined once softly and snuggled a few inches closer as if he knew his presence would pass comfort through the quilt and into her very bones.

Time passed by softly and slowly as Cerys sat beside the bed. How many more of these passings would she be here for? She'd never wanted to do another after her own mother's, but she was thankful she was here for Dilys's because otherwise, she might be alone when she passed. Cerys had been grateful neither of her parents had died alone, and it would have broken her inside if she'd come down from that hill today to find Dilys had gone with only the dog here with her.

The old woman's hand was cold in hers and she rubbed it lightly to warm it and then pulled the covers up closer under her chin. Soon nothing would warm her again. Cerys wondered if she could feel cold now or whether she was beyond that. She'd said it didn't hurt. That was a blessing.

"A good way to die," that's what Dilys would call this if she could speak now. No tubes, no hospital buzzers, no frantic whir of hospital and medical procedures. Dying as she had lived, quietly and in the place she loved, in her home, with that poor faithful dog by her side.

She noticed a corner of paper peeking out of the bedroom drawer and she opened the drawer to see what it was. An envelope, which must have been lying under the DNR notice. It had her name on it. Rhys mustn't have seen it when he picked the DNR sheet up, but it was dark in the room with the tiny cottage window and a dull sky, and the writing was faint.

Cerys took it out of the drawer and glanced at Dilys, who slept on, her lungs battling to breathe while the rest of her began to surrender. The name was written on it in the shaky hand of the old with failing sight. She opened it. There was a letter inside written in the same wobbly hand.

Dear Cerys,

Thank you for everything you have done for me. It is more than you can ever know. I wish we could have had longer together but know that you have made my last days brighter and happier than anybody else could have. And you brought Lily and Sammy with you, and you have all given me a chance to have a family even if it was only for a few months, but it has been a blessing I had not looked or dared hope for.

I want you to know, as you enter this new stage in your life, that things are not over and not ended. These are new beginnings. Look out for them and do not be afraid that good things will not come now. It is a hard change sometimes to move into that last third of life and know there is more time behind you than ahead, but do not fear it. We learn wisdom in the life before, that carries us through the life ahead if we let it. It is not the end, but a new time to grow. Change feels hard but, when we look back after, we realize it was good for us.

I wish I could stay to walk through this with you for a few more years but I know you are a strong woman and you will do it without me. I want to give you a little gift to help you though, and I know you will do the right thing with it. It is your choice what to do with it and it is a gift freely given. You know I never had a daughter and I always wanted one. I would have been so proud to have one like you and, for the last few months of my life, you have given me that gift I have always longed for. To me, you have been that daughter. When I asked for my lawyer to visit a few weeks ago, it was to draw up a new will. I have left you the farm, to do with as you please.

I have left my land and property to my daughter, as I always wished to be able to. I have given instructions to the lawyer to make sure I am buried in the churchyard beside my husband. You can just see the farm from where the grave is.

I hope this gift will bring you joy and freedom, however you use it. Please look after Kip for me. He will be happy with you.

With all my love,
Dilys

Cerys put the letter down on the quilt in astonishment.

She let the words sink in slowly, each one feeling as if it etched across her skin and into her memory. A gift indeed, but while the legacy Dilys left her was of huge value in itself—joy and freedom indeed—her words of wisdom were perhaps the greater gift. She knew that deep inside her, a chord that resonated through every fiber.

And to have that unconditional support and wisdom and humor ripped away so soon, just when she felt it had saved her as much as meeting Lily had—the sense of loss steamrollered into her. She felt the breath slam from her, leaving her winded and barely able to stay upright. She wanted to fall to her knees and scream.

But she did not, because that was not what Dilys needed now. No, now wasn't the time to give in, not yet.

"Thank you," she said, taking Dilys's hand. "Thank you!" Dilys's eyelids fluttered, and she seemed to smile before drifting back to where she was beginning to journey. There was nothing more Cerys could say right then. She had a job to do, as a daughter, and she held Dilys's hand and talked softly to her about the farm and the sheep. The mundane and beautiful things of the farm and the hills. Rhys glanced in on them, and Lily appeared in the doorway at one point. Cerys shook her head at her because she could tell from Lily's face that she would break down if she came in, and that wasn't how Dilys wanted to go.

So she held her hand and talked about the beauty of the changing season and the moods of the hill, until the rattle grew stronger and louder. And then it eventually stopped entirely, and the dog froze and then let out a low mournful howl.

52

IT WAS OVER, THAT LITTLE dream she'd had, her space carved out in time here at Bryn Terrin. All of that had ended.

Cerys lay in bed in the cottage the day after they'd lost Dilys, thinking of the letter. Cerys would honor Dilys's wishes and contact the lawyer and make sure she was buried as she wished.

And then what for her?

She still didn't know the answer to that, and she'd been too busy dealing with the practicalities yesterday to think about it until now. She'd been acting like this could last forever, like she could turn it into some kind of new life, and of course that couldn't happen.

You still could, a voice inside said. It sounded strangely like a whisper from Dilys, but that was just the fancy of grief. Her last confidant torn away and she felt the loss like a hole punched through her. She felt as if that was visible to the world, as if they could see through that great gaping void in her that Dilys had helped to patch up for a short time. Too short. And she was alone again. She couldn't survive that.

Now it was yawning open again—the hole of who she was now she was no longer a mother, no longer a daughter.

She was nothing.

She didn't even have tears to cry. She was empty of them. This grief was a hollow, cold thing, an arctic desert. She could feel its chill right down into the tips of her fingers, freezing her.

Killing her.

There it was waiting and laughing softly, the blackness. It always knew it would be back and she had no defenses against it. All of that tenuous hope was exposed now as the nonsensical ramblings of a middle-aged woman who had lost the plot. Stupid bitch. It was always coming for her and she was an idiot to think anything else. And this time, as it folded her into its deathly embrace, there would be no escape.

She could feel its hands on her now.

"I'm sorry, Katie," she whispered into the night. "I think I nearly made it back but I couldn't quite do it. I'll leave a note this time so you understand I love you. And Matt and Alex." She almost said Gavin, but that was too bitter a pill. It would take her under soon and then she wouldn't be herself again. Best to write the note while she still had some semblance of who she was remaining. She would hang in there until the funeral because that was what she did, but she also knew watching Dilys laid under the earth would be the final nail in her own coffin. The grief would give her back to the blackness, and that's why it was grinning at her now. She knew how this played out. She'd been here before, after all.

She dragged herself out of bed to get a paper and pen to prepare a letter to her daughter. Lily didn't need her now. She had Rhys, and she would be fine. It had all only ever been a delay. She'd known that at the start of this. Fool to think that had changed.

As she went to the drawer in the kitchen to see if she could find something to write on, she noticed headlights coming up the farm track toward the house. She expected the vehicle to turn off at the fork up to the next farm, but it didn't. It continued heading to Bryn Terrin and stopped at the farm gate. Cerys peered through the window as the engine was turned off and the lights killed. A figure got out of the car. She could just about make that out. She felt the soft brush of fur on her legs as Kip came to stand beside her. The dog was tense and listening intently.

She strained her eyes to see through the gloom and the figure appeared to turn on a small light. A flashlight or a phone, she wasn't sure.

As soon as the hand went on the gate, Kip let out a flurry of barking and flew at the door, scrabbling to get out, snarling. She saw the figure check but then the gate swung open, and the light came toward the cottage.

It wasn't Rhys. He would have driven straight in, and Kip might have set up some woofs to alert her, but not like this. She regretted that the shotgun was still in the farmhouse.

She heard Lily's door open and her call out "What's going on?" over the dog's barking.

"There's somebody outside," Cerys called back, trying to keep her voice low but struggling to be heard over the dog.

Lily paused to check she'd heard correctly and then banged the light on. Cerys saw the terror in her eyes. "Who?"

"I don't know. I can't see."

And then there was a thunderous banging on the door. Not just knocking; Cerys would have sworn it was kicked too. Lily shrank back against the wall.

Cerys went to the door and grabbed Kip's collar and hauled him back. "Who's out there?" she shouted. "Watch out or I'll let the dog out on you!"

There was a second of silence, broken only by Kip's frantic snarls.

"Who the hell are you?" came the shouted reply in an unfamiliar voice. "And where's my bloody wife?"

Cerys turned to Lily, who fled into Drew's room and slammed the door shut behind her.

53

CERYS LOOKED THE MAN UP and down. "And who the hell are you?" she said with icy politeness. He was much older than Lily. Cerys wasn't old enough to be his mother, but she was certainly old enough to take no crap from him. He was around forty, she estimated, and lean with a face she could imagine some women finding very attractive. It did nothing for her. There was no warmth or kindness in those eyes.

But some women looked for that bad-boy edge, and he had that in bucketloads. Though at his age, she thought scornfully, he should have well grown out of that, but she supposed his type never did.

She could imagine the casual cruelty he could inflict without any conscience at all.

He paused at the chill in her tone. She made it very clear she wasn't fazed by him in the slightest, and Kip, still struggling against his restraining collar, helpfully snarled and showed his teeth to emphasize this point.

"I'm Danny," he said, with a smile that didn't meet those rather unpleasant blue eyes. "I'm Drew's father and Kayleigh's husband."

She raised an eyebrow at him. "Well, then you need to keep your voice down and your temper in check! And have some respect for the fact that at this time of night, your daughter is well asleep in her bed, and unless you are some kind of lunatic, or psychopath—" she paused for effect "—you'll not want to disturb her now and frighten her half to death with the racket you've just made."

He was fuming. He couldn't hide that, though he appeared to try. He gave her that smile again. It was more wolfish than appeasing, and she wondered if he knew that. "I haven't seen my daughter in months. I've missed her. I wouldn't want to do anything to upset her, but it has been very hard for me, very hard. You obviously know she's been taken from me. You must appreciate how worried I've been. It's difficult to keep a proportionate reaction after all this time."

Oh, she could see now why Lily feared him so much. She could imagine how some people believed the act. Even now, raging inside, he was trying to turn on the thing that he would call charm. Unfortunately for him, Cerys had been around enough to have seen his type, even among some of Gavin's business contacts. The men with the slightly loud voices and the over-jovial bonhomie, with the little wives in the background who never looked quite settled, always thought of as having nervous dispositions. She'd come to understand what that façade meant when she saw it. And this was a particularly nasty variant standing in front of her, although who indeed knew what those other women endured behind closed doors.

The key thing now was to get rid of him. They were up here alone and Lily was cowering in a room with Drew. He'd be less threatening in daylight when the two women weren't in nightclothes. She smiled politely, in control. She already sensed he wasn't quite so good at handling women like her. "Of course, but really, it's the middle of the night, and you've arrived without warning, making an enormous commotion. And now is really not the time to be having these conversations. I suggest you come back tomorrow when people are actually dressed." She allowed an aspect of her annoyance to show there. It would do no harm. "No matter what has happened, it's important to deal with these things in a civilized manner, especially where children are involved."

He snarled like the dog. "What? So she can leg it in the night again? I've been to court, you know. A judge has said she has to return Drew to my care. All I have to do is call the police and they'll come and take her."

She regarded him steadily. "I think you may find that if this is the approach you take, it's no wonder she 'legged it in the night,' as you put it, last time. You may want to rethink. And *if* what you have said *is* true, then go on and call the police." Not for nothing had she dealt with Gavin's stroppy suppliers and retailers in those unregarded stints, where she'd supported the business too before he'd been able to get a full office staff complement.

❧

Lily couldn't stop shaking. Even the sound of his voice, never mind what he said, the way he'd booted the door, set up that chain of terror inside her that made her disintegrate.

How had he found her? How?

She looked round for her phone, but it was back in her bedroom. Incredibly, though Drew had turned over and muttered restlessly, she was still asleep despite the noise outside.

Lily could hear low voices outside but not what they were saying. But even though she couldn't make out the words, she recognized Danny's as one of them. She'd heard those quietly menacing tones so many times that they haunted every dream and poisoned every memory. They were lodged into her bones. A visceral reflex of fear whenever she heard them, no matter what she'd done or not done. Even his voice flooded her with adrenaline. Her heart pounded as her body prepared itself for flight. But there was nowhere to run and no escape here.

And that bloody phone was in the other room.

Who had told him where she was?

She strained her ears at the door to hear. The voices were low and quiet as if far away now, and she realized Cerys was outside. She could hear Kip's low, continual snarl, which made it harder still to make out any words.

She took a deep breath. Think, think…

And then she caught a few of Danny's words: "What? So she can leg it in the night again? I've been to court, you know. A judge has said she has to return Drew…"

Had he got a court order yet? Because if he had…

Oh God, the thought made her sick beyond bearing. If he had the right to take Drew with him…

She was frozen, deaf for a second to Cerys's response, until something of what she said registered, "Call the police."

But he said he had a court order. That meant they'd take Drew straight away. Rhys said that's not how it worked, and Danny wouldn't be believed. Too late for that though—in her absence, he'd got a judge to believe him. He was plausible like that, and Cerys and Rhys didn't know him or what he was capable of. She'd seen people fall for his lies over and over again. She couldn't risk thinking that it would be different this time.

By the time they did believe her anyway—even if she could convince them—he'd already have Drew back. That's what that judgment meant. He could just take her now. She couldn't let that happen to Drew, couldn't lose her, and couldn't let her be taken from her mummy. She'd do anything to stop that. She already had, and she'd keep on until she won.

He would not take her little girl. No way.

⁓

Danny wavered between exploding with fury at the attitude of the woman in front of him—Cerys had no doubt at all that he had issues with being spoken to like this by a woman, because that was written all over him—and deflating and retreating because she was, of course, absolutely right. If he bullied his way past her and into a house he wasn't invited into, she would have every right to call the police and have him removed. And that would do his case no good in the courts. He needed to at least appear to be the reasonable one in the marriage. He knew that and so did she.

In the end, he chose the latter. He nodded slowly, but it wasn't without an air of menace, and nor was that tight, lupine smile. "I'll come back tomorrow," he said, and then shouted a threat to Lily that made Cerys slam the door behind him.

He sat in the car for a while before noisily reversing it back down the track, tires screeching against the rough surface.

"Well, you really are a charmer," she breathed as she watched him go.

⁓

Lily heard Danny's voice call out: "I'm coming back for you in the morning, Kayleigh, you be sure of that! And I'm taking Drew with me."

And then the door closed, and the dog's snarling quietened.

She had to leave. She had to get out of here now before he came back. Because when he did, he would take Drew, he would take her, and there would be nothing left of Lily when he did that.

And she was gripped with terror at what he might do to Drew when she wasn't there. If Drew cried or annoyed him, and he didn't have his usual punching bag around to take his frustrations out on.

She had to run.

54

WHEN SHE WAS SURE HE was well clear, Cerys went into Drew's room. Lily was sitting beside the bed, curled in a ball. Cerys couldn't see her clearly in the dark and didn't want to disturb the little girl by turning the light on.

"I told him to go," she said softly. "Are you okay?"

"He'll be back," Lily replied after a moment.

"Yes, I think he will, but we have time to plan for that, so don't worry about it now. Go back to bed and try to sleep."

Lily got up from the floor and kissed her daughter gently so as not to wake her, and went back to the bedroom. Cerys knew she'd struggle to get any sleep now, but she needed her to try because she needed to think how they were going to get out of this without the distraction of Lily panicking.

As she would be, of course, and Cerys could clearly see why now. He was a nasty piece of work, as her mother would say, dressed up as something better.

She made Lily the hot chocolate and took it through. She was sitting up in the bed and Cerys could see her shaking. "Drink that and try to get some sleep," she said. "We'll work out how to deal with him, don't worry." She wished Rhys had been here, not to confront Danny as that would probably have made everything far worse, but at least to be with Lily now. He was in A&E tonight though, and there was nothing he could do to swap out at this time.

She patted Lily's arm. "We'll sort it out. Sleep now."

Lily didn't answer but Cerys needed to think and Lily did need to sleep so she left in the hope that the girl might calm down and get some rest. She wasn't wildly optimistic about that but she had to hope.

She herself lay awake trying to work out how they should manage this now. They were going to need a lawyer if he wanted custody, but how would they afford that? Lily's wages wouldn't cover it, and she had no money of her own. It had been subsistence levels and accommodation for her job on the farm and, now Dilys was gone, she didn't have a wage coming in. It would take months to sort Dilys's estate out, and they didn't have that kind of time. Cerys really doubted he had got a court order—she was almost sure he was bluffing—but Lily wouldn't see it like that. Thankfully she mustn't have heard him or she would have said something by now. Best not to say anything to her until Cerys had an answer to the problem.

Rhys might help, but she didn't really want to put him and Lily in that position when they were so new together. It seemed to be going so well, but she didn't want either of them to feel trapped.

So really there was only one solution and one source of money. It was a huge risk. Huge. In fact, it was more than a risk. It was the end of the line for her, and there would be no coming back from it, but Lily needed her.

She got up as quietly as possible and exited the cottage silently. Creeping across the cobbles to the farmhouse, shivering inside the coat she'd shrugged on over her nightdress, she let herself into the farmhouse.

And then she made a phone call.

55

LILY MADE HER MOVE AFTER first light when Cerys had gone to the sheep. Cerys had looked in on her and told her to lock the door and she'd be as quick as possible and then she'd gone off.

As soon as Cerys was safely out of sight, she packed a sleepy Drew in the car and headed off down the track away from the farm. She had no plan. All night she'd been thinking about this, but there was no solution other than to run. She couldn't go back to him, not now. Not when she knew what a better life was. And he wouldn't stop, he would keep coming.

She couldn't go to Rhys because she knew what Danny was capable of. She couldn't put Rhys in that situation. Even if he fought shy of physical revenge, he'd make some kind of sly allegation that could cost Rhys professionally, and she wasn't going to let that happen.

Nor could she pull Cerys into her mess. Cerys would try to talk her out of it. She would think they could fight it, and maybe they could if he didn't have that order. But Lily was out of time and he was not separating them from each other—this was the only way she could keep Drew safe now.

So, with tears streaming down her face as she drove, and Drew's sleepy, confused voice asking, "Mummy, what's wrong?" she sped down the track away from the farm.

She couldn't answer, just shook her head, and hoped Drew would stop asking.

Then she got down to the bottom of the track and there was his car, blocking her exit.

He was parked and waiting. He'd known she'd do this.

He'd dozed off in the car seat. Even seeing him like that made her shake so much, she could hardly steer the car. She slowed gently to a halt so the noise didn't wake him.

"Be very, very quiet," she said to Drew. "We're walking." She pulled the car quietly onto the shoulder by the field gate. If he did wake and see her run, he wouldn't be able to drive the car in after her.

She could see Drew's terrified eyes looking at her through the rearview mirror. "Is that Daddy?" she whispered.

"Yes, super quiet... Come on." She killed the engine and crept out of the car. She didn't even close the doors for fear of alerting him, just put them to slightly. She and Drew slunk back up the track to a stile into the fields, and she lifted the little girl over and then followed herself. "Come on, we're going for a little run," she whispered. And holding Drew's cold little hand in hers, she began to run as fast as the small girl could manage. She headed down the footpath, with little idea what direction she was headed in, just that it was away from him, and that was the most important thing.

Never going back. Never.

56

CERYS LOOKED IN CONFUSION AROUND the cottage. Where were they? And then a horrible fear assailed her. He couldn't have come back yet. She'd hardly been gone.

She went to the farmhouse but it was still locked up, and Lily's car was definitely gone. When she returned to the cottage, she noticed a little scrap of paper by the kettle.

I'm taking her somewhere we'll be safe. I'll do what I need to do to protect her. I'm not letting him take her. I don't care that he has a court order. He's not having her. I'm sorry I couldn't say goodbye.

Lily

Cerys sat down in a slump of the arm of the little sofa.

That's why she'd been so odd last night; she'd thought it was because Lily was scared, which of course she was, but it was much more than that. She'd heard what he said about the court order, but why hadn't she spoken to Cerys about it? She could have told her he was lying.

Why didn't she talk to her?

Cerys cursed herself for not raising it, for not checking, but if she hadn't heard then the disclosure would just have caused Lily more worry. What a mistake that line of thought had turned out to be. She had to get hold of Lily quickly, before she got too far.

Cerys ran over to the farmhouse and unlocked it, cursing that she'd been stupid enough still not to have got a mobile phone, and they hadn't put fuel in Dilys's old car. She picked up the landline phone and dialed Lily's number. It went straight to a message saying the phone was unavailable. She must be out of signal. Cerys texted quickly.

"Please get to somewhere safe and then call me. Let me help you. I've got some money on the way to pay for a lawyer for you. Stay safe, Lily, and call me when you can. I will help you. He's not going to take her."

She paused.

"I love you both."

She'd never said that before.

She phoned Rhys next, but there was no answer so she left a message.

"Is Lily with you? Danny came here last night, and now she's gone and taken Drew with her. Please call so I know she's okay."

And then she had to hang up and wait. Kip rested against her leg.

Now what?

She still couldn't believe how Lily hadn't spoken to her before running after all they'd been through together.

Don't be so stupid. She's been let down all her life by everybody. She's hardwired not to trust anyone. Of course, that's how she reacts. It's all she's ever known until recently.

And then all Cerys could do was wait.

Except no, there was one thing more. She could find where Dilys hid the key to the gun cupboard.

57

LILY HUNKERED DOWN BEHIND A drystone wall, wrapping her arms around Drew in an attempt to keep them both warm. She had no idea where she was—somewhere out in the hills. The mist was down, and she couldn't see far beyond the hill they were on. With a sinking feeling in her stomach, she realized how dangerous this was. Neither of them was dressed for being out here in this weather.

"I'm sorry, Mummy, I can't run anymore," Drew whispered, though they must be a long way from Danny's car by now.

"It's okay," she whispered back, though it really wasn't, and she had no idea what to do next. She could feel Drew shivering. They were high up, she thought. She'd imagined she was heading down to the sea, but it felt as if the temperature had dropped too much for that to be correct. The mist swirled around them, like sitting inside a cloud, and she guessed they'd been so disorientated that they'd gone higher into the hills than she'd intended.

Cerys had told her often how dangerous hill weather could be.

Reluctantly, she took her phone out of her pocket. There was no signal. Her heart sank. This had been her last resort, to call for help. She'd avoided this for the last two hours, wandering around in this fog, hoping the sun would rise higher in the sky and burn it away as it sometimes did but that didn't look like it was going to happen.

A chill of fear ran up her neck.

She got up. "Come on, let's just go a little way further and see if I can get a phone signal."

The fact her little daughter didn't even question why they were running blindly into the hills away from her father said it all really. *Damn you, Danny, you're not going to get us now. Not after we've come so far.*

58

THE PHONE RANG, AND CERYS snatched it up.

"Cerys, is that you? Where is she?" It was Rhys, panicked.

She was just about to answer when a thunderous hammering started on the front door, which she'd locked as a precaution. Oh, so Danny was back.

"Where's my fucking wife?" he bellowed through the door. It was almost a scream of pure rage.

"Cerys, what's that?" Rhys asked urgently.

"I don't know where she is. I was hoping she was with you. And that's her husband outside. He's just come back."

"Call the police," he said. "I'm on my way now."

"I can't," she said to his hung-up phone. "They're looking for me too." She knew that from her call last night, and actually she must have known that anyway. She did. She'd just ignored it. She was a missing person and that had been inevitable. Of course the police would have been alerted and would have started a hunt.

Her bracketed space in time was coming to a conclusion, as she had known it would, no matter how much she had ignored that reality.

She went to the door and shouted back at him as he continued to bang and scream. "She's not here, you lunatic. Go to hell!"

She was rewarded with a volley of abuse and more kicking at the door. But that door was good solid old wood; it would withstand that kind of thing with ease. It'd take more than him to kick it in with those thick strong iron bolts buried deep into the stone lintels around the frame. It would hold.

God knows what would happen when Rhys got here. She still hadn't found the key to that gun cupboard. Where could Dilys have put it? Another kick to the door sent her to check the kitchen drawers again.

"Pack that in right now and get out of here! I'm calling the police," she yelled. "I've told you, she's not here!" She refused to be intimidated by him. He was a bully and needed standing up to. Another kick to the door lit her fuse, and her temper flared.

She shut Kip in the hall and marched over to the door and unbolted and unlocked it. He burst the door back before she could open it and exploded, red-faced, into the farm kitchen.

"How dare you?" she snapped, furious herself now. "How dare you enter this house without permission? The police are now on their way, and I suggest you leave immediately, before they arrive and remove you!"

He glared at her, all but frothing at the mouth, she thought. For a second she wondered if he might hit her, but her temper was so risen by now that she didn't stop to care. She was not his poor, terrorized wife. Let him just try!

Kip barked and snarled through the hall door.

"I'm not leaving without my wife and child!" he yelled at her, spittle flecking her face as he shouted.

"I've told you, they're not here. She's gone! And no wonder because you've certainly shown your true colors, haven't you? Wait until the police get here! And don't try telling me you have a court order. If you did, you'd be at the police station right now."

"She's hiding here and I know it!"

"Take a look, you maniac—her car has gone—"

He laughed unpleasantly. "Her car is at the bottom of the track where I blocked it in. She's run back up here."

A chill spread through Cerys and she stared at him in dawning horror. "Her car is...?" She took a step back.

Where was Lily now? She couldn't have sneaked into the cottage and hidden there? She had to protect her if so.

But the cold feeling spreading through Cerys told her that Lily wouldn't do that.

She'd run on foot; that was what her instinct would have told her to do. She was terrified of this man, and she'd run and run and keep going.

Cerys took a deep breath in and dragged up every ounce of icy dignity she possessed. "I have told you that she's not here and neither is Drew. Now you need to leave."

He spat full in her face. "I'll be watching and I'll be waiting, bitch!"

He turned on his heel and left, storming out of the farmyard and back down to his car.

Cerys went to the kitchen sink and washed the spit from her face with trembling hands. Kip's frantic barking subsided to a low, anxious whine, and after shutting and bolting the door again, she went to let the dog in. He rushed through and licked her hands in relief.

"You know what?" she said to him with renewed determination. "I really need to find that key. Now, where would she have put it?"

59

OUT ON THE HILL, LILY was still stumbling around trying to get a signal, and the mist was still bewildering them both. Drew had started to cry softly and her little fingers were so cold. She couldn't stop shivering. Lily was getting really scared now. What the hell had she been thinking?

Actually, she didn't know what she was thinking, but when she saw Danny her reaction wasn't logical—it was a reflex born out of pure fear. Out of what he had created within her. And the adrenaline made her run. It would probably have carried her through this mist and cold and miles of hills and out the other side on its own. But she wasn't alone—she had Drew. When was she going to learn? She'd thought she'd made progress to being a less shit mother, but look at them now. This just proved Danny's point about how incapable she was.

And then finally, she got a bar of signal. One tiny little bar. She froze.

It held—yes, it was still there. Not daring to move, she dialed Rhys.

"My God, Lily, where are you? We've been so worried."

"I don't know," she said, her voice shaking with cold. "Out on the hills. The mist is down, and I've got hardly any signal. I don't know where I am, and Drew is freezing. I-I'm—"

But she couldn't say she was scared because Drew was listening and she would not let her down and frighten her—she would not.

He could hear it in her voice anyway. "Okay, I'm on my way. Try to take shelter. We'll find you somehow. Get out of the wind—down near a wall. Get her inside your coat. I'm coming."

"Rhys, he's found me. He's got a court order. He's going to take her."

"I know—Cerys called me. Don't worry—it's going to be okay, I promise."

A message bleeped through on her phone as she was speaking, but she couldn't see it. Then the reception cut out and he was gone. She could have wept, but there was a chilled little face watching her too intently to allow herself to do that.

"Okay, we're going to find somewhere warmer to wait, and Rhys is going to come and pick us up," she said cheerfully, through numb lips. She led Drew to the edge of the field they were in and crossed the wall to find a small corner in the lee of the wind. As Rhys had said to, she hunkered down and pulled Drew inside her coat as much as she could. The little girl shivered against her.

"How will he know where we are, Mummy?" she asked.

"Probably track the phone location," she said. Now what would Cerys do to try to distract Drew? Think like Cerys, that was her default setting in times of emergency. She had to try.

60

CERYS OPENED THE DOOR WITH relief as Rhys pulled up outside the gate. He didn't bother opening it and driving in, just clambered over and ran up to the farmhouse.

"Did you pass him?" she asked urgently. "He said he was down on the track by her car."

"He's still there. I whacked the horn at him to move the car and he pulled it onto the shoulder by Lily's. I think he's waiting for her to come back."

"He probably thought you were plainclothes police. I told him they were on the way. She won't come back. Not while she thinks he could be there waiting."

"She called me. She's out on the hill in this," he said, waving at the fog. "I need to find her, but she's totally lost and freezing and had hardly any phone signal. I have no idea where to start looking. She could be anywhere by now."

Cerys looked anxiously out at the mist. Where would they even start? "Try calling her again," she said as she ran to drag boots and a coat on, and she grabbed a blanket too as an afterthought to wrap poor Drew in when they found her.

He was still trying to get a phone signal when she got back. "Nothing," he said in despair. "We could go down to where she left the car and start from there. If that shit has moved, of course. But she could have gone in any direction."

"Don't worry about him, I've had an idea," Cerys said. "As long as you don't mind playing policeman."

Rhys had a moment of confusion and then grinned as he caught on. "Oh, I see. No, I can do that. I see enough of those guys at work to know how to fake it. But once I've got rid of him, what then?"

Cerys sighed. Yes, indeed, what then? And just then, a cold, wet nose nudged her hand.

61

CERYS WATCHED FROM A DISCREETLY hidden vantage point as Rhys approached Danny's car.

"Can you get out of the car, sir?" He gestured to Danny in case the car window muted his voice.

Danny opened the door. "Who are you?"

Cerys rather thought from his voice he suspected Rhys might be a police officer, and certainly he'd aped walking like one. He hadn't been kidding when he said he had plenty of practice observing the police.

"Detective Constable Carver of the North Wales *Heddlu*...Police," he replied, in consideration of Danny's English accent. "I'm going to have to ask you to move your car, sir. We've received a complaint, and when I passed earlier you were blocking the road. This lane is private property, and the owners have requested you leave."

"I'm looking for my wife," Danny said, drawing himself up as if readying for a battle he didn't quite understand.

"I'm sure you can look for her from down there," Rhys replied, gesturing back down at the public road.

"My wife is reported as a missing person!"

Rhys nodded slowly. "Well, sir, if you have reason to believe she's in the area, I would advise you to drive over to Bangor and discuss that at the police station. Let's do this properly, sir, not cause upset to local folk with threatening behavior. Now move along, please."

Danny blustered for a moment and then got into the car, sullen-faced, and drove back down to the road. He was soon out of sight in the mist.

Cerys hurried to Rhys's side. "Right. I knew it—he hasn't got a court order at all! I bet they turned him down. Come on, before he tries walking back or something like that." She hopped over the stile that Lily had used hours earlier and clicked her fingers to Kip to follow. "Good lad, find them, Kip. Find Drew!"

The dog gave her a quick quizzical glance, then got his nose to the ground sniffing. She could tell he picked up a scent without much trouble and started to follow it. She'd seen him do this with sheep often, so she could read the set of his tail and the stance of his shoulders perfectly by now.

She and Rhys followed behind silently. "Don't call out to her unless we absolutely have to," Cerys said to Rhys after a while. "I don't trust that man not to double back when we think we've got rid of him. And if he's out there and he hears us calling her, I don't want him getting there first."

The dog followed the trail patiently for a good half hour until they were toiling up a hill, and Rhys said, "Didn't we come this way already? Does he know what he's doing?"

"She's lost," Cerys said, "so quite possibly she's been moving in circles. Trust the dog—this is his job."

"I'm just worried," he muttered. "They've been out here ages."

He tried the phone again, and this time it rang and Lily answered. "I think we're close by," he said. "Are you both okay?"

"Yes," she answered in a wobbly voice. "How do you know you're close?"

"Guessing from the signal improving, though it could be this fog lifting too that helps. We've got the dog—he's tracking you. Hang in there."

"Keep talking to her for a few minutes," Cerys said. "Try to chat to Drew."

He chattered away quietly into the phone in what Cerys guessed was his positive doctor voice as they wended their way up and over the hill.

"No, I can't see much ahead of us, but don't worry—Kip is definitely on to something."

A blast of wind took his breath away as they followed a turn the dog took back downhill again.

"Must be facing the sea," Cerys said as the mist swirled around them like an angry ghost.

The dog leaped a wall and Cerys glanced around for a stile but couldn't see one, so they had to scramble it.

"Damn!" Rhys said, glaring at the phone. "I've lost reception. Are you sure he's going the right way and not further from her?"

"He might be," Cerys said grimly. "He's following a trail on the ground, so she's not close enough for him to air scent her yet. Let him get on with it."

"He's going round in circles on this bloody hill!"

"Trust the dog!" Cerys snapped at him. "Or have you got a better idea?"

He shook his head and tried to call Lily again but there was still no reception.

They trudged along, barely able to see more than a meter in front of their faces at times.

Rhys glanced anxiously at his watch, marking how long they'd been out here looking. "We need to hurry up."

"If we rush him, he could miss the trail," she replied. "He's a dog, not a machine."

And then his phone rang. "It's her!" Rhys answered. "Hi, hi, we're back in reception." He paused. "We are coming, as fast as we can. Hang on, please hang on." He moved the phone away. "She's getting desperate," he hissed to Cerys.

"I know. Keep talking to her."

The dog suddenly picked up the pace, and they had to jog to keep up. They took a sharp left and then Kip froze and his nose went up in the air, scenting the breeze.

Cerys paused too, watching. The dog cast a look back at her, in that silent communication they both understood, and then he trotted briskly down the hill, air scenting and heading toward the wall.

"He's found them, come on!" Cerys said and broke into a jog after him.

"Hang on," said Rhys into the phone. "I think we're nearly there."

They hurried down the hill and over the drystone wall at the base, and then the dog picked up even more pace.

"Can you see us?" Rhys said urgently into the phone. "Where are you?"

The dog raced down the next field and leaped clean over the wall at the end of it.

"No, I can't see you…oh, oh!" And then they heard the dog whining and snuffling on the other end of the phone and Lily beginning to cry in relief.

Rhys accelerated down the field after the dog and vaulted the wall with Cerys running behind, less athletically but as fast as she could. As she scrambled over the wall, she found Rhys crouched down beside Lily and Drew, his arms round them and Lily trying to rub her face dry so Drew didn't see.

"Here," she said, passing Rhys the blanket. "Wrap Drew in that, and let's get them out of here."

He helped Lily up and cocooned Drew in the blanket like he was swaddling her, then he lifted her into his arms. "She's cold but she's okay," he said, "but we need to get back as soon as possible. Which way back?"

Cerys paused to fondle the dog's ears in thanks, as she had seen Dilys do so many times. Her hand trembled for a moment on his shaggy head as the barb of grief caught her unexpectedly. The pain from losing someone was like that—you never knew when it would strike, sudden and swift like a rattlesnake's bite.

The dog nudged her hand softly, almost as if he knew. "Kip, home!" Cerys said, and the dog checked behind him to see they were all ready before he trotted off.

"He does know—" Rhys began to ask. He'd been about to set off in another direction entirely.

But Cerys cut him off. "Better than anyone," she replied firmly. "Follow him." She put her arm round Lily to help her and the girl looked at her anxiously. "Of course he hasn't got a court order," Cerys said to her. "He was lying. You've told me how good he is at that, haven't you? Well, there, you see—he even had you convinced."

Lily swallowed, still not entirely sure she could believe that, which was understandable given how many times she'd been lied to by the people she should have been able to trust, but she was too cold and exhausted to argue now, and Cerys was content to wait to convince her. She gave her an arm to help her along, and they walked on behind as fast as they could. Rhys strode ahead, checking back. "You go on," she called. "If we lose sight of you, Kip will double back for us."

And the dog did, as he guided them off the hills and back to the farm, he yo-yoed back and forth to steer both Rhys walking ahead, and Cerys bringing up the rear, back to safety.

Lily sighed in relief as she saw the farmhouse through the shroud of fog. "Has he gone?" she mumbled to Cerys through numb lips.

"Yes, Rhys pretended to be the police to get him to go."

"He'll come back," she said and Cerys felt her shudder.

"We'll be ready if he does."

Fortunately, there was no sign he'd returned, and Cerys decided it was safer for them all to be in Dilys's farmhouse. The door was stronger there if he did come back. She heard Dilys's voice in her head in the old woman's irascible tones: *And if he does come back, you tell him what for. I would if I could be there, make no mistake about that.* She smiled wryly at the thought, despite how it made her eyes suddenly sting.

She ushered them all in and got the fires lit while Rhys ran a warm bath for Drew. In the end, Lily got in with her too, as there was only enough in the tank for one bath, and Rhys made hot drinks while Cerys bustled over to the cottage for changes of clothing. An hour later, and with hot soup and sandwiches inside them all, Cerys packed them off into the sitting room, where there was a good blaze going in the hearth, and she put the TV on. She strongly suspected Drew would doze off soon after the shock of the day, and she needed to talk to Rhys with Lily out of the way so she didn't get anxious. Sure, they'd have to discuss it with her later, but she'd been through enough so far today. There'd be time for that when she'd taken a nap herself and recovered.

"So what now?" she said to Rhys in the quiet of the kitchen, with Kip curled up on her feet wearing the expression of a dog with a job well done.

He shrugged. "She's going to have to come clean and face it; there's no way round that if she wants rid of him for good. But she's got us, so she'll be okay. She's just not going to like it. She'd rather run."

"That's understandable, having met him."

"The mistake he's making though is thinking he's getting anywhere near her now," Rhys replied firmly. "He's not. Any interaction will go via lawyers—that's what I need to talk to her about."

"Me too," Cerys said. "I sent for some money to cover the cost of hiring one. I'm expecting it to be in the bank by tomorrow."

He looked at her curiously. "And what's the deal with that? You know, I've never asked you this because, to be honest, Lily told me to mind my own business. She said people have all kinds of reasons for not wanting to be found and yours was nothing to do with me." He grinned. "She was really quite strict about it. But I couldn't see it being a similar reason to hers—you just don't seem like that's something you've had in your life. I said as much to her, and she admitted she didn't know either because she'd never asked you and she never would. Said if you trusted her enough to tell her of your own accord, that would be the best thing."

Cerys nodded. Well, it was all nearly up now, wasn't it? So keeping secrets was a waste of words now, and a waste of trust. If she needed to move forward with Lily, maybe it was time to tell her. She couldn't expect Lily to trust her if she didn't accord that same respect to Lily, after all.

62

"SO, WHO ARE YOU REALLY?" Lily asked Cerys. They'd tucked Drew up in bed early, even though she'd napped part of the afternoon. Lily sat on the sofa with her feet folded under her, a pose she generally found made her feel safer though she didn't at all know why. Rhys sat at the other end of the sofa, giving her space. Or giving her and Cerys space to find each other maybe. She wasn't sure which. She was just glad he was there.

Sometimes she looked at him and couldn't quite believe he was actually there. Especially after he'd met Danny. Rhys must think she was an idiot to have been taken in by him.

"My name really is Cerys," the older woman replied. "Cerys Anderson. I have three children—Alex is twenty-seven, Matt is twenty-three, and Katie is just nineteen. And that's the most important thing you can know about me, that those are my children and I was a mother. Nothing more than that—a mother. I didn't have a career. They were my whole life."

"You say it like it's over," Lily said. Cerys looked so sad. She'd never seen that expression on her face before and it shocked her. Beyond sadness actually; a deep, bone-deep, melancholy.

"They left," Cerys said, and to Lily, those were the most despairing pair of words she'd ever heard. There, in those words, was Cerys's whole life gone... Lily suddenly understood that. She understood because she knew what Cerys had been to her, how she had looked after her and Drew, how she so entirely and completely embodied motherhood to Lily. So it made sense that when she lost that, she lost everything.

She didn't know how that felt inside, but she knew how that would devastate Cerys.

"They left," Cerys repeated. "They were gone, and then what was I?"

"What about their dad?" Rhys asked quietly.

Cerys swallowed as if it gave her difficulty. "Gavin. We've been married for thirty years. I met him at university. He runs his own business—a very successful one, making storage crates for removal firms." She shrugged her shoulders. "He's worked hard on it, really hard, to give us a good life and everything we needed, but somewhere in all that he and I lost each other."

"You were still with him until you left?" Lily asked.

"Yes, but it was getting harder and harder." She seemed to struggle to find words to explain and stopped for a while, but Lily waited patiently and shot a warning glance to Rhys to do the same. She knew that feeling, the attempt to express the inexpressible you didn't even understand yourself. "I didn't understand at the time, not until I spoke to Dilys about it really, but I think I wasn't too well in the end." It obviously hurt her to get the words out. "I think I may have been depressed. What scares me is that I could still be, that it's just there waiting to come back. Dilys said I should have seen a doctor. Perhaps she was right."

Rhys frowned. "I'll find you a good one if you need to."

She nodded. "Maybe you might need to, maybe I am over it. I suppose time will tell. Anyway, when all that started, whatever it was, it made things much worse between Gavin and me. Then, one night when I was feeling low, we had a huge row, and he said some things that hurt badly, at a time when I just couldn't take more. I left that night and I drove to my old home, my father's farm. It's all sold off now, broken up in pieces. I set fire to the car, and I sat in the cold and waited to die. I wanted to die somewhere I felt close to him and Mum."

Lily, who hadn't really known the detail, was still shocked by this, but Rhys looked horrified, and she glared at him meaningfully to warn him to mask his face. Cerys didn't need to see that.

"It didn't work. I woke up and I wasn't dead. The weather had changed and the frost didn't happen. So I walked to the next village and got a bus to the coast. I wasn't sure whether I'd kill myself or not. Something had changed in the way I was feeling, but I wasn't sure what it was. But how could I go back? I couldn't, and I still couldn't think straight about it. I only knew I still wanted to run."

"I understand that—needing to run," Lily said. "I really do."

Rhys looked like he found all of it incomprehensible, but Lily suspected it was the massive gap in what he knew of Cerys now and what he was hearing. She knew firsthand now what being a mother meant to Cerys, so it was less of a surprise it had had such an impact. She was cross with Cerys's stupid kids though. How could they not have seen this coming? They'd had it all and not even realized how lucky they were and how precious but fragile it all was. They were idiots. People like her would have given all they had to be in their shoes, with a mother like that. Unconditional love—if you had it, you didn't realize what power it brought you. It was only when you hadn't that you understood.

"I ran to the sea," Cerys said softly, "and I thought I might walk into it at one point. Walk into it and keep walking until the waves ended it for me. And then I met you." She met Lily's eyes. "You saved my life; you and Drew. You didn't know it, but you did. I would never, *ever* let anyone hurt you."

63

AS LILY FLEW ACROSS THE room and flung her arms round Cerys, she knew that this bond they had formed would never be broken. Something now lay between them as strong as blood. Maybe even stronger because they had freely chosen each other in this mess.

"*You* saved *me*," Lily said, her face buried fiercely against Cerys's hair. Lily, who was never fierce, hugged her like she could imprint that understanding into her bones. "You have given me more than anyone ever has. I just didn't understand anybody would really ever do that for me."

Cerys stroked Lily's back gently, finding those calming circles that soothed her, that soothe all sad and lost children. "I know, and I understand." Those words would have a power beyond their measure—she knew that as she said them. A mother's love for a child had to be unconditional, and that was what Lily needed.

"You do, and I should have told you instead of running off," Lily said with force. "I'm just stupid, and I get scared and that takes over."

"I know, it's okay," Cerys said, still circling on her back, circling peace back into her.

When you'd saved each other, that was something nobody could ever take away from you. It was something beyond friendship, beyond blood even. Cerys knew that, whatever happened after this, she couldn't walk into the sea now; she couldn't walk away from her time here, because somebody else needed her, and that wasn't a role Rhys could fulfill. She'd chosen to play this part for Lily as Lily had chosen to accept it.

She hugged Lily back. No, no regrets now, no matter where or what this led either of them into, no matter what came of it.

"I called my family," she told them. "In fact, I called a little while ago to let them know I was safe, but I left a message and didn't actually speak to them. But this time I called my husband and I told him I would be taking money from my savings to pay for the legal fees to make sure you get full custody of Drew. He knows where I am now."

"How did that go?" Rhys asked. He was clearly surprised, but he nodded in a supportive way too.

Cerys wasn't quite sure how to answer. It really wasn't clear to her how it had gone either.

❧

Gavin had answered the phone immediately. "Hello?"

She had paused, but barely, because she had a job to do. "Gavin, it's me."

"Oh my God, oh my God." And she could hear to her horror that he was crying, "Are you okay?"

"I'm perfectly well, yes, thank you," she said, and she thought as she said it that she sounded ridiculous. Like someone from a BBC period drama. Why on earth had she said that? Except that in their decades of marriage, she'd actually never heard him cry like that. He was the kind of man who hid tears, and if he was going to do it at all, he went away behind closed doors, or for a long, private walk where he wouldn't be observed by anybody—as he had done when their last dog had died. And Gavin was the kind of man who gave the appearance that it was acceptable to cry privately about a dead dog, but not a missing wife.

"I'm so sorry," he sobbed down the phone, and she was appalled.

Not that he was crying, because to her there was not and never had been anything wrong with that. If anything it was a frustration that he was so unemotional, and she'd accepted it as part of him even if she didn't celebrate it. No, she was appalled that he was in such a state at all. She honestly hadn't expected this.

"I'm sorry," he repeated. "I didn't mean it, not any of it. I'm so, so sorry—"

And the rest of what he said was incoherent. She didn't know what to say. She'd expected him to be angry possibly, curt and distant maybe—that would certainly have fit with the mood of their marriage toward the end. But he sounded…broken, and she wasn't prepared for that.

She just didn't know what to do or say next, but she had a script she had to stick to.

"Gavin, I called to tell you I'm safe and not to worry. I do need to access some of my savings, so I called to tell you that too and not to be concerned when I take the money out."

She could hear voices in the background behind the desperate sobbing, and then the clipped tones of her youngest son, who tended to speak as if he was a machine gun firing rapid action—she'd always loved that about him as a child, and it still amused her when he grew up. There was never any hanging about or small talk with her Matt.

"Mum, where the hell are you? We've been worried sick!"

"Matt, I'm fine. I just called to tell your dad I need to access some of my savings."

"Well, it's a good job you did call. The police have got a watch on your bank account. You're a major missing person case, you know."

It shouldn't have been a surprise, but somehow in that closed-down pocket of world she'd chosen to inhabit, it still was. "No, I haven't followed the news, Matt."

He went off on a staccato rant about all they'd been doing to look for her, and it was too much to take in.

"Matt, you need to tell them to stop. I'm quite safe and well," she interrupted.

"Then come home!" he exploded.

There was some frantic conversation and then Gavin had obviously taken the phone back. He seemed to have pulled himself together a little when he spoke again.

"I'll make sure the bank releases the money without a fuss," he said. "But I want your address. The police will want to know to reassure themselves and I need to know you are safe." He hesitated and then went on. "I do think they'll insist and they won't just take my word for it. When you vanished, they questioned me for some time in case I'd murdered you, so—"

"Oh my God, Gavin, I'm so sorry!" She felt tears start in her own eyes. She'd never intended to put him through that. Of course, she'd read about cases where that happened, but she'd conveniently managed to block all of that out of her mind when she had chosen to run and hide.

"It doesn't matter now," he said, and he really did sound as if he didn't care about any of that at all, but of course it must have been hell for him. "What matters is that you're okay. I'll get you whatever you need. I'm just so sorry, Cerys."

He was struggling again and passed the phone back to Matt with an instruction to get the address so he'd witnessed it too. Cerys had given it, but she'd also got the name of the police contact and would phone them to reassure them she was completely safe and that no further action was needed.

"Why can't you just come back and sort it out?" Matt demanded.

"I just can't right now," she replied.

She'd called the police station and booked a callback with the officer in charge to confirm her safety.

"I was with an old friend of the family, caring for her, and she's passed. I can't leave the farm yet as there's no one to take care of it, but I assure you I am quite safe." She'd given identifying details, and they said an officer would come out and visit to confirm if that was more convenient, but she could tell on the phone that they believed her.

"No, I'm not going back," she said, "or yet. I'm sorry for all the upset caused, but I wasn't entirely well and I am getting medical support now. I need more time. It's a very remote spot, and I've been busy. I hadn't realized all the trouble I've caused and I do want to apologize for it. As I said, I've not been myself lately but I'm a lot better than I was, so you really don't need to worry about me anymore."

She was deliberately as cautious as possible so as not to jeopardize any further position for Lily.

"I know it's caused you an awful trouble," she said, "and if I'd been well, I would have realized sooner, but I didn't want to be found. You see, I just wanted to disappear."

"That must have been hard for your family," Rhys said. "What will you do now?"

"I don't know, honestly. I need time to process it all, and now isn't that time. I need to be here for Lily and Drew." Lily shook her head and, as she started to speak, Cerys said, "No, I really do. I've committed to that and it's important to me. I have to do this, Lily. I'll deal with…home…after."

In the end, she called the local station, and she borrowed Rhys's car to go down there. She repeated her apologies and reassured them that she was of sound mind now. "I'm not ready to see my family," she said. "I need time. Please."

The officer was actually very helpful, she found. She had a perfect right, he said, to withdraw from contact if that was what she wanted. He understood there were marital difficulties, and as long as Cerys was safe, they were satisfied. They would put out a statement that she'd been found safe and well, and that would be the end of their involvement. "Good luck, though," the officer said to her as they parted. "I hope you work everything out somehow."

Cerys nodded reassuringly. She needed to get back to the farmhouse and think. She needed the solitude to process all of this. Her head was a whirl, and she was operating on autopilot right now—her established pattern of a mature and capable woman who always, always coped with everything, who navigated her way through all life threw at her with ease and aplomb.

But she'd broken, and she was not really that woman any longer.

Or was she?

Maybe she actually was. The thing was she no longer knew. It was all happening too fast, and she needed to pause and breathe and take stock.

And for that, she needed the hills, and quiet.

The farmhouse was peaceful on her return. She could just about hear the faint hum of the TV from the sitting room, so she guessed they were in there resting still, and no wonder because it had been a dramatic kind of day. She crossed the yard and leaned on the gate to look out over the dark hills.

It was unthinkable now to go back to her old life and how things were. She just couldn't do it. But she couldn't turn her back on Gavin entirely either— the phone call had taught her that. Whatever had happened that evening she'd left, she hadn't been herself, and he'd said things while lashing out—she knew that. What she didn't know was how any of this could be fixed.

She'd found a level of peace and happiness here that she hadn't felt in years, and she didn't want to give that up. As she felt the cold, quiet hilltop air on her face, she knew she didn't want to go back. Dilys had given her a great gift here, and she'd trusted her to know what to do with it. She knew now that she didn't want to give that gift up, but that meant giving up her way back to her old life. She couldn't have both, and the latter hadn't made her happy in a long time. Dilys had given her other gifts too, and she owed it to her to make the best use of this one. She wished she'd had longer with her, to make her know how appreciated she was, and, yes, how loved, so that her last years could have been enriched by that instead of just a few months. Every time she feared moving outside of those conventions of life that she'd been so trapped by, she'd remember Dilys with an exultant surge of joy that would always be matched equally by a tide of grief. At the moment that was so strong that it threatened to take her breath from her and overwhelm her completely.

Let it wash over. Let the waves wash over and ebb. You don't have to fight it. You can let it flow, let it be what it is.

Grief was not to be battled, she thought. Because grief was part of love. And suddenly she felt calmer, as if she would not be washed away by this.

The thing was, you could want to give a way of life up, but that didn't mean you wanted to leave behind the people in it. She hadn't stopped loving Gavin, and she certainly hadn't stopped loving her children. She'd had moments where she hated Gavin, really hated him for how much he'd hurt her, but she still loved him. He wasn't like Lily's horrific husband. He had never intentionally set out to hurt her or make her feel bad. He'd been ignorant and careless and blind, but never cruel.

She realized that what she wanted most of all was for him to understand her. But was that possible, even now? Perhaps not, and that was their tragedy. Two people separated by a lack of common ground. What a way for a marriage to end after all these years. Probably the fate of many marriages if she really thought about it.

But what a terrible, terrible waste of love it was.

64

CERYS WOKE TO A THUNDERING crash and Kip barking frenetically and furiously.

"Where's my fucking wife?" she heard from the kitchen and she leaped out of bed and ran through, shutting a furious Kip in the bedroom. She wouldn't put it past Danny to kick the collie if he started barking at him, and she didn't want Kip hurt.

Danny was standing in the kitchen, swaying slightly, words slurring, and she recognized with dread that he was drunk.

How had he got in?

She held her hands up to try to calm him down, but calming a drunk and enraged man was different from dealing with him daytime and sober. She didn't know what he was like when he'd been drinking, but from the level of fear he'd instilled in Lily over the years, she wasn't optimistic that he was the cheerful, happy kind of drunk.

"Look, she's not here," she said.

"Yeah, you've said that before, you lying bitch," he shouted. "Now where is she? She's coming back with me now!"

"I've told you, she's not here. She's gone to stay with some friends."

He laughed. "Liar! She doesn't have any friends."

"She does now," she retorted. "Now she's away from you."

He swung his hand at her and she ducked away but he still caught her. The blow knocked her backward into the kitchen cupboards and pain shot through her jaw. The shock silenced her for a moment as her face throbbed. He hadn't even hit her full force and yet it was agonizing. Never, in her entire life, had a man hit her in the face, and God, it hurt.

Out of the corner of her eye, she saw Rhys sneak into the kitchen behind Danny. He'd skirted through the back of the hall and in through the scullery that connected both. She kept her face impassive so as not to give Rhys away, but, as he came in from the yard behind Danny, his foot crunched on a piece of broken glass from the window Danny had used to gain entry.

Danny froze and then whipped round.

"Who are you?" he snarled. And then he looked Rhys up and down and his face tightened with rage. "You're with her, aren't you? You're fucking my wife!"

He swung at Rhys who ducked back more successfully than Cerys had and blocked him. And then he charged with a roar that sent Kip barking hysterically from the other room.

"Bastard!"

Rhys dodged out of the way and gave him a cracking blow on the back as he charged past into the wall. He was too drunk to respond as rapidly as the younger man, and he thudded painfully into the stone. But the alcohol numbed the pain as well as made him slow, and he turned and charged again. This time, Rhys was trying to get across the kitchen to check on Cerys, who was still clutching her jaw, and he caught hold of the doctor round the waist while he was distracted and flung him to the ground under him. Rhys was pinned to the stone flags for a second until he brought an elbow back sharp into Danny's stomach.

"Ooof!" he huffed out, winded as Rhys bucked and partially threw him off.

The doctor rolled over and grabbed Danny by the throat, flipping him onto his back. She saw the red mist of fury descend in Rhys's eyes and she guessed, as she had, that he was remembering everything Danny had done to Lily as he swung punches at the man's head.

Cerys ran for the phone and called the police but as the connection was going through, the wire was pulled out of the phone and the line went dead. She whipped round to see Danny there, his eyes glittering and his face dripping with blood from a cut on his head. She couldn't see Rhys. She edged backward to try to get to the scullery door so she could loop round out of the hallway and escape, but she saw his eyes follow her direction of travel and he guessed what she was up to.

"Where's my wife?" he hissed. "Is she back there? Is she?"

"I told you, she's not here. I wasn't lying. Do you think we'd let her stay here with you on the loose? I know how you've treated her."

This was a dangerous game, and it could go badly wrong, but at this stage she had little choice. If she could get him to take his eyes off her escape route and lose his temper enough to go for her, she could weave and feint and maybe, just maybe, get enough space to get down that passageway into the scullery. But she needed him to charge at her for that, so she needed him to lose control.

A very dangerous game indeed, and she didn't know now what had happened to Rhys, but there was still no sign of him, so that didn't look good, not at all. A chilly hand clutched around her heart—was he dead? She couldn't hear a sound from back there.

"You know nothing," Danny spat at her. He wasn't going to budge yet. He was playing with her, like she was prey. He probably got a kick out of this kind of behavior, she thought, drunk or not.

"I know you treated her like garbage, you made her feel like she was nothing, and you tortured that girl until you drove her away," she replied, her voice rising to a shout. She hadn't lost control at all, but it wouldn't do him any harm to think she had, or to possibly think she was calling out to Lily.

What he didn't know was that Lily really wasn't there, and neither was Drew. They were back in Bangor in Rhys's little flat, safe and out of the way. She'd wanted Rhys to stay with them, but he wouldn't leave her up here alone in case Danny did come back, so after he'd taken them to safety and a peaceful night's sleep, he'd come back up here to make sure she was okay too.

She had to get to safety somehow and get help. The only way was possibly to get to the car.

Or…maybe, just maybe…

Because he wasn't falling for her first plan.

He took a step forward, sauntering now and laughing.

She grabbed the old telephone receiver and chucked it at his head. He dodged, swearing, and it gave her enough time to run back and fling herself into the understairs cupboard. There was no lock on the inside, but she wedged herself against the door and braced her legs against the wall. He shoved the door violently and the door pounded against her back but she managed to hold on.

He stopped after a moment.

"Stay in there then! It'll be easier to find my bitch wife!"

He still believed Lily was in here, which meant he thought Drew was too, and he didn't care that she would have been able to hear all this. He didn't deserve that child at all. And he'd had the gall to call Lily unfit.

She heard him clumping unsteadily down the hall. She prayed he didn't open her bedroom door and hurt poor Kip—the collie would try to protect her as he would have done Dilys, and she couldn't stand to think of Dilys's dog being hurt, not when the old woman loved him so much—but the best way to stop that now was to execute her plan. At the moment he was searching the rest of the house, so Kip was safe for now, but she needed to be quick. It had to be in here somewhere. She'd looked everywhere else. If she was wrong, she was in real trouble, but this was the only place she hadn't had a chance to search yet.

Now, where would Dilys have put it?

She looked around the small storeroom frantically, trying to channel the old woman's logic. It'd need to be somewhere easy for her to have been able to reach, but not anywhere an intruder would think to look. The light from the ancient bulb overhead was good enough to see by in the small space.

It was then she spotted the dusty packet of old-lady incontinence pads on the shelf above, torn open and half-empty. She could almost hear Dilys's chuckle. No burglar would look in there. She grabbed the packet and rifled inside.

At the bottom was a small key. She dropped the packet and tried the lock on the gun cupboard. It clicked open, and she sent a silent thanks to Dilys, wherever her spirit was now. Inside was a shotgun and another key that opened the cartridge safe on the floor.

She filled her pockets with cartridges, then broke and loaded the shotgun. It had been years since she'd done this, but her dad had taught her well.

She cracked the barrel back into place. There was a snarl and a shouted voice as Danny obviously opened her bedroom door a crack and then slammed it closed again as Kip launched at him. She froze, listening, but then heard him walking away and Kip still barking, unhurt. He must have seen enough to know Lily wasn't in there.

He walked right past her hiding place and out to the kitchen.

Going to check the cottage, she guessed.

Cerys hurried out of the cupboard and plugged the phone back into the socket, but when she tried it, it was dead. She prodded the socket on the wall and it had come loose. Damaged wiring, but she couldn't afford the time to mess around with it. She ran through to the kitchen, shotgun pointed ahead. She hadn't shot one of these since she was a girl, but she still knew how. Rhys was lying on the floor, a broken kitchen chair over the top of him. She tucked the gun under her arm and crouched down next to him and shook him gently. He shifted and moaned.

At least he was still alive.

"Stay there," she said. "Where's your phone?"

"By the bed," he mumbled.

She cast an anguished look at the door. What if Danny came back while she was getting the phone? Rhys was helpless and she didn't know what Danny might do.

But she needed to phone for an ambulance. He was obviously concussed and needed help.

And, moreover, she needed the police. Though if Danny did come back, they wouldn't get here in time to be of any help.

She made a dash to the spare bedroom that he'd been using. His phone was on the bedside table, and she ran back to the kitchen with it to get the passcode, but before she could make a call, she saw a car pulling into the farmyard through the gates that Danny had left wide open. She ran out to see who it was—*please let it not be Lily!*

Danny had smashed his way into the cottage and discovered it was empty. He'd obviously had the same thought as Cerys and was running across toward the car. To her horror, Cerys saw he was carrying a large kitchen knife, and in the same instant, she recognized the car and the driver.

"No!" she screamed, running at the car and waving. "Get out of here! Go! Go!"

Danny heard her and turned in fury toward her. He ran at her, knife raising as he descended.

This could not be happening, not now. Please not now, not with them here! She'd put them through enough.

This would have to end here one way or another.

The car headlights glinted off the long metal blade as it came toward her. The car tires screeched on the cobbles, with the stench of burning rubber as it pulled up suddenly to avoid hitting her as she ran at it.

She had to stop them. She could die here, she knew that. But worse, so could they.

Dear God, what had she done to them?

It wasn't the figure of Danny she focused on any longer, but the blade coming toward her, slashing through the air.

There was a shout as the car door opened and a figure launched at Danny, taking him down.

She screamed as there was a desperate scrabble on the ground and she heard her husband cry out in pain.

"Gavin, no!"

And then Danny rose up, knife in hand, blood dripping from it in the car headlights, and she heard Katie scream too from inside the car.

A mother would die to save her children, her family. But she could also kill too. This would end here. This man had caused enough misery. All the pain of the last few years had made her strong, she discovered in that moment, not weak. She collected that together, and the borrowed pain from Lily's suffering at his hands, and she pulled it into an action that didn't care about the consequences.

He came toward her with the bloodstained knife, spewing screamed hate at her as he lurched forward.

Cerys raised the shotgun and fired. Danny dropped like a stone.

65

CERYS RAN OVER TO DANNY'S prone body, in fact hurdled him, without stopping to check if he was alive. She fell to her knees next to her husband, who was gasping in pain and hanging onto his leg as blood oozed out.

"Katie, call an ambulance!" she shouted. "Now!"

As she looked up, her daughter was beside her, dialing frantically.

"Gavin, Gavin..." she said, and then she didn't know what to say. *Please don't die* seemed stupid and useless, especially given that she hadn't even had the chance to say sorry yet.

She hadn't known how she'd feel when she saw him again, but it certainly hadn't been this—this rush of terror that he was going to die.

"Gavin, I'm sorry." Because that really was the most important thing to say, in case he didn't make it. She could hear Katie on the phone, her panicked voice telling them to hurry up.

"Did he get you?" Gavin asked, teeth gritted through the pain. His face looked ghastly under the glare of the headlights.

"No, no, he didn't, you stopped him," she answered, and she gave him her hand to grip on, then realized she should be stanching the blood.

A swaying figure appeared above her, and she looked up in horror—expecting to see that Danny had risen from where they'd left him.

But it was Rhys, his face smeared with a trickle of blood oozing from his forehead. He stumbled down next to her. "Let me see," he said groggily, and then to Katie, "Is that nine-nine-nine? Put the phone to my ear."

He moved Cerys out of the way slightly, looked down at Gavin's leg, and warned, "This will hurt," before he grabbed around the wound in a far more effective way than Cerys ever could have.

And then he spoke into the phone. "I'm a doctor. We need support up here quickly. There's a man here with a knife wound, possibly to the femoral artery, but it's too dark out here to tell properly, and I have a head wound and concussion. I'm applying pressure but we need an air ambulance fast. We have another casualty with a gunshot wound. I don't know what condition he's in. He was an intruder—shot in self-defense." He glanced at Katie. "Take the phone back and keep talking in case he comes round over there. I can't let up with this pressure."

Cerys moved round and cradled Gavin's head in her lap and Rhys gave her an approving nod, then winced as it jolted his wounded head. She brushed her fingers across her husband's face lightly, feeling perhaps she had no right to touch him now. He closed his eyes as though it soothed rather than annoyed him though, and she could see him trying to breathe through the pain.

"Try to keep him talking," Rhys said in a low voice.

"Gavin, stay with us," she said. "An ambulance is coming. You're going to be okay. Rhys is a doctor. You just need to hang on for us until the ambulance gets here. Everything's going to be fine."

She saw Rhys look up at Katie and jerk his head back to where Danny lay. "Is he dead?" He didn't sound as though he much cared, other than in the practical sense of dealing with a dangerous man.

Katie took a few steps over and looked down. "He's breathing," she said. "I think Mum's shot him in the shoulder. He's bleeding quite a lot."

"Do you know any first aid?" Rhys asked her. "Ever done a course?"

Katie shook her head. "No, sorry."

Cerys saw the deliberation flash over Rhys's face—the A&E doctor, the practical decision-maker on life and death if that was needed. "Leave him then. I can't stop what I'm doing here, and this needs my full attention. The ambulance crew will pick up when they get here."

One pair of hands, no choice.

Cerys looked back down at her husband. He'd lost weight and he looked a mess. She'd done that to him, she realized. In her imagination, he'd been happy she was gone, buried himself in work like he always wanted to do, and her not being there was really a great relief.

His appearance now didn't reflect that. He said the police had thought he might be responsible, but when she thought about how he'd broken down on the phone...

It was more than that, more than his stress over the police investigation. It was grief, and nobody knew better than her how to recognize that.

And now he might die, and that would be her fault too, for being here and putting him at this risk.

He'd run out to save her, after she'd left him and put him through all of this.

He reached out and squeezed her fingers. "I love you. I missed you. I'm sorry. I need you to know, it was always only ever you. I did it all for you and the kids. I'm sorry I didn't make that clearer."

He meant it. She'd known Gavin long enough to know that. He meant every word. He wasn't a man for fine words and speeches, or for words at all really.

She also recognized he was telling her this in case he didn't make it.

"Is he okay?" she demanded of Rhys.

"He will be as long as this ambulance hurries up," said Rhys grimly with absolute focus on stopping the bleeding. He wasn't dissembling that he had no time to deal with Danny. He was saving his patient. "Keep talking to him."

This could be her last chance to explain, and if it was, she couldn't let him leave thinking he was to blame for all this. For her.

"Gavin, I've done a lot of thinking while I've been here. I've come to understand that though there were things I was unhappy with—the kids leaving, us growing apart—it was much more than that, and nobody was to blame. Not you, not the kids, not even myself. It was simply all too much at once and, on top of that, I wasn't well. I can see that now."

Rhys leaned over so Gavin could see him and interrupted. "Mate, I don't know you but I am a doctor, and I can tell you this is true. You're in no position to understand the whys and wherefores of that now, but trust me on this. Listen to her."

Gavin nodded.

"It wasn't that I didn't love you all," she said, her eyes filling up. "It was that I loved you, all of you, so much. And I was in such a lot of pain inside, Gavin. I just couldn't stand it so I had to get away."

"I was scared you'd hurt yourself," he said in a voice raspy with pain.

"When I went, that's what I thought I was going to do," she admitted. "But then that didn't work, and I met someone."

"What?" he croaked, jerking as if he was trying to sit up in shock, and she realized what he thought she meant.

"No, not like that! God, Gavin, I'm fifty-three and menopausal and—just no! No, I met a girl who needed me, who had never had a mother and who needed one. And she saved me, Gavin, and I saved her." She felt the tears rolling down her cheeks and he reached up, wincing in pain, and brushed them away. "That bastard over there that I shot, who you stopped from stabbing me—that's her husband."

"Can I just interrupt to say—" Rhys leaned over again "—that if I'd known the gun was there, I'd have shot him first myself and saved her the trouble?"

Despite the pain and blood loss, her husband gave a snort of laughter. Had she stopped to think about it, Cerys would have put money on him liking Rhys. He would get Rhys's dry sense of humor.

"Now I can hear a chopper coming—Gavin, isn't it?" Rhys continued. "Okay, Gavin, hang on in there, and we're going to get you out of here to the hospital. All right, mate?"

The next minutes were a whirl of activity. The air ambulance came down in a nearby field and a crew came hurtling out and over to the farmyard, directed by Katie, who ran to meet them. "This one first!" shouted Rhys. "Serious bleed here, and you need to get him out of here."

A paramedic dropped to his side. "What about the other one?"

"Don't know, couldn't get to him—he's the assailant. Injured in self-defense. Come on, this man needs out of here now. This is his wife—take her with him."

Someone put their arm round Cerys and led her to the helicopter. "Don't leave him behind," she said, beginning to shake and her head was spinning.

"We won't, just getting him stable," the voice beside her said, and she turned her head to see a policewoman guiding her toward the chopper. Cerys hadn't even seen her arrive in the melee going on behind them.

"My daughter?" she said, "Katie...I need..."

"You need to sit down," the police officer said firmly. "Come on, let's get you in here and let them sort the rest out. They'll have your husband here in a few minutes. Just stabilizing him to move him."

Katie appeared by her side as she clambered into the helicopter. "Mum, I'll drive to the hospital. I'll see you there."

"Are you all right?" Cerys asked, reaching out a hand that shook violently to touch her daughter's face.

Katie grabbed that trembling hand and held it firmly. "Don't worry, I'm not hurt," she said and tears began to stream down her face. "He could have killed you, and now Dad…is he going to be okay?"

"Enough for now," the policewoman said gently, detaching them to help Cerys get into the chopper. "Let your mum get some medical attention. She may be in shock, and we need to get your dad to the hospital. Try not to worry. You drive carefully down there—no more injuries tonight, do you hear?"

Cerys looked at the officer with a vague question as she slumped into a seat in the helicopter.

"I've got one that age myself," she said, as she wrapped a blanket round Cerys.

"You don't look old enough," Cerys said, and then she closed her eyes because everything was spinning.

She heard more noise and voices around her. She thought she heard Gavin cry out in pain, but that was drowned out by the whirl of helicopter blades in a cacophony that made her wince for it to stop until she felt the helicopter lift and take off and the din seemed to quieten.

"Gavin?" she said faintly.

"Right here, he's fine," a soothing voice replied as they were whisked away.

66

LILY SQUEEZED RHYS'S HAND IN relief as he opened his eyes and spotted her sitting by the hospital bed and smiled.

"Oh, hello," he said. "Where's Drew?"

"One of the nice nurses took her off to give her breakfast and take her to the playground," Lily replied, clutching his hand tighter. "Her name's Sioned. She said she knew you. Said she'd finished her shift and she'd help out."

"Oh yeah, she's married to a friend of mine," he replied. "She was really pleased when she found out I was seeing someone. Said it was about time I got my act together."

Lily grimaced. "I don't think she'd think I was much of a catch if she knew everything."

He pulled her hand to his mouth and kissed it. "Yes, she would. And she'd be right."

"How are you feeling?" Because changing the subject was the only way to deal with the emotion that surged inside at his words. The kind of emotion that still frightened her, and maybe always would.

"My head hurts a bit but otherwise okay." He touched the dressing on his head. "How's everyone else?"

"Cerys's husband is much worse than you, obviously, but they said he'll be okay. They said it could have been very different if you hadn't been there, but he's going to recover." She grimaced. "Danny is going to make it too, but they airlifted him to another hospital, they said, as he needed specialist treatment—the shotgun shattered his shoulder. The police have been pretty kind so far. I think Cerys's daughter spoke to them about what happened."

"They'll want to talk to me," Rhys said, "to substantiate it all, but that's okay. You know he'll never get Drew now, don't you? He's got no chance."

She took a deep shuddering breath in. "I guess so," she said wonderingly as the impact of that sunk in. Danny and his actions would hang over them like a storm cloud until Rhys and Gavin were fully recovered, but at least the sun had come out for Drew and her. She smiled, and it felt like a rainbow spreading across her face.

"Trust me," said Rhys. "It's over—she's safe with you."

She looked at him as if seeing him for the first time, the thin, clever face, serious dark eyes that could laugh and then flash back to sober in a second, all so quick she could think she'd missed it. The kind of man you wouldn't notice walking down the street, but exactly the kind of man you *should* notice if you had any sense.

"I can get a bigger place," he said, with that sidelong look that wouldn't meet her eyes that she knew meant he was nervous and didn't know how to say this. "On the island, if you'd like. Big enough for all of us."

"Is that what you want?" she said carefully. She could feel that familiar fear rising inside her, the chill on her skin, the pounding heartbeat she could hear even up in her ears. She'd sat here for the hour she'd been waiting for him to wake up and lived with that fear. She'd put it aside briefly when he woke, but it was back now with a vengeance, choking off the breath inside her chest.

He gazed at her with that intense look she knew meant he was struggling, but she couldn't help him—she was frozen. "Yes," he said firmly in the end, staring intently at her as if he could get her to understand that way, in a way he couldn't with words. "I want to be with you. I want us to be together."

"Why?" she asked. Because that little girl inside her who had watched her mother leave her, even though she'd screamed and cried after her—that little girl needed to know. She didn't understand.

Lily didn't understand, even now.

He closed his eyes tightly in frustration, his face screwed up as if in pain. "I love you," he said, opening them again. "I love you. You are who I pick out of everyone on this planet. I want you to pick me back."

She swallowed hard, feeling tears brewing because despite how strongly she'd come to feel about him, and how, in those quiet times before she fell asleep each night, she dared to imagine a future together could be possible, she knew she was going to have to lose him.

"I'm not a good person to pick," she said. "I'll let you down. You deserve someone better. Someone who isn't messed up inside like I am."

"I pick you," he said with a steely determination. "And I know who I'm choosing."

She shook her head at him. She was giving up the best thing here she'd ever had, but it wasn't fair to him and that broke her even more than she was already broken. "You can't fix me, Rhys. There's too much damage. I'll never be like other girls."

He sat up straighter in the bed and glowered in a way that would have made her laugh at any other time, a less charged time. "Can you remember I'm a doctor, please? You don't need to explain trauma response to me. I know I can't just love you better. I wish I could but I know that's not how it works." He shook his head in frustration at her and then looked like he regretted it. "But I do know how to get you help and how to be there for what you need to fix yourself when you get that help. And I know I can stick at it for as long as it takes, and be there for you and for Drew. I know all of that and I choose you. Absolutely you—nobody else."

She opened her mouth to argue.

"And don't bother to tell me you're not a good mother, or a good person," he cut in heatedly. "Because that's your mother leaving you talking, and that's Danny talking. Listen to me, listen to Cerys—listen to the good people in your life."

It was only a few words she needed to say. But it felt like a chasm to cross. She couldn't do it. She couldn't get those words out. She wasn't brave enough to be this person who wasn't a failure anymore.

And then Drew burst into the room, clutching a cookie. "Are you better?" she said excitedly, seeing Rhys sitting up. The nurse, Sioned, followed her in.

"She wanted to see him," Sioned said to Lily. "Is that okay, because I can take her out to play again if you're not ready?"

"It's fine," Rhys said as Drew perched on the bed next to him.

Sioned nudged Lily gently in a conspiratorial way. "He's kind of an idiot but probably worth the effort, you know. He needs someone like you."

"Someone like me?" Lily said in shock.

"Yeah, someone real. Not a pampered princess." She snorted. "We see too much in our jobs to put up with anyone like that, me and him." She grinned at Lily. "Give him a chance." And she waved to Drew, who waved back, and she left.

Rhys watched Lily steadily over Drew's head.

And Lily couldn't be a failure anymore because that little person there was relying on her not to be. And for the few months in her life where she'd not been that useless waste of space, it'd been with Cerys and Rhys in her life.

"We believe in you," he said softly. And he held his hand out.

He'd said she was brave. She didn't feel brave. Not one bit, but this now felt like the most courageous thing she'd ever done.

Choose this. Choose him. Choose to trust.

Choosing this means being able to be hurt. Being able to be disappointed. Being able to be destroyed.

And Cerys's words came into her head. *I'm prouder than I've ever been of anyone in my life that you did what you did for your little girl—you are a fantastic mother!*

Lily reached out and took Rhys's hand.

"I pick you too."

67

CERYS HELD A CUP OF water for Gavin to sip. He swallowed gratefully, and she sat back down on the edge of the hospital bed.

"I want you to come home," he said hoarsely. "That's what I came up here to say. I know you've been unhappy and I know it's my fault. I wanted to tell you I never meant for any of this. I never wanted to lose you, Cerys. I just wanted you to be happy. I worked so hard to make all of you happy, and when I couldn't—" And he stopped suddenly.

She knew why. He didn't know how to say it without it sounding bad, so she finished it for him. "You wanted me to be who I used to be again." She held up her hand when he started to protest. "No, Gavin, it's okay, I understand. I haven't been that woman for a long time, and some of that has been because our relationship hasn't been right. But not all of it, and that's not your fault. It took me being away to see that, and to see who I was and who I am now."

"Do you want to come back?" His voice cracked. "You sound like you don't."

"I don't think I can because it'll never be the same again, and I don't want to go back to who I was there before I ran. I've left that behind and that's where I want it to stay." She nodded slowly at him. "But that doesn't mean I don't want you or the kids in my life in some way."

"How?" he asked. "I don't understand."

"I don't know, Gavin, and I don't understand either. But now isn't the time to work it out. You need to get better and then we can try to figure out what's next."

He nodded, gray-faced and exhausted already. "Can you stay for a while though? Please?"

She pulled up the chair closer to the bed and sat beside him while he drifted off back to sleep. She really did have no idea what would come next, but what she knew now was that one end led to a beginning, no matter how unlikely that might seem. She'd learned she could make that happen. Even if it felt like a bitter end, it need not be.

She shook her head at the seeming impossibility of sorting this tangled mess out, but a flare of spirit inside told her she would. And for now, she'd sit beside Gavin while he slept. It didn't matter how far apart they'd been from each other. They had three kids together and he'd just taken a knife to save her. Their roots were intertwined after all these years. Their branches might have grown toward different sources of light, in different directions, but, right down, in the bones of her, she knew that roots mattered more.

If it were her lying there injured and sleeping, she'd want him to sit beside her too, so here she would stay until he woke.

68

LILY ROUNDED THE CORNER TO the coffee machine and saw a girl, younger than her, who looked so like Cerys that it made her stop in her tracks. The girl was filling two cups and glanced up at her as she approached again.

"Cerys's daughter, right?"

The girl nodded, startled.

"You look like your mum," Lily said.

The girl put the cups down. "Are you Lily?" she asked, suddenly hesitant.

"Yes," she said, and that sudden fire that she hadn't felt since she stood up to Rhys in the hospital filled her belly again. "And you're an idiot! You and your whole family. I need to tell you that."

"I beg your pardon?" The girl looked stunned, and Lily could feel herself burning with frustration.

"It's Katie, isn't it? Well, Katie, I need you to understand something."

"Excuse me! What gives you the right to speak to me like this?" And Katie looked cross, but the girl's eyes flinched away from Lily at the same time.

"You had everything," Lily told her. "You had everything somebody like me ever wanted. I would have given anything to have a mum like yours. Anything! Someone always on your side, someone there for you no matter what. Because you know what, we don't all get that! Some of us have to make do with nothing, so when we see someone like you, with so much, who doesn't even know, who just doesn't take care of that, it makes us mad. I just want you to think about it—"

"Don't you think I haven't?" Katie snapped back at her, drawing herself up in a way that reminded Lily again of Cerys. She had that same assertive look too that only came with the confidence of security. "I've thought about it every day since Mum disappeared. Whether it was anything I'd done. Whether I could have stopped it. Whether I should have spotted signs I just didn't see! Me and my family have been through hell since she went, so don't you dare lecture me."

Lily was about to retort, and then she thought of that moment at the Christmas Fair in Beaumaris, that moment when she knew Cerys had a family wanting her home for Christmas. And she'd ignored that to keep Cerys for herself.

Her anger burned away as suddenly as it had arrived. She wasn't really good at righteous fury. And actually, was it anger anyway? Or was it jealousy now Katie was back on the scene? With a sullen nod of acknowledgment to Katie that she'd back off, she knew the answer to her own question and it wasn't pretty. "She just wants to be loved like she loves you, like she matters," she mumbled at Katie.

The girl's eyes filled with tears. "And she is loved. I just didn't see how she was struggling. She hid it well, you know."

"I'm sorry I shouted," Lily said. "I'm not like you—I'm not smart and I'm not good at this stuff but your mum saved me. She showed me everything I'd missed all my life and helped me turn it round. I owe her big-time. So now I need to fix things for her."

"And that's what this is about?" Katie asked. "Well, thanks, but I already worked out for myself how dumb I've been not to see how bad things had got."

Lily passed her the cups of coffee. "I wish she was my mum."

Katie took them, her face relaxing in sympathy. "Oh, I don't know—maybe you got your wish after all. I know my mother, you see, and I think she might actually have found a second daughter now." And she left Lily standing by the machine as she carried the cups carefully down the corridor.

⁓

When Katie entered her dad's room, balancing the cups carefully, Gavin was still asleep, but Matt had arrived and was slumped in a chair looking tired from the journey. Cerys went to give him her cup, but Katie shook her head and handed over hers instead. "I'll get another in a minute. I met your friend Lily at the coffee machine."

"Oh?"

Katie smiled. "She clearly thinks a lot of you. She read me the riot act."

"*Lily* did?" Cerys looked incredulous. "She's usually very quiet!"

"She wanted to make sure I wasn't stupid enough to lose you again." Katie put her arms round her mother. "I'm sorry. I've regretted so much every day since you left that I didn't see what you were going through. You deserve better, and I do blame myself for not being around more when I did know how much you missed me. I did know and I was being selfish. But it was never because I don't love you. Never that." She shook her head at herself. "I just wanted—"

Cerys pressed her finger to Katie's lips. "I know what you wanted. And it's nothing I didn't want too at your age. Don't blame yourself that I didn't tell you how I felt either. If I'd been more honest, if I'd said what I wanted, then maybe it would have been better all round. I think I've learned that while I've been here." She smiled ruefully. "I met someone who taught me that sometimes it's best to be blunt and get what you feel out there."

She hugged her daughter back, closing her eyes tightly so the tears of relief that she could do this again wouldn't escape, because her middle child looked frankly horrified by all the female emotion on display and he wouldn't cope with all this much longer. She looked up over Katie's head buried in her shoulder and dredged up a smile for Matt.

"I wasn't there either when I should have been," he said in a hurried way. "Sorry." And then as an afterthought. "Love you. Obviously."

And she knew, because Gavin had told her earlier, that her eldest son was beavering away at the family business, holding it all together so she had a quality of life to come back to. And she knew better now how love showed itself in different ways. She'd been too lost in herself to see that, but with that black drowning tar cleared, she could realize that again and rejoice in the different ways her kids loved her.

Because they did. And even though it hadn't been enough then, it was now.

You couldn't control how someone else loved you. You couldn't make it the way you loved them yourself. You could only appreciate them for what they were and accept the gift they gave you.

And actually, she was okay with that. She really was. Finally.

69

LILY WAS JUST LEAVING THE hospital when a white-faced Angharad stumbled over to her, her belly so large now that she was struggling to walk. "Oh my God, I've found you," she said and grabbed Lily's hands in hers. "I'm so sorry, are they all okay? Oh God, I'm so sorry! I heard the news about Cerys and Rhys being attacked—it's on the radio and all around the island now. Well, you know what it's like here, I heard first thing that morning from my neighbor whose cousin rang her because she heard from…" She shook her head in confusion, "…someone, I can't remember who now. I shut the salon up for a week as soon as I heard—I knew you'd be needed over here. Are you okay? Are they okay?"

Lily released her hands and patted Angharad's arm in confusion. "They're all going to be fine. Cerys's husband is still in there, but he's pulling through well. Should you be here though? You look like you're going to give birth any day now. Shouldn't you be resting? Or have you come in for an appointment?"

"No, I came to find you." Angharad burst into loud, noisy tears. "I need to apologize for what I've done. I thought it was for the best but I was wrong."

A horrible realization began to strike Lily. "Angharad, what did you do?"

The hairdresser's face was streaming with tears, tracks of mascara running down her face. "It was me who told your husband where you were. I didn't realize. I thought I was doing something good. I saw him on the news, you see, doing an appeal."

"Oh, Angharad! Why didn't you speak to me?"

"Oh, God, Lily, I wish I had. But he was so convincing about being worried for his little girl, and scared for you. And I have to be honest, love—when I realized it was you he was looking for, and I knew that you were pretending your little one was a boy... Well, it made me uncomfortable to talk to you about it." She held her hands up in apology. "It made me suspicious, okay, and I just wanted him to know you were both safe. I didn't tell him more than that. I don't know how he found you. I didn't even go to the police. He was outside his office on the news so I rang there—I saw the name on the sign."

"He'll have traced the phone," Lily said with a sigh. "He's not what he seems, Angharad, and he knows some nasty people. And he'd only have to trace it to Beaumaris and then ask a few questions in the shops, and he'd have found me."

"I had no idea, love. I am so sorry, please believe me. You never talked about him, and I didn't know what kind of man he was or I would never have done it. And all of this is my fault. I mean, I understand now why you were trying so hard to hide from him. I'm sure I'd do the same to keep my kids safe. I feel terrible."

Lily caught her arms. "Look, it's okay. You shouldn't be rushing around and getting upset like this in your condition. There's been enough trouble caused by Danny, and I don't want this hurting your baby. Please!"

Her face crumpled again as she clutched once more at Lily's hands. "Okay, but I'm going home right now and ringing the flower shop to make up some bouquets to say sorry to you all."

Lily smiled. "Angharad, that's lovely, but you don't have to do anything more to apologize to me. I know how easy it is to be taken in by Danny, believe me. And you've given me so much already with that job—"

"And that job is yours, don't you worry! But I will get the flowers. I need to, you see. I have to do something."

Lily smiled. There was no point arguing with her in this mood and if it calmed her down—and, well, Cerys would like it because after all, it was Gavin who'd been on the worst end of all this. "Daffodils are Cerys's favorite," she said as she hugged Angharad. "Now you just take care of that baby."

70

CERYS ARRIVED AT THE HOSPITAL midmorning after tending the sheep to find Gavin being checked over ready for discharge later. She took a deep breath. This was the moment they'd been waiting for after all, but a week on from him being injured and she still wasn't ready and there was no plan for what they would do now.

"I was wondering," Gavin asked tentatively, "if I could stay with you for a few days and see what it's like up there."

She wasn't sure where he was going with this, but she could see he was trying to meet her where she was on safe ground, so she nodded. "Yes, probably a good idea not to travel too far at the moment, and some fresh air will do you good. The weather forecast is good for the next few days too, and it's beautiful up there right now. The daffodils are coming out, like little bundles of hope."

"That's my Cerys," he said wistfully, "right there. I've missed her."

"What do you mean?"

"You always saw things I didn't. I loved that about you. You saw daffodils and saw hope. I just saw yellow flowers. Being with you made me see the world differently, made it a better place."

She nodded, remembering that girl he'd met, the woman she had been before the blackness came and swallowed her up. But she was up and swimming free again, and that's where she was going to stay. She didn't always know how, but she was going to do it. "Yes, come back with me and stay."

❧

She made up the guest room at the farmhouse. She'd left Dilys's room untouched for now. She'd hesitated for a few minutes about where to put Gavin, but he was still in a lot of discomfort, so logically having his own bed was best for recovery, and it saved the awkwardness of them being together when that time and that decision just hadn't come around yet.

They had an awkward supper around the kitchen table. Katie had wanted to stay, but Matt had stern words and told her to get out of the way and give them space for a few days, so she'd driven home on the pretext of collecting Dad's stuff.

The time apart hadn't made it any easier for them to make small talk, and Gavin focused on eating his food. But then he always had. Had never understood dinner table conversation and lingering over a meal. Eat and get on, that was his way. She wondered if she disliked that about him or accepted it as one of his idiosyncrasies. She really wasn't sure. But what she was sure of now was that her opinion mattered and was not to be pushed aside as if her views didn't count as long as the kids were okay.

She was past that now. She watched him eat. It seemed insignificant perhaps, such a small thing, but it was important to her to know how she felt. To analyze those feelings and not suppress them.

He irritated her by not lingering and chatting. She could feel that emotion. But what to do about it? What to do? She drummed her fingers on the table in thought.

He looked up, startled. She smiled to herself because her thoughts mattered now.

In the back of her mind, she heard Dilys chuckle approvingly.

"I always regretted that we didn't chat over meals," she said. "In a Continental way. Katie used to, so I got over it, and then she left and it went back to silent meals again."

"I'm not good at small talk," he said, and for once there was no defensive tone to his response, just a sadness.

"I know," she said. And perhaps it didn't matter so much. Perhaps it wasn't a deal breaker.

"But I don't mind you talking," he said. "Just because I don't, it doesn't mean I don't listen."

And that was a shock. Oh, how much time had they wasted because they'd never had this conversation before? The death of a thousand tiny cuts to their marriage, but how many were real and how many imagined? Truly, perception was all relative. There was no absolute reality in the space that lay between people.

"I missed your cooking," he said suddenly. "Not someone to cook—not that—but *your* cooking, the way *you* made things. Because it's how we like our chicken roasted, and even how you always do carrots in batons. All those things. They were *us*. You made them our things—everything you did, the way you did them and nobody else could do in the same way. Nobody else would ever be you."

And she smiled because it was absolutely typical of Gavin to express himself through his stomach. And she felt a surge of warmth and affection at both the familiarity of that, and the complete simplicity of the mind he had sometimes. It might drive other women to distraction, but she had loved that about him—his lack of complexity.

"And then you were gone and nothing felt right then. It was like my whole life was gone. And that's right—it was." He stopped, struggling for words to express himself. "Because you *are* my whole life." And then he clammed up again, confused about how to manage the emotion welling up as he spoke.

She was touched, despite his clumsiness—or perhaps because of it. The fluency of his words didn't matter; it was what lay beneath that counted. There was no subtlety to Gavin. He would say it himself—a simple man of simple tastes. Her dad had approved of that—"a good lad, no ponciness about him," she recalled him saying the day she'd told him she was going to marry Gavin. Ponciness was a great weakness in her father's eyes. She laughed aloud at the thought.

"What?" Gavin said, still looking at her in a confused way.

"My dad always liked you," she said, and she got up and cleared the plates away. She turned the radio on so there was no pressure to fill the silence themselves.

As she washed up, Gavin pulled up a stool beside her to take the weight off his injured leg and wordlessly began to dry the plates. Branches apart, but roots connected. Was it enough? Maybe.

She scrubbed a stubborn stain on the oven tray as an advert came on the radio between the tracks of music.

"Could you help a young mother in North Wales? Mentor Mums is a new project connecting new mothers with experienced mums who can give advice and support. Help end the loneliness and stigma many young mothers feel."

Cerys froze, listening. Gavin, noticing, grabbed his phone and punched in the website details as they were read out. Then he handed her his phone. She dried her hands and scrolled through the site.

"It's a charity. It says they're especially interested in hearing from mature women who can give practical support as well as emotional help." She stopped, her brain whirring. "They're open twenty-four seven. I'm going to call them."

She didn't ask Gavin what he thought. Once, she would have checked it was okay with him, but not now. And he didn't object to that at all. In fact, as she dialed, she realized that Gavin never had objected to her taking the initiative and just doing something. It was her who'd needed the validation of asking. Almost asking for permission. No, she couldn't blame Gavin for that. It was her own silly fault, wanting him to agree with everything she did and then if he didn't, taking that as him denying her.

There were mixed faults in this marriage.

She went through to her bedroom to make the call, and when she returned, she found Gavin watching a TV show. Or at least staring at the TV. She wasn't convinced he was engaged by it.

She sat down beside him. "It's a habit I got into," he said, muting the sound. "Sometimes I can't even think what I've watched. But it stopped the silence and kept me from dwelling on it."

He didn't ask her about the call, but he didn't say anything else either, so she filled the gap herself. "They were really interested in meeting me. They even asked me about a paid position with the charity and invited me to an interview next week!"

"That's great," he said. "You'd be amazing."

"Would I?"

"You made the best mother imaginable for our kids. Of course you would." And then he sank his head into his hands.

"What's wrong then?" she asked with a large dose of irritation. Even now, couldn't he want her to have something for herself?

"It means you're not coming home. I should have known you wouldn't.

Stupid of me to think you might want to, but I'd hoped anyway." He rubbed his face. "I'm sorry. I'll get Katie to pick me up tomorrow. You've got a new life here, and I'm in your way. I can see that."

"No, I'm not coming home," she said, "or at least not going back because this is my home now." She could see Dilys's grin in her mind's eye. "Someone special to me gave me this gift because she knew I would love it as she did, and I'm not throwing that away." Cerys took a deep breath. Was this really what she wanted? Was she sure? She reached out and took Gavin's face in her hands. Lined hands now, weather-beaten too. But they fit around the familiar angles of his face as if they belonged. Roots, still.

"But you could stay if you want. For as long as we need to work this out. Maybe we can find a way through this. I don't know. I only know I haven't stopped loving you, not really. We may never work our way through this, Gavin. We may be too far gone—"

He held his finger to stop her. "We won't know if we don't try. I only ever did it all to make you happy. If you're not happy, then there's no point to it. I learned that while you were gone. So let's try something else, eh?"

71

IT WAS AN AUTUMN WEDDING, and Drew made a stunning brides-maid with a wreath of red berries and dark-green foliage lighting her blond hair. Lily had used the curling tongs on it, as it was starting to grow out now, and she looked like a little faerie creature in a dress that matched her mummy's. They got ready at the farmhouse under Cerys's supervision, although Lily and Rhys now had a cottage they were renting in Beaumaris, where it was easier for him to get to work, and Drew had started school there that September.

They married in the village church on the hill, where Dilys was buried. Cerys gave away the bride. "Because why should it be a man?" Lily said. "The only person who's ever earned the right to do this is you."

She'd decided to keep the name Lily, she said. She liked the sound of Lily Jones, and it had happy associations for her. Kayleigh was someone she wanted to leave in the past. This here, these people, they were her fresh start. So while she was changing her surname, she might as well make the forename official too. Drew was happy to be able to be herself again. "Being Sammy was fun," she told her mother solemnly, "but not forever." She crinkled her nose up. "And I never want to have to dye my hair again. It stinks, Mummy."

Lily had laughed. "You might change your mind about that when you're older." But if that was her main complaint from her months as a boy, then Lily could breathe easy.

They'd thought at first the vicar might say no to a church wedding as she'd been married to Danny, but he remembered the events of the spring, which had been big in the local news. "No hesitation at all," he'd said to Rhys when he approached him. "It'd be an honor."

Cerys's family came, and along with them Rhys's family and friends packed the church. "There's loads of them," Lily had laughed to Cerys when they'd been sending the invites. "I always wanted that you know, a big extended family, a husband, kids. Nothing flashy. Just that." And her face flushed pink as she suddenly leaped up and hugged Cerys. "And a mum."

The first of Cerys's Mentor Mums girls came too—Shannon—and her baby boy. She'd stayed in the cottage over the summer and into September. A thin, nervous girl, a child in the welfare system like Lily. "She's no idea what to do with a baby, Gavin," Cerys told him that first night Shannon arrived. "And she's exhausted and he won't sleep. I'll stay over in the cottage tonight." And she had done for two weeks until she'd got little Tyler into a sleep routine and the great dark shadows had disappeared from under his mum's eyes. She saw the gleam of pride in Gavin's eyes when she finally came back to the farmhouse to sleep. He didn't say a word but it wasn't needed. That day, their branches touched again.

Shannon had been nervous about attending a wedding with so many family members there, but Lily had delivered the invitation personally to her and said, "I want you there. I've been where you are. Remember that." And so she'd accepted Cerys's help to find a nice dress and an outfit for Tyler and promised to be there on the day to be part of it all.

Gavin had found his stride again but at a different pace. Alex had taken over a large chunk of running the company, and Gavin kept in touch remotely. To everyone's surprise, they both enjoyed it that way, and it seemed to be working, so Gavin was content and he'd learned to value the peace and quiet around him and the long walks he had time for now. Matt had laughed and said Alex had always wanted to be in charge but never thought he'd get the chance, so really it had worked out for the best for everyone.

The wedding reception was down in Beaumaris. Angharad had pulled out all the stops to make up for her part in this and had gotten the hotel at a good rate. She knew the manager, and it was the quiet season so she'd cajoled him round, plus all those guests coming over from the mainland, and he'd all but given the venue and the grand dinner away.

Before they left the church on the hill though, Cerys and Lily walked in the glints of the autumn sun to where Dilys lay at peace.

"I didn't know you'd had the gravestone done," Lily said as she looked at the marble slab with the second inscription fresh and new under the name of Dilys's husband.

"Last weekend," Cerys replied. "Just in time. I wanted it to be here for the wedding. It took me a long time to think what I wanted for her on here but I finally decided."

"Dilys Matthews, devoted wife, beloved *periglour*, and completely her own woman," Lily read. "What does *periglour* mean?"

"It's a Welsh word meaning 'soul friend,'" Cerys replied. "I think she would have liked that."

"She would," said Lily, and she bent to place her wedding bouquet on the grave. "It's beautiful. And I love the last part too."

Cerys smiled. "Ah, she was, wasn't she? I wanted something that honored her properly."

"It does, it really does."

As they turned to go, Lily hesitated. "Can I tell you something?"

"Always."

"I'm a bit scared about this next part—the reception, I mean. Everyone expects a good party and they'll get one because Angharad has gone to town on it. Like her guilt trip knows no bounds, and she's determined to make it up to me. But the thing is, I'm not really a party person. And what if all Rhys's family think I'm miserable or boring?"

Cerys set her hands on Lily's shoulders. "You don't have to be a party person. This is your wedding and you enjoy it in the way you want, and if anyone tries to bully you into being otherwise, I'll head them off. You be yourself and that's all you need to be."

Lily nodded. "I just don't want to let anyone down."

Cerys pointed back at the gravestone. "One thing that woman taught me, and a thing I wished I'd learned years ago, is we don't have to be anything other than who we are. We don't have to pretend, or put on an act."

Lily smiled and took Cerys's hand. "You're right. But then you always are."

And Cerys laughed, a sound that echoed out as far as the hills. "I haven't always been, but I am about this." She touched her fingers to her lips and then touched them to the gravestone. "Bless you, Dilys."

Together they turned and walked back toward the waiting wedding cars.

Cerys tightened her grip momentarily on Lily's hand. "*Cariad*, always remember, you and I are enough just as we are."

READING GROUP GUIDE

1. Compare Cerys and Lily. How are they similar? How are they different?

2. Lily lies to Cerys and Dilys about Drew to keep her safe. At what point do you think keeping secrets becomes unjustifiable?

3. Think about why Cerys chose to run from her family. Do you agree with how she did it? What would you have done differently?

4. Initially, Danny easily turns law enforcement and the media against her. Why do you think that is?

5. What originally draws Lily and Cerys together? What ultimately keeps them together?

6. Dilys, Cerys, Lily, and Drew become a makeshift family. Count the number of mother/daughter relationships in the story.

7. Discuss why Cerys found herself wanting to commit suicide. Why do you think she never sought professional help?

8. Explain why Lily is able to trust Rhys.

9. At the end of the book, Cerys agrees to try to fix her marriage with Gavin. Do you think they will be happy?

ACKNOWLEDGMENTS

As ever, thank you to my fabulous agent, Ariella Feiner. We've been together a long time now, longer even than I've been married. I still use her wedding present for my coffee every morning a decade later, and she remains the calm voice of good sense in my publishing journey. Thanks to her assistants, Molly Jamieson and Amber Garvey, for taking care of me too.

At Trapeze, my thanks for this book go to Sam Eades and Zoe Yang for their editorial input and promotional support and enthusiasm. Also to Laura Gerrard for further editorial work. To Donna Hillyer, my gratitude for finding all my errors in the copywriting stage and for some great insightful editorial work to further improve the book, and to Rosie Pearce for being my project editor again. A lovely team of people and a pleasure to work with.

At the wonderful Sourcebooks, I'd like to thank Theodore Turner for copyediting. Also on the design front, my grateful thanks to Heather VenHuizen and Stephanie Rocha for the cover and Holli Roach for internal design.

This book has been written in the strangest of times and between three different houses as my family relocated just after the first COVID-19 lockdown ended, hated it, and then came back again as the second lockdown was released. It marks a period I think most of us never want to go through again. We went on an adventure, I told my daughter. We just didn't like this one and that's sometimes how it goes. To my husband, I quoted the saying, "If you don't like where you are, move—you are not a tree." So to Paul and to

Orlaith, my love and thanks for putting up with me during the various stages of my writing process with which they are now so familiar, including the inevitable part where I declare the book is rubbish and nobody will ever read it. At this my husband calmly responds, "You always says that" and goes out and buys me a bag of Haribo, which miraculously helps. Why it does is one of life's great mysteries, but it is a truth recognized by my family that it will.

A thanks goes to my in-laws, Allan and Alison Holdsworth, for all their help and support in the weirdest and toughest of years. Thank you for being there for all the emergencies, both of you.

I don't tend to thank huge lists of friends because I rarely share much of the process or plot with anyone other than my agent or family, but I do want to thank two. My unending thanks go to Victoria Roberts for a couple of minor points of legal advice but mostly for being the best of friends—that is, a friend in need. You kept me standing at times this year, and that's something I will never forget. I also want to thank Jayne Thane for her encouragement and for making me laugh and for her loyalty and understanding—I hope you like this one too.

And finally, the book is dedicated to my mother's memory. She was my greatest confidant and I miss her every day.

ABOUT THE AUTHOR

Laura Jarratt is a Carnegie Medal– and Waterstone's Children's Book Prize–nominated author. She lives in Cheshire with her husband and their two children. She works in education and has written four YA books and two adult novels to date.